Wolf's Baja

Other books by Craig MacIntosh

The Fortunate Orphans
(Beaver's Pond Press, 2009)

The Last Lightning
(Beaver's Pond Press, 2013)

McFadden's War
(Pugio Books, 2015)

Wolf's Vendetta
(Pugio Books, 2015)

Wolf's Inferno
(Pugio Books, 2016)

WOLF'S BAJA

ISBN: 978-0-9913611-6-8

Cover design by Kent Mackintosh
Book design by Belldog Media and typeset in Janson Text

Printed in the United States of America
First Printing: 2017

19 18 17 6 5 4 3 2 1 0

Published by Pugio Books
13607 Crosscliffe Place
Rosemount, MN 55068
www.cjmacintosh.com

ACKNOWLEDGEMENTS

Another book and another debt to my collaborative team. Editor, Cindy Rogers, put her usual perfect touches to my words. Without her input there would be no coherent story. Thanks to brother Kent Mackintosh for the striking cover artwork as always, Jeff Wechter, who handled the interior, Molly Miller's proofreading skills, and Liz Royce's translations. I continue to mine retired Navy SEAL Captain Chuck Wolf's limitless store of adventure tales as well as former FBI Special Agent Jerry DeWees's forensics expertise. My indebtedness includes gratitude to Linda for her unflagging support.

*"Let your sharp arrows pierce the hearts
of the king's enemies..."*

—Psalm 45:5

In memory of
Patty Connole

Chapter 1

San Diego, four years ago

An aging Honda sedan, its headlights two piercing cones of light, felt its way through thick coastal fog hugging Sunset Cliffs Boulevard. At the wheel, Sam McFadden peered into the cotton wall confronting him.

"Can't see more than twenty feet."

In the passenger seat, former Navy SEAL Tom Wolf, cellphone glued to his ear, lowered the window. He stuck his shaggy blond head into the mix of salt air and fog, searching for an open parking spot.

"Whoa, end of the line, Sam. Better pull in behind this white van before someone else comes along."

McFadden spotted the vacancy and crept to the tail end of a line of pickups and vans. He killed the lights and engine and got out. "Stretching my legs, Wolfman." Stepping over the low guardrail, McFadden crossed the hard-packed dirt trail to a row of chained wooden posts lining the edge of a cliff. Eyes closed, he leaned back, breathing in salty air. The morning's only sounds belonged to surf washing rocks below.

Wolf grabbed a foam cup half-full of hot coffee and got out, joining his friend at the chain-and-post barrier. His phone's irritating dial tone ruined the moment. "Snuffy's not picking up," he complained, cellphone in hand. "Maybe he's on his way."

McFadden squinted at his friend. "Huh, and this is your trustworthy longboard buddy from college days?"

"So he's late," grumbled Wolf. "Cut him some slack, Sam. Snuffy's good people. Third-generation waterman." Puzzled, he ended the page and sipped his coffee. "Not like him to ignore my call, though."

"Maybe he's sleeping in."

"Not him. The man's wired to wake at first light."

McFadden turned his back to the ocean, his eyes scanning fuzzy dawn outlines of beachfront homes lining the street. "If he can afford to live here he must be doing okay."

Following McFadden's eyes, Wolf pocketed the phone. "Grandparents bought right after the war and Snuffy's folks lived here all their lives. He grew up at this stretch of beach. Man, we spent a lot of time in the water here during our college days." He turned to gaze at the shrouded ocean. "Snuffy dropped out his senior year to take care of his folks until they died. Never went back. Stayed. Took up carpentry. Custom builder. Got married. Got divorced. Wife didn't surf and he wouldn't leave the beach."

"Never thought about moving? Taxes alone could probably kill you."

Wolf shrugged, "What the hell, house was paid for. Had an inheritance. What can I say? Snuffy loves the water. Works when he wants to these days. Can't blame him." He looked seaward. "Might already be out."

McFadden ran both hands through thick black hair salted with gray and looked over his shoulder at Wolf. "He could be anywhere out there."

Wolf grinned. "All we have to do is find the biggest peak. If I know Snuffy he'll be alone, sitting outside, waiting for the biggest wave in the set." He finished his coffee. "Getting lighter, Dawg. We should paddle out and look for him."

"Needle in a haystack, Wolfman. There are at least a half-dozen peaks up and down this stretch."

"True, but if he doesn't show in the next ten minutes let's go out. Hate to waste all those good waves."

McFadden thought of his wife. "I should call Reggie."

Wolf snorted. "Let her sleep, Sam. She knows what we're doing."

"All she knows is that I took the morning off to go surfing with you. I didn't tell her which break we'd be at."

Wolf pointed with his cup. "See, right there is a prime example of the dark side of marriage." He warbled in a high-pitched voice. "Sam. Oh, Sam, dear. Where are you?"

McFadden scoffed. "Yeah, spoken like an authority on matrimony."

Draining the cup, Wolf shrugged. "Okay, Mister Married Man, let's warm up." He did leg lifts and knee bends at the railing to loosen stiff muscles. McFadden followed suit with windmills. The fog began to thin, revealing a skirt of huge boulders piled at the base of the furrowed brown cliff. A stopgap action to fight erosion, the glistening rocks poked above hissing whitewater.

"Tide's still out," said Wolf. "Long paddle ahead of us."

McFadden rubbed sleep from his eyes. "All the more reason to go out," he said. "I can hear the surf but can't see it." He lowered his head, straining to pick up booming sounds of waves one quarter-mile offshore. Two surfers trotted out of the fog, anonymous alien twins in matching black, full-bodied wetsuits, short, leashed boards under their arms.

Wolf watched them navigate the stairs to the rocky beach and then kneel on the narrow strip of gritty sand to wax their boards. "Gonna get crowded before the sun shows, Sam."

"Don't these people have jobs?"

Wolf said, "Cutting school or coming off the night shift."

McFadden huffed. "Could also be trust-fund babies like Snuffy."

"A lot you know. My man works for a living."

"When he wants to, you said."

Another two cars parked, disgorging a quartet of surfers who began waxing boards. Wolf griped, "More competition."

"So, we going out or waiting?" said McFadden. "Time's a wasting."

Wolf said, "Snuffy's AWOL. Let's go out."

He went back to the car, tossed the coffee cup, and shucked his gray fleece pullover in the back seat. McFadden did likewise. Already wearing booties and full wetsuits, the two worked the upper half of the neoprene suits over their arms and torsos. They pulled tight fitting hoods over their heads and tucked the collars inside their suits. Tugging at nylon straps, they sealed the suits with zippers the length of their spines. McFadden loosened straps holding their surfboards to welded racks on the Honda's roof and lowered the boards while Wolf did windmills. Leaning on the hood, McFadden balanced his board on both knees, adding yet another layer of wax. He tossed the wedge to Wolf, who did the same to his eight-foot board, then tucked the scrap under his sleeve.

"Keys?" Wolf said.

McFadden patted his hip. "Trunks, right side. Got your spare?"

"Roger that."

"Okay, last call for Snuffy, Wolfman. Lead on."

McFadden locked the car and followed Wolf to switchback stairs clinging to the worn bluff. Stainless steel railings led to the sand and rocks below. Reaching the launch point at the base of the cliff, they fastened board leashes around their right ankles and waded into frigid waist-deep foam alongside their boards. Three eager newcomers descended the stairs behind the two, passed them, and paddled toward a horizon lined with dark walls and exploding whitewater. Wolf, kept pace with McFadden as they stroked from the boulder-strewn beach. Glancing back, he spotted yet another surfer on the stairs. *When the surf's up, word travels fast.*

Chapter 2

The fog broke apart, moving out to sea courtesy of an early morning offshore breeze. Wolf and McFadden fought through lines of incoming whitewater. The competitive trio was far ahead of them, the latest arrival behind them, gaining.

"You in any hurry?" Wolf yelled to McFadden.

"Not trying to win a race with the younger set if that's what you mean." The two laughed. A dark-green wave riddled with scraps of kelp rose in front of them. The two punched through the feathering breaker, boards held nose down to escape a pummeling. Icy water seeped into their suits, flushing what little warmth they had. Halfway to the takeoff point a wall of foam came marching at them, an orphaned board dancing in its grip. Reaching out, Wolf snagged the trailing leash and held on. Flailing in the chop ahead, a swimmer yelled, arms overhead. Wolf and McFadden closed with the surfboard's owner, a curly-haired blond who looked to be a third their age. The boyish swimmer took the leash and clung to the short board, exhausted.

"Thanks, man," he gasped. "Dude dropped in on me. Pushed me. I went over the falls. Lost my leash."

"Pushed you?" said McFadden. He got a weary nod in answer.

"It happens," said Wolf. "Glad we came along."

"No lie, man. It's a long cold swim."

"You a regular here?" said McFadden. He got a nod.

"How come you're not in school?" said Wolf.

Flashing a conspiratorial grin, the towhead said, "Surf's up."

The three resumed paddling outside. Wolf said, "Got a name?"

"Connor."

"I'm Wolf and that's Sam."

"Okay, Connor, who's the biggest badass local out here?" said Wolf.

The youngster snorted. "Definitely Teddy Limmer. Nickname is Tank. Looks like one. Guy's an asshole."

Wolf laughed. "Kid's got a potty mouth, Sam."

"Well, ask anyone, they'll say the same thing."

"He the one who pushed you?" said Wolf.

"Nah, that was Foster, one of Tank's enforcers."

"Enforcers?" Wolf said. "Guess we'll have to watch our manners, Sam. Hey, Connor, do us a favor and point out Tank when we reach the lineup."

"Hard to miss," said the youth, "he's got a Billy goat beard and red-striped longboard. Guy pumps iron. Give him plenty of room. He doesn't like strangers at his break."

"We're friendly sorts," said Wolf. "We get along with everyone."

"Uh, huh. Not Tank. I've never seen you guys here before."

"I'm a friend of Snuffy's," said Wolf. "You know the name?"

The three crested a threatening swell and kept paddling.

"Snuffy's cool. A regular. Laid back, you know? Old dude."

Catching McFadden's smile, Wolf said, "Yeah, practically ancient."

"Well, Connor, let's go meet Tank."

"Don't say I didn't warn you."

Chapter 3

A new set like dark corduroy rippled the distant kelp bed. McFadden nodded. "Outside, Wolfman. Big." He began digging deep, heading to open water to avoid the incoming waves. "I could be home in bed right now," he yelled over his shoulder.

Wolf followed in McFadden's wake. Connor passed them both, thin boyish arms pumping like pistons to take him out of the impact zone. The first wave grew into a wall, rising in a feathering peak. A dozen surfers scrambled up the wave's face, scratching for safety. A lone figure turned, took too strokes, and dropped into a near vertical takeoff and impossible bottom turn. The wave's lip curled from top to bottom, exploding in a thunderous roar of white-green foam. The rider carved a radical cutback and dropped down the wave, racing the building wall. He went airborne over the back of a collapsing section, his board tethered to him by the leash.

"Nice moves," said Wolf to McFadden.

Connor's reedy voice followed them. "That was Tank," he yelled.

Wolf and McFadden, trailed by the kid, crested the next three waves, spectators to acrobatics by those lucky enough to take off and survive the bottom turn. Bobbing among increasingly larger waves, Wolf looked toward shore. The incoming set had cleaned out most of the surfers. Undeterred, scattered paddlers regrouped in the kelp and headed back out.

Following protocol, Wolf and McFadden waited their turn. Rotating into the lineup, McFadden caught two medium-sized waves. Both were classic ruler-edges waves. On the second one, he faced collapsing sections due to an anonymous surfer who snaked behind him both times. Burying his anger, Sam paddled back out. Wolf fared no better. Biding his time, he caught two waves, twenty minutes apart. Both times, his ride was short-lived. The same hulking rider dropped in twice, forcing him prone on his board to avoid losing it. He was buried in angry whitewater until it turned him loose. *So that's Tank*, thought Wolf.

Paddling to the lineup, Wolf and McFadden sat off by themselves, studying the wave patterns and grumbling about interlopers. What scraps of fog remained rolled away; revealing ragged blue holes in drifting clouds. The sun made a brief appearance before ducking behind more clouds. Thirty minutes passed, the main body of surfers fighting over head-high waves. Huge sets poured through, each time thinning the herd, the waves marching from the horizon as if produced by machine.

Wolf and McFadden waited. Finally alone, they were rewarded with ominous humped shapes heading their way. Jockeying into takeoff position, they let the first wave sweep through. The next wave seemed to draw the entire remaining ocean to itself, creating an endless wall in both directions.

"Sam, you want it?" yelled Wolf.

McFadden nodded, turned his board toward shore and began paddling. The wave built, taking him with it as the peak grew. Two final strokes and McFadden was racing the feathering lip toward the shoulder. The wave thundered, its backside peppering Wolf with spray like buckshot. Facing his own immense wall of green, Wolf turned toward shore, eyeing the wave over his left shoulder as he paddled. Picking up speed, the wave lifted him. He pushed into a crouch and braced for the drop. Hurtling down the wave's face ahead of the angry lip, he carved a graceful bottom turn, climbed the steep wall, and prepared for another turn.

Ahead of him, a surfer on a red-striped longboard paddled into the wave's shoulder and dropped, forcing Wolf to cut back to avoid a collision. Chased by the collapsing curl, Wolf readied for the crushing blow. The section threw itself on him with all its force, burying him, snapping his leash. Not done with him, the wave held him down, tossing him shoreward like a rag. He surfaced without his board in a boiling whirlpool of foam. Finally released by the spent wave, Wolf dog paddled in angry chop to get his bearings.

"Dude, you rock! What a ride!" Connor, whose board Wolf had saved, was also adrift, a grinning blond head in the foam.

"Seen my board?" yelled Wolf.

Connor pointed to the cliffs. "Mine too," he said. "That was a cleanup set for sure," he babbled. "Dude, you were robbed."

Cresting a swell, McFadden arrived. He paddled toward the swimmers, two boards trailing him, one foot planted on the nose of each surfboard to tow them. "How long do I have to keep saving your ass, Wolfman?"

Wolf swam to McFadden to reclaim his board. The kid did the same, thanking McFadden profusely for the repeat favor. He pushed Connor's board to him. "Your skeg's broken."

Connor flipped his surfboard and studied a splintered stump held by a scrap of fiberglass. "That was Tank's doing."

Wolf straddled his board. "He broke your fin?"

"Yeah, I'm not the only one he's done it to."

"That was uncalled for," said Wolf, fuming. "Hell, he's the one who dropped in on you."

Connor shrugged, righted his board and lay prone, sapped.

"It's getting sloppy out there," said McFadden.

Straddling his board, Wolf glanced seaward. "Your call, Sam."

"The break can't hold this size, Wolfman. I'm going in."

"I'm done, too," said their dispirited tagalong.

Wolf said, "Fine with me. Watch the shorebreak, might be tricky."

The three headed in, one eye on the ledge beneath the cliff, another on the incoming surf. Battling the current, they scrambled ashore during a break in the waves. Helping each other reach the stairs, they climbed to street level, boards tucked under their arms.

Chapter 4

Wolf unlocked the car and handed McFadden one of three thermos bottles filled with lukewarm water. Both pulled off their neoprene hoods, rinsed salt from their eyes, and poured the tepid water through the collars of their wetsuits. "Oh, man, that hits the spot," cooed McFadden, his limbs warming. "Love it."

Wolf handed Connor the third thermos. "Take it, kid. You earned it. Warm up."

"Thanks." Connor doused himself. "Righteous, dude," he said. "That was one sweet ride you had going."

"Would have been nice to have finished it," grumbled Wolf.

"That was classic Tank," Connor said. "No way he was gonna let you get the ride of the day. Typical."

"Tank, huh, Wolfman? King of the hill."

Connor handed back the thermos. "Pretty much does what he wants. What can I say? I told you he was an asshole." Wolf and McFadden slipped their boards into covers and strapped them to the Honda's racks.

"We played by the rules," said McFadden.

"Doesn't matter. This is his spot. If he doesn't know you, he makes sure you pay for invading his space. He gives localism a bad name."

Wolf peeled the wetsuit from his upper torso, "I can understand one wave, maybe two, but every wave? No way."

"I had the same thing going on my rides," said McFadden.

"That was Foster," said Connor. "He does what Tank tells him."

Like Wolf, McFadden stripped his wetsuit to his waist and donned a sweatshirt.

"Hey, Boys!"

Wolf and McFadden turned at the sound of the voice. Pushing a bike, a dismounted, wild haired, bearded cyclist in workman's overalls and heavy boots crossed Sunset Cliffs Boulevard, dodging traffic. He leaned his bike against the walk's guardrail and embraced Wolf.

"Snuffy. Where the hell you been?"

"Neighbor's car broke down halfway to work in La Jolla. Had to do some quick on-the-spot repairs. Sorry 'bout that. Couldn't be helped."

Wolf turned to McFadden. "Sam, meet Stu Larson."

"Snuffy to friends," said the tall, broad-shouldered cyclist. The two shook hands. "Looks pretty heavy out there, huh? How was your session?"

Wolf tightened the straps on the Honda's rack. "Cut short by some of your local boys."

Connor, unnoticed until now, piped, "Tank and Foster at it again."

Larson tousled the youth's hair. "Hey, Connor, how you doin?"

"Good, Snuffy." He nodded out to sea. "You coulda kept the peace."

"Anybody get hurt?"

McFadden said, "Came close. But no, nobody hurt."

Larson jammed hands in his coveralls. "Good. Yeah, Tank can be a problem. Sometimes he just gets a wild hair." He shrugged. "I guess every spot has someone like him."

"That's what kills the fun of surfing for me these days," said McFadden.

"We were low-key," said Wolf. "Best I didn't meet the gentleman on shore."

Stroking his cinnamon-colored beard, Larson glanced past Wolf. "Well, now's your chance. Speak of the devil."

Chapter 5

Two lumbering figures crested the stairs, one of them stocky and bearded, carrying a red-striped longboard. The pair stopped at a pickup at the head of the line. Wolf stared at the two men. McFadden knew the look.

Snuffy caught the look as well. Changing the subject, he held out his arms. "You guys want to dry out at my place? How about I whip up a little breakfast?"

Connor, brightened. "That'd be cool, Snuffy."

"Sure," said Wolf, "Right after I have a little talk with Tank."

McFadden grabbed Wolf's arm. "C'mon, let it be, man. So the guy's an asshole, no argument there. But we don't need this."

"Need what?" Wolf glanced at McFadden. "What we don't need are guys like Tank calling the shots. I'm just going to reason with him. Maybe a little attitude adjustment."

Releasing his grip, McFadden shrugged. "Yeah, I can imagine your version of reasoning. Let's take Snuffy up on his offer of breakfast."

"Good idea. You go ahead," said Wolf. "I'll catch up."

"I'll wait," said McFadden. "Okay, I'll watch your back."

"This won't take long," said Wolf, grim. He headed toward Tank, now loading his board in the pickup's bed. McFadden tagged along, six steps behind. Larson put out his arm to hold Connor back. Two of Tank's acolytes, reading Wolf's body language, drifted away from the truck.

"Tank!" boomed Wolf.

Aware of Wolf, Limmer ignored him, instead, busying himself with cushioning his surfboard in the truck bed by wrapping it with a worn quilt. Wolf left the cliff's path, ending at the truck's tailgate.

"I was told you were the big man in the lineup. Heard you keep the peace out there."

Propping elbows on the tailgate, Tank spoke without looking at Wolf. "Do I know you? I don't think so. You're just another one of those assholes that thinks they can do as they please, go anywhere they want like they own the place...and fuck with the locals. Not in my backyard."

Wolf caught Foster grinning from the sidelines. McFadden moved there, to the left, behind Wolf. There would be no threat from that quarter. A knot of surfers gathered at the top of the stairs, close enough to hear Wolf's challenge, far enough back to remain spectators.

"Normally I don't go out when it's this small," said Wolf, gesturing to the ocean. "But hey, it looked like it might be fun. Only what do I find? A bully on a longboard. That's old school, man. What gives?"

Tank threw a disgusted look at Wolf and resumed his nothing task.

Wolf taunted, too loud for the curious to ignore. "What's it gonna be, Tank? Your homies are watching. Rep's on the line. Gotta do something, man. Shame to lose your spot in the pecking order because a stranger calls you out."

"I got no quarrel with you," said Tank. "Fuck off."

Wolf bristled. "But I've got a quarrel with you. You played the big man out there today. I practice etiquette at every break I surf. From Waimea Bay to Makaha, the Pipeline, and Steamer's Lane."

"Am I supposed to be impressed?"

Raising his voice, Wolf played to the growing gallery. "That's just to let you know you're out of line. You just couldn't let it be, could you? You drop in, play the big shot with your friend there, and bully anyone you want to."

Finally facing Wolf, Tank glared. "Back off, sonofabitch. I got no reason to hurt an old man like you, dude."

Wolf heard tittering laughter from those watching. He raised the stakes. "You broke the kid's fin for no reason. That pissed me off."

Rising to the bait, the big man said, "So I snapped the kid's skeg, so what? He dropped in on me. So you're pissed off. So fuck you."

"For the record, you dropped in on him, not the other way around."

An audible gasp escaped from the growing crowd of surfers crowding the top of the cliff. Tank reddened, rage in his eyes. He leaped at Wolf, his arms wide to trap his tormentor. Wolf easily danced aside, letting the big man stumble into the car behind the pickup. Tank recovered and charged Wolf again, swinging his fists, trying to connect. Wolf ducked aside, delivering two stinging slaps to Tank's face in rebuke.

Foster moved to intervene. McFadden yelled, "Don't even think about it!"

Wolf moved at Tank, feinting, weaving, keeping the bully off-balance. Tank lunged again and missed. A quick foot sweep and the big man went down on his backside. Laughter burst from the crowd, enraging Tank. He rose, glaring at those on the sidewalk, silencing them.

Wolf backpedaled before Tank's blundering charge, slapping his opponent repeatedly with open hand. His back against the tailgate, Tank groped behind him for a weapon, anything he could use. Gripping a tire jack's steel shaft, he swung it at Wolf and missed, taking out a headlight of the car parked behind his truck. Wolf barreled inside, gripping Tank's wetsuit and head-butting him. His nose bloodied, the steel shaft useless at close quarters, Tank rained ineffectual blows on Wolf's shoulders and arms.

Wolf knifed his opponent's groin with a knee, ending the brawl. Dropping his weapon, Tank fell to his knees, out of breath, writhing in pain. Wolf picked up the jack and tossed it in the pickup's bed.

Towering over the groaning Tank, Wolf said, "How about that, I had no idea you had a pair, little man. Imagine my surprise." The crowd whooped at the insult. Turning to Foster, Wolf challenged, "You want a piece of this?" Tank's man shook his head, retreating to a chorus of hoots. Wolf leaned over the prone Tank, pointing to seaward. "If I hear about you busting another skeg or going after someone out there I will personally come back for you. You understand? You hearing me, Tank?"

A weary nod of surrender and a wave but Wolf wasn't through. He slammed the heel of his hand against the upturned skeg on Tank's board, snapping the fin. "That's a reminder, asshole."

Wolf rejoined his stunned friends at the Honda. "What were you thinking?" said McFadden.

Arms folded, Wolf leaned against the car. "Dunno...I just...I can't stand schoolyard bullies."

"It wasn't even close," said an awed Connor. "I never thought I'd see Tank fold like that."

Snuffy held up a cellphone. "Got it all, Wolfman. He started it. He could have done some serious damage with that jack. Say the word and this goes viral on YouTube."

"Keep it unless he calls the cops," said Wolf, calming. "Now, what about that breakfast you promised?"

Chapter 6

Snuffy Larson pocketed his phone. "All are welcome. Better drive your car to my place. I'll meet you there, Wolfman. You know the way. I'll leave the garage door open. Don't leave your boards sitting out here for the picking, especially after whipping Tank's ass." Mounting his bike, Larson crossed the street, followed by a grinning Connor, who trotted after him, crippled board under his arm.

Later, in Snuffy's kitchen, he and Wolf regaled McFadden with big wave stories while Connor listened in wide-eyed worship. "Is it true," he asked, "you know, what you said about surfing Waimea Bay and Sunset?"

"Yeah, it's true," said Wolf. "Another week here on the coast and I'm heading to the North Shore for the winter."

"He keeps a quiver of boards at a friend's house in Haleiwa," said Snuffy. "He's a wild man, Connor. Now stop asking the man questions and let him eat his breakfast." Wolf and McFadden finished eating and opted for coffee, while Connor asked for seconds.

"Kid possesses the proverbial hollow leg," said Larson from the stove. "This might be the only decent meal he gets all day." He pointed with a spatula. "Say, why aren't you in class anyway?"

"And miss today?" said Connor, his mouth stuffed with sausage and toast. "No way." He shrugged and returned to his hash browns and eggs.

Snuffy joined his guests at the kitchen table. "Connor's incorrigible when it comes to surfing," he said.

"Reminds me of someone I knew in college," said Wolf.

"Yeah, I guess he does have that look." Snuffy tousled the boy's hair. "In addition to skipping school he thinks I'm part of his meal plan. Probably would trade high school for full-time surfing if his mom would let him."

"You won't tell her will you?" said Connor, mopping his plate with a crust. "I only missed my first two classes...and one of them is study hall." He finally pushed from the table. "Thanks for breakfast, Snuffy."

"You're welcome. Now clear your dishes and get outa here. I wanna catch up with these gentlemen."

"Can I leave my board with you? Beats having to carry it home."

"Sure. Stow it in the garage rack with mine. We'll fix it later."

Connor dumped his dishes in the sink and was gone. Wolf poured himself a second coffee. "Who's the kid?" he asked.

"Connor Ware. Only child. I know his mom."

"Know her in a biblical sense or as a friend?"

Snuffy blushed, not answering.

Wolf glanced at Snuffy then McFadden. "Give it up, Snuffy. You playing father figure to cuddle with the mom?"

Snuffy blushed. "Aw, c'mon, Wolfman. Kid's lonely. You know, single working mom. If I'm not on a job I'm usually around or out in the water. He started tagging along about two years ago."

"Uh, huh. Describe the lady."

Arms behind his head, Snuffy leaned back, smiling. "What can I say? Quintessential California girl. Fun-loving, blonde, blue-eyed, killer body. Loves her kid. Great lady."

McFadden helped himself to more coffee.

Wolf kept going. "Divorced? Separated? Status check."

"Widowed. Connor's dad was second-generation Army. Iraq."

Wolf's smile faded. "Sorry to hear that. Glad you're around, Snuffy."

"Yeah, me too. Connor's a hoot. Great little surfer. His mom is really special. We make time for each other." He got up from the table. "Now, if you're done with the third degree I'll clean up."

"Just checking up on you and trying to keep you out of trouble," said Wolf.

"Ah, that's good coming from you. Guess I'll have to steer clear of Tank for a while thanks to you."

"I'll make another house call if you need me to," said Wolf.

At the sink, Snuffy said, "I think he'll go quiet for a while. Nothing like rubbing a man's face in it in front of his friends."

"Scratch one bully," said McFadden.

"You call, I'll come," said Wolf. "I want to know more about this lovely widow."

"I've said enough already. She doesn't need to meet you at this point, Wolfman. I'm just getting her to trust me. Meeting you will set me back."

"She have a name?"

"I'm not saying another word. Let's talk about the old days."

Wolf took the hint. Nursing his fresh coffee, he and Snuffy replayed college surfing days, amusing McFadden with embellished stories of adventures gone awry and those that had succeeded—the latest one, the morning bout on the cliffs now immortalized on the carpenter's phone.

Chapter 7

San Diego, three months ago

Despite the hour, the planet's busiest border crossing was awake. Barely visible through the hovering marine layer—a seasonal coastal cloud cover trapped by the Peninsular Range—dawn announced itself as a rosy sliver above the San Diego Freeway. A fast-moving river of lights belonging to Tijuana-bound traffic filled southbound lanes. East of the highway's concrete divide, northbound headlights clogged the border station's incoming lanes like swarming fireflies. In addition to cars, buses and trucks, a shuffling nose-to-tail line of foot traffic descended on San Diego, drawn by the promise of shopping or a day's wages.

One half mile west of the freeway, on American soil, a frustrated Wayne "Mo" Morton perched atop his Land Rover in the nearly deserted Plaza Major Shopping Center parking lot. The growing light was a reminder to Morton of tardy friends. What little patience he still possessed was eroding by the minute.

Rubbing sleep from his eyes and cursing under his breath, the barrel-chested Morton dropped down to pace beside his battered Land Rover. Stuffed with tents, coolers, wetsuits, spare clothing, bins of food, camping equipment and two spares, Morton's overloaded vehicle sat under a slender light pole in the middle of the huge lot. Four bulging surfboard bags, secured to racks by wide nylon straps, rode the roof.

In the passenger seat, "Pinky" Connole, Morton's traveling companion, slept undisturbed, his breath fogging the window, his ragged snore rasping like a chainsaw. Blissfully unaware of Morton's building temper, the whippet-thin Pinky was taking advantage of the cool, pre-dawn darkness to catch up on sleep. For the past two hours, he and Morton had waited for friends due to join them on a long-planned, two-car surf safari to Baja. In light of the delinquent couple's no-show act, Pinky elected to sleep, Morton to pace and rage.

Grumbling, soft at first, then louder, Morton howled at the delay in his well-laid plans. Pounding the hood in frustration, he broke Pinky's reverie. Morton followed his banging with a string of volcanic curses. Flinging open his passenger door, a disgruntled Pinky stumbled into the chilly morning air, unkempt red hair bristling, his sleep ruined.

"What the hell, Mo. A guy can't even get ten minutes of sleep?"

Throwing up his hands, Morton roared back, "Ten minutes, my ass, Pinky. You been sawing logs for an hour like some berserk lumberjack on steroids."

"What? If you can't sleep, I can't sleep?"

"Damn right. Where the hell are they anyway? I've got half a mind to leave."

"That's right. You got half a mind." Steadying himself against the open door, Pinky retaliated by relieving himself on the Land Rover's right-front tire. His act prompted a pained outburst from Morton, which Pinky ignored.

"Try calling them again," said Pinky, zipping up.

Morton put his nose to the offender's. "Do not, I repeat, do not piss on my car," he growled. "I'm warning you..."

Unbowed, Pinky turned away. "Yeah, right. Try 'em again."

Morton fished his cell phone from his jacket just as a horn sounded from the freeway's last southbound off-ramp. The two glanced across the parking lot. A pickup camper, swollen board bags riding on top, exited the freeway, blinked its lights twice, and made a right on Camino De La Plaza. Taking another right at the lot's entrance, the truck aimed for the Land Rover. As the truck closed, a figure thrust halfway out the passenger window, waving both arms.

Chapter 8

Billy and Connor had finally arrived but Morton was not amused. The missing pair had thrown off his timetable. Before the truck came to a complete stop, the grinning man in the passenger seat rode the swinging door. "Ho-yah, boys! Better late than never!"

Arms crossed, Morton planted his feet, showing a disapproving scowl. "Took your own fine time getting here," he said. "We coulda been across an hour ago."

Billy, the truck's bearded driver, got out. Bathed in the headlights, he sauntered to the Land Rover. Wrapped in a fleece-lined jacket, Billy wore jeans, boots, a checkered wool shirt and a leather-flying helmet from another era.

"*Que pasa*, Mo? How ya doin?" Ignoring the chilly reception, the new arrivals waved away Morton's smoldering anger and exchanged greetings with Pinky. "My man," said Billy, "you actually with this frowning dude?"

His anger having no effect on the latecomers, Morton folded. "What happened, Billy? We were beginning to worry you guys weren't going to make it."

Lanky, helmet-wearing Billy turned on the charm. "Hey, what can I say? Connor here is a hard man to roust. His mom 'bout took my head off when I came by this morning."

"Too much partying?" a grinning Pinky asked, prodding Connor.

"Nah. I had to stay up late writing a final school paper before I could leave. Then, there was packing, saying good-byes. You know, stuff like that. All is cool, right? Let's do this. You good, Mo?"

Morton had mellowed by degrees. He shrugged. "I'm good."

Billy said, "Well, okay. Let's get this wagon train on the road."

The four returned to their vehicles. Across the parking lot, early shift drones come to wake a sleeping Walmart trudged across the expanse to the chain store.

Though a stubborn dawn gloom lingered on the coast, the sun broke clear of the hills. In an hour, clouds hugging the shore would scatter as well. Morton led them out of the lot, turned left on Camino De La Plaza and drove to the second left, an on-ramp leading back to the freeway.

Staying on Morton's tail in one of the five lanes separated by white concrete barriers, Billy jockeyed with early traffic. Slowing at the ninety-degree turn where the old San Ysidro border crossing sat neglected, he tailgated Morton toward the temporary El Chaparral entry. Paralleling the border, traffic swept down a sterile corridor of concrete and fencing. Ahead of them, on the left, a huge Mexican flag hung limp in the gray morning.

Land Rover and pickup drifted to the far right's *Autodeclaracion*—Something to declare—lane and passed under a MEXICO sign spanning the road.

They made a tight left turn at the flag where the first checkpoint stalls spread across pavement dotted with embedded yellow steel bumps. Morton and Billy got the once over from gatekeepers and were waved through to the secondary vehicle inspection station.

Morton and Billy parked and left their passengers behind to watch their belongings. Both men took passports, car papers, drivers' licenses and cash to the immigration stop. They got visa forms, paid the fee, and got the required stamps. They returned to their vehicles and chatted amicably while waiting for Pinky and Connor to repeat the process.

Chapter 9

Waiting at the parked camper and Land Rover, Billy was teasing Morton. "Easy as one, two, three," said Billy. "You owe me. Always better to cross in daylight."

Morton flashed back to earlier attempts, one of which had turned ugly during an ill-advised pre-dawn border crossing the two had made as high-schoolers. "Yeah. How many years we been making this trip? Five?"

"At least. What's the plan? We still picking up the trailer and bikes in Ensenada?"

"Already made the arrangements. Sebastian's expecting us." Morton added, "All set to go. We'll test ride the bikes to make sure. But he knows what we want. Sebastian's cool. It's better this way."

Billy leaned against his pickup, checked the tension on the straps holding the boards. "Yeah, no reason to attract attention at the border with something shiny for the locals to think about. Don't care what the bikes look like as long as they run."

"Trust me. Sebastian knows bikes. You'll love it, man."

"Hey, still pissed we showed up late?"

Shrugging, Morton threw up his hands. "For a while. When you didn't turn up I thought maybe you had changed your mind. Backed out without telling me."

"No way, man. Wouldn't miss this for the world. Might be the last hurrah."

"You know me, I get bent outa shape sometimes. I'll get over it."

Billy smiled, a sly disarming grin. "You over it now? We good?"

They bumped fists. "We're good."

"Here come the boys," said Morton.

Pinky and Connor sauntered to the waiting two.

"Any problems?" asked Billy.

Both shook their heads. "*Nada.*"

Once in their vehicles, the four headed across the concrete apron, joining traffic streaming south. The customs officer who had sent the four Americans on their way with a welcoming smile left his post to step outside as they drove away. Cellphone to his ear, he described the quartet, their cargo, and their vehicles, then returned to his post.

Clearing the border station, Morton and Billy played tag with a line of aggressive drivers eager to claim the far right lane. Passing under a fenced pedestrian bridge filled with stragglers, they followed green overhead signs for Tijuana/ Ensenada and got separated by more weaving traffic. Spotting the Land Rover with its cargo of boards, Billy kept Morton in sight on the sloping serpentine incline curving alongside the Tijuana River's ugly, parched concrete channel. As they merged with the *Avenida Internacional*'s concrete ribbon leading to the coast, a rusting, aged, yellow Mercedes sedan with two men in the front seat, joined the parade heading south without being noticed. The Americans, oblivious to their tail, drove on toward Ensenada.

With Morton at the Land Rover's wheel, Pinky buried his head in a pillow and drifted back to sleep. In the pickup-camper, Connor played with the radio dials until he found an abrasive mariachi station to his liking. Followed discreetly by the yellow Mercedes three car lengths behind, the Americans kept pace with the traffic.

The glorious Mexican sun finally made an appearance, banishing the remnants of the cloudy coastal hangover. The sea, hinting of turquoise, sparkled beyond stacked white blocks of housing and industrial buildings hugging the highway at Tijuana's fringes. The deserted bullring's profile poked above the crowded skyline, a reminder of the past. Ensenada, where Sebastian waited with the promised trailer and dirt bikes, beckoned to the two-car caravan. Beyond that lay their goal—the real Baja.

Chapter 10

Three months later

"Sam, you want your salsa hot, or extra hot?"

McFadden had come in from the patio's outdoor kitchen to find his wife, Reggie, attacking a growing mound of tomatoes and onions next to the sink. He plucked a glistening jalapeño from the cutting board. "The hotter the better," he said, twirling the pepper. McFadden threw his arms around her waist and nuzzled her neck. "I like my salsa like my women—extra hot." Reggie rolled her eyes and shrugged. "Careful, I'm cutting jalapeño." Knife poised over the mix, she smiled. Behind her, a small flat screen TV droned on with scraps of San Diego's midday news—fender benders, a shoplifting ring's arrest, a hotel groundbreaking, a rumored tuition hike at area colleges, and a teaser about weather.

McFadden broke free and snagged a can of beer from the refrigerator. He ran the chilled can across his forehead and popped the top. Sipping the beer, he turned to the counter, his eyes caught by a flashing report from the noon news. A "Breaking News" announcement filled the screen with the image of a surfer going airborne over the back of a wave. McFadden's eyes caught the clip. Back to Reggie, he planted hands on the granite countertop and leaned close to catch the robotic male anchor's voice.

"The FBI today joined with San Diego police detectives looking into what has now apparently turned from a college graduation excursion into a three month-old missing persons case. For a live report we go to Crystal Hamm at the border crossing."

Reggie put down her knife and joined Sam in front of the television. "Isn't that Tom Wolf's girlfriend?" Nodding, he waved her into silence and turned up the volume.

Taking the handoff from the anchor, Hamm, a buxom blonde, microphone in hand, strolled on a sidewalk along the San Diego freeway's last fenced overpass prior to the border. Mexico-bound traffic flowed non-stop behind her. "What was originally thought to be a case of four young Americans overstaying a Baja surfing vacation has now escalated, with anxious family members demanding answers. San Diego law enforcement officials turned to federal authorities for help two months ago. So far, no progress has been made solving this disappearance. The FBI confirmed they are assisting in the search but still have no comment."

After a filmed news conference with strutting, overconfident Mexican police officials—a session more photo op than informative—the report cut to stock video of border crossing lanes, lines of cars and trucks. Crystal Hamm's voiceover continued as the screen filled with shots of border guards talking to drivers and a shot of the Mexican flag waving about the El Chaparral entry station. The image morphed into a photo lineup of the four missing young men. An FBI phone number crawled across the screen.

"Hey, I know that kid!" said McFadden, pointing to the screen.

"Which one?" said Reggie, rinsing her hands and the knife.

He answered without looking at her. "The last one on the right. He's the youngest. Connor...forgot his last name until now."

The news report ended with a live shot of Crystal Hamm on the freeway overpass, reading from notes. Next, the anchor tossed out a bland scripted question. Weather followed. A blaring car dealer ad popped up and McFadden muted the image.

"You know, Wolfman and I met that kid a few years ago when we surfed Pacific Cliffs."

She frowned. "When Tom got in that fight?"

"Yeah," McFadden said. "Your memory amazes me sometimes. But let's be clear, the Wolfman didn't start it."

"So you say."

"It's true. Guy threw the first punch, his last."

McFadden, eyes on the floor, said, "Connor was a nice kid. Hope they find him and his buddies."

"Not the best place to go," said Reggie. "The Philippines is safer."

"That's debatable. You know, Wolfman and I did a Baja safari once."

She put her arms around his neck. "When you were younger."

"True. He was stationed here and I was passing through town on a thirty-day leave."

"And single," she scolded. "You both were such risk takers."

"Youth does that to you, Reggie." He nodded to the silenced television. "Like these college kids. Invincible. Not a care in the world."

"Imagine what their families are going through," she said.

"A nightmare," agreed McFadden.

Reggie changed the subject. "Does Tom still date the reporter, Crystal Hamm?"

McFadden shrugged. "When he's in town, I guess. I don't follow his love life."

"Jealous?"

"Never." He made a playful lunge for his wife and the two embraced.

"Don't forget," she said, "Carl and Karen Frey will be here for dinner at six."

"The grill is spotless, lady. You just pay attention to your salsa."

"I know...make it extra hot, like your women."

"Woman," he corrected her. "I can only handle one at a time."

Chapter 11

Kearny Plaza, McFadden's Gun Range

The incoming call was an unfamiliar number but McFadden gambled and picked up the phone in his office and hit the speaker button.

"Sam McFadden? Snuffy Larson. Remember me? Tom Wolf's friend."

"Yeah. Pacific Cliffs. Been a couple of years."

"Yeah, the fight," said Larson. "Guy named Tank tried to clean the Wolfman's clock. Got his ass handed to him. I still have the phone video."

"Sure, I remember you, Snuffy. Long time. How you doing?"

"Hanging in there. I'll get right to it. You been following the news about those college students missing in the Baja?"

McFadden's heart skipped a beat. He had half-expected the call.

"Yeah, a tragedy. To be honest, I hadn't paid much attention until two days ago. Recognized Connor's picture. Didn't realize he was part of that. Thought of that morning when we first met. Assume you're involved."

"I am. I'm close to Connor's mother, Sara."

"So I remember." McFadden sighed. "Close as in—?"

"Close. Sara's a terrific woman. Great single mom and all that means. She's taking this hard."

Trying to stay neutral, McFadden said, "I can only imagine. What's the FBI telling her?"

"Good out of the gate but now not so much. They're going through the motions, you know? I mean she gets updates from time to time. Used to be daily."

"And now?"

McFadden sensed anger and resignation in Larson's voice. "Now Sara and the families go for days without hearing."

"The feds probably have a lot on their plate," said McFadden.

"True, but so much bullshit comes Sara's way she has a hard time separating fact from fiction these last few weeks."

"Why the call, Snuffy? What can I do? I know a couple detectives in with San Diego Police Department but that's as far as my connections go. They're likely following the FBI's lead on this."

A pause. Hearing a woman kibitzing in the background, McFadden guessed it was Connor's mother. "What can I help you with?" he said. "I'd probably depend on the FBI to solve this."

"But we're getting the runaround," said Snuffy. "Seems simple enough. Follow the money. See where these kids went. Talk to people."

McFadden, elbows on his desk, hand to his forehead, said, "Isn't that what they're doing? Aren't the Mexican authorities cooperating?"

"Who knows?" said Snuffy. "We get the company line but it's wearing thin. She just wants Connor back home."

"I can appreciate her frustration," McFadden said, "but it's more of a waiting game, isn't it? I mean, what can you do?"

Snuffy's voice took on a conspiratorial tone. "Last week, out of the blue, Sara got a phone call from some lawyer in Mexico."

"I can guess where this is going."

"Yeah, some guy's saying he's seen Connor."

Sitting bolt upright, McFadden said, "He's alive?" and instantly regretted his choice of words. "Sorry, didn't mean to sound surprised. It's just that...with no leads in the story...look, I don't mean to appear pessimistic, Snuffy. Maybe this is a good thing if it's true. A lead, right?"

"Our FBI liaison thinks we shouldn't get too excited about the call. They think it's fake. A feeler to make some quick cash off a desperate parent. Crazy, huh?"

"Huh, what about the other families? What have they heard?"

"*Nada.* Sara's the only one who got a phone call."

McFadden got up from his desk and closed the office door to muffle sounds from the indoor range. He paced. "Let me guess, Snuffy. A ransom demand, right?"

"Of course. It's a cottage industry down there."

"I've heard that," said McFadden. "What does the FBI think?"

"Said the same thing. Told Sara not to get her hopes up. The Mexicans told them they've never heard of the guy."

"So, you're at a dead end? Sorry, bad choice of words. What do you do now?"

"We can't wait. Sara wants to go to Mexico to meet with this lawyer. He said he can negotiate with the people holding Connor."

McFadden sat on the edge of his desk. "Noooo. bad idea. That's a no-brainer, Snuffy. Like trying to rescue a drowning man. Pretty soon you have two drowning victims instead of one. Tell her not to do that."

"Tried. She's determined. Remember, this is a desperate mother."

"You can't even be sure this guy's legit. Stick with the game plan, Snuffy. Let the FBI handle this."

"She's losing patience, Sam. Won't listen to me. Certainly not hearing what the feds are telling her."

"I hate to say this, but Connor may not even be alive at this point. Have you considered that?"

"You try telling her that."

McFadden backed up. "Not on your life. You called, I answered. I'm telling you to stick with the game plan. The

FBI is her best hope, Snuffy. They have hostage negotiators and trained rescue teams."

"I hear you, Sam. But we're talking about Mexico. Anyway, my main reason for calling is to see if you and the Wolfman are interested in helping."

McFadden covered his eyes with his free hand. "Mexico? You kidding? Even the Wolfman would tell you Beirut is a picnic compared to Mexico these days. And the Baja is off the grid, Snuffy. That's outside my area of expertise."

"That's overplayed, Sam. Thousands of Americans go there every year. Hell, some of them live down there half the year."

"Ask Wolf about that. He'd confirm what I'm telling you. Stay the course."

"But that's the problem. There is no 'course' at this point. We have to do something, especially in light of this call about Connor."

"Do not do this, Snuffy. I say again, let this go."

"At least let me talk to Wolf."

"He's in Hawaii. Somewhere on the North Shore, I'd guess. Probably will be there through March. I haven't talked to him in two months. He prefers it that way."

"Can you put me in touch with him?" said Snuffy. "For Sara's sake? For Connor's sake?"

"This lawyer's call is a pretty thin thread to hang your hopes on, Snuffy. I'm speaking for myself, not the Wolfman."

"It's worth a shot. We...Connor's mother and I...would be grateful for a chance to talk to him. Work with me on this, please."

"I dunno. The risks are huge."

"How about you tell his mother that? I can put her on, Sam."

McFadden rose from his desk, one hand in the air as if holding back the inevitable. "No. Do not do that. I don't need to talk to her about this."

"She's right here. Sam."

"Don't put her on." Won by the anguish in his caller's voice, McFadden yielded. "Look, I'm not promising anything, okay? I'll run up the flag and see if Wolf responds. I don't think his take on this will be any different than mine, Snuffy."

"But you'll try, right?"

"I will. Don't expect anything. I'll try to reach him but be prepared to be disappointed."

"As long as we get a chance to make our case. That's the important thing right now."

"Give me seventy-two hours."

"I can only promise twenty-four. After that, we head for Mexico."

"Don't do anything stupid, Snuffy."

"Twenty-four hours, Sam."

"Snuffy, listen to reason—hello?" The connection died. McFadden slumped at his desk, drained from the call. He picked up his cellphone and tapped the number Wolf had given him two months ago—along with a sworn oath of privacy.

Chapter 12

McFadden finally caught Wolf in Hawaii after three tries, the last one from home. He put him on speaker, and closed the doors to his den. Wolf was in a foul mood. Had been a spotty winter, he said. Too few truly big days, too many weeks of moderate surf and a scarcity of perfect conditions. And too many people in the water. The crowds, Wolf griped, were worse than ever and growing at each of his favorite breaks.

"Never seen it this bad," he complained. "A dozen guys going for each wave. Even Pipeline and Waimea. Suicide. Everybody hoping for a photo in the magazines.

Takes the fun out of it. Might have to come back just to avoid the fights. And when it's flat for more than one day everyone goes nuts."

McFadden leaned back in his leather chair, arms behind his head. "Some things never change. Still scrapping, huh?"

"Hey," boomed Wolf, "I never start the arguments."

"But I'd bet you never back down."

"What would be the point? I'm not anyone's punching bag, Sam. So what's the reason you're calling? Better be good."

Bowing, McFadden laced his fingers together and moved on, explaining the situation with Snuffy Larson and Sara, the mother of the missing Connor Wade. To his surprise Wolf confessed to being out of the loop. He had not seen the news, had not talked with Crystal Hamm for months. Frustration, then anger, in his voice fueled a promise to return as soon as he could book a flight to the mainland.

McFadden tried a reality check by adding his opinion. "You realize this could be an exercise in futility, Wolfman."

"Maybe. But it's a no-brainer, Sam. Tell Snuffy he can count on me."

"Knew you'd say that. Email me with flight details. I'll pick you up. You've been missed, Wolfman."

"And I've missed a certain blonde reporter."

"Still here. Still working for the dark side. Check out the station's website for her reports about these missing guys."

"I'll do that. Let her know I'm heading back."

"You do it. And work on your social skills before you call. Not talking to her for months probably didn't win you any points."

"Yeah. I'm probably in the dog house, huh?"

"You can stay with us. I'll have Reggie turn down your covers."

"How's she been?"

"If you're asking about her adjustment to life after the shootings and the fire, I'd say she's coping well, considering."

"Good. But don't even think about going to the Baja, Sam. She'd never let you out of her sight."

"Who says we're going to the Baja?"

A pause. "You kidding? That's where Connor and friends are."

"It's been ninety days and counting, Wolfman."

A resigned sigh. "We'll see. I just hope it's not too late."

"I'll be waiting to hear from you."

"Amen. Gotta go, Sam. I need to check on flights."

Chapter 13

Reggie was waiting when Sam returned to the living room. She paced in front of the fireplace, arms crossed. He knew the signs.

This is not going to go well, he thought. *She's on to me.*

McFadden dropped to the couch, threw an arm across the back and waited for *Typhoon Reggie* to make landfall in the living room.

She feinted. "How's Tom?"

He wasn't fooled by her calm. "He's heading back."

"Why?"

"You know why, Reggie. Those missing students."

"He'll go to the Baja to look for them won't he?"

Sam backpedaled against the ropes. "That would be my guess."

She pivoted in front of the fireplace. "And you want to go with him."

He parried. "Haven't made that decision yet."

"But you're thinking about it."

McFadden rose from the couch, heading for a neutral corner—the kitchen. "How about some wine?" he said over his shoulder.

She followed on his heels. "No way can you seriously be thinking of going." Reggie was up in arms and Sam was in her sights. McFadden fished in the cooler for a bottle of Zinfandel, her favorite. He opened it, poured two glasses, and offered her one. She waved it away.

"Nothing's been decided," he said. McFadden backed against the granite countertop and sipped, his eyes watching her over the rim of his goblet. She circled the island, as if to trap him. McFadden put down his wine. "Even Wolfman said it's dangerous. He calls it The Wild West."

"If he thinks it's crazy why would you even consider going?"

"I haven't agreed to anything, Reggie. But a mom is pleading for help. She's at her wit's end about what to do. Time's running out. The longer the wait, the worse this situation becomes. Every minute that goes by lessens the chance that these boys will be found alive."

She faced him, hands on hips, brow furrowed. "What can you do that the FBI hasn't been able to do? Even the Mexican government hasn't been able to find these guys. Sam McFadden, are you listening to me?"

"I am," he said, retreating to the leather sofa. He stretched his legs in front of him. Waiting for an opening, McFadden let her simmer. He found one when she took a breath.

Leaning forward, elbows on knees, he gestured as she paced. "Let's at least hear what Tom has to say. He might be just as reluctant to get involved as—"

She turned on him. "As what? As reluctant as you are? I don't hear you saying you won't try to help."

"Wait a minute, Reggie. I didn't commit to anything. Snuffy called me in a panic. He wanted to get hold of Tom. I made the call. It was the least I could do, honey.

Connor's mom was about to head off to Mexico with her life savings to try to get her son back."

"Probably a setup. People are kidnapped all the time down there."

"I know," he admitted. "That's why Snuffy wanted the Wolfman's help. Thought he could talk some sense into Sara before she drove across the border." It was a flimsy defense and McFadden knew it.

Reggie ran out of steam and sank into a wingback chair opposite. Her eyes filling with tears. Avoiding Sam's stare, she pressed the heels of her hands against closed lids. Silence filled the room.

"You'll go. I know it," she whispered.

"I made no promises."

"I know you, Sam McFadden. You'll go." She fell silent.

Ceasefire, he thought. A draw, he hoped.

"I'll take that wine now."

Relieved, he went to the kitchen, safe for the moment.

Chapter 14

San Diego, Present Day

Deep in conversation, Wolf and McFadden nursed two beers in a corner booth while ignoring a raucous scrum of alpha males at the far end of the hotel bar. The group, Special Forces and SEAL vets attending a reunion at the hotel, had driven away more timid guests with their alcohol-fueled storytelling. A lone waitress, a stunning blonde with a Teflon hide, suffered the group's leers while delivering another round of drinks.

Brow furrowed, Wolf finally glanced up, his concentration broken by the catcalls and laughter. "Some guys never grow up, Sam."

McFadden chuckled. "Yeah, right. They're probably too young to have heard of 'Tailhook.' Don't be too hard on them, Wolfman. There but for the grace of God go you."

Wolf corrected his friend. "No, there but for the grace of age and wisdom, go I."

"Age I'll buy, wisdom, maybe. You're just lucky I'm with you," said McFadden. "I'm keeping you focused. Truth is, you'd rather be bellying up to the bar with those guys."

Hoisting his beer, Wolf said, "Not at all. I'm right where I need to be at the moment. Now, you were saying?"

"I was saying, 'How many guys do you think we'd need for this Baja thing?'"

Wolf frowned. "I put a bug in Preacher's ear after I booked my flight to the mainland. Aside from you he was the first one I thought of. Preacher didn't need much convincing to come out here. And having this reunion going on is a blessing. Told him to do some recruiting when he got here, told him to be discreet. He's already looking. Said he'd see us before tonight's banquet and pass along names of the willing."

"Have a number in mind?"

"I do."

"Care to share it?"

Wolf stared at the bar flies. "I thought about it on the flight over."

"And?"

Drawing wet circles on the table, Wolf said, "First reaction was to put together a small army and go in with a big footprint." His eyes caught McFadden's. "But the more I thought about it, two, maybe three guys at most would be better."

"That's your thinking now?"

Wolf nodded. "Right. You, me, Preacher, plus one, maybe two."

"That enough?"

"Wouldn't attract attention."

McFadden said, "There is that."

Warming to his scheme, Wolf said, "Works for me. You'd have to sweet talk Reggie into letting you go, but I have a plan to fix that."

"Love to hear it. She put her foot down hard."

"How's this? Snuffy has a deep-sea fishing boat, a forty-footer. You two could go down the coast in support. Preacher and I would go overland."

"Huh, maybe that could work."

McFadden gazed at the loud group at the far end of the room. " A Baja trip's not an easy sell, Wolfman. Mexico's toxic these days. You know I'd be gone already if it weren't for Reggie."

Wolf waved away the excuse. "Don't give it a second thought, Sam. I didn't expect you to jump into this one. I knew she'd dig in her heels."

"She doesn't wear heels. Used her claws this time. I can show you the scars to prove it." McFadden finished his beer, signaled the besieged server for two more. "Thanks for offering me a pass, Wolfman. But the boat angle might work. I think I could get her to agree to let me to handle logistics offshore. She wouldn't be happy about it if she knew what we're thinking, though. In my book that would include getting you back across the border if you stepped in it."

Wolf's eyebrows rose. "I'd be counting on it. You'd be on the water. We'd run down the coast in tandem. Question is—will she buy it?"

"Put that way, yes. We'd have to get sat phones in case things got touchy. Plus, we could stow a lot of extra stuff in the boat for backup."

"Roger that," said Wolf. "At this point I can't go back to Connor's mom and say, 'Sorry, Sara, couldn't round up enough guys to take this on."

"We'll get the guys we need."

Wolf said, "I'll go it alone if I have to."

"You won't need to. We can make this work."

Wolf paused as the server arrived with a pair of chilled San Miguels. He thanked her, dropped a ten on the tray, and said, "Any of those guys get outa' line and start playing grab ass, just tell 'em your older brother is sitting here keeping an eye on you."

"Hey, I grew up with three older boys. I can handle it."

Wolf saluted her. "Just in case, I got your back." She smiled and retreated, her place taken by a muscular figure in pressed khakis, a dark green golf shirt, and a reunion badge draped around his neck.

"Commander Wolf?"

Glancing at the stranger, McFadden pointed to Wolf with his beer bottle. "He's your man, friend."

Chapter 15

The new arrival, red hair clipped short, a square sunburned face with gray-flecked goatee and intense blue eyes, stood at parade rest, hands clasped behind him. "Sergeant Michael Parvin, sir."

Wolf said, "You with that group of barflies?"

Looking over his shoulder, their visitor said, "Negative, sir."

"Okay. At ease, Mr. Parvin," said Wolf. "Do I know you? More importantly—how do you know me?"

"By reputation, sir. Word gets around. You know, people talk, tell stories."

Wolf smiled. "Can't believe everything you hear."

"I heard enough." Parvin relaxed, but only slightly. "I served with the Twentieth Special Forces Group, sir. My old company and some of the SEALs we worked with in the sandbox are here as part of the weekend reunion."

"Hope you're enjoying yourself. By the way," said Wolf nodding at the bemused McFadden, "this is Major Sam McFadden, one of your own."

Parvin extended a beefy hand. "A pleasure, Major."

McFadden shook hands. "Likewise. Do I hear Georgia in your voice?"

"Alabama, sir."

"Close enough," said McFadden. "Whereabouts?"

A proud smile. "Oneonta."

McFadden blanked but Wolf rescued him, saying, "You look like you played ball, Parvin. Crimson Tide, Auburn?"

"Oneonta. High school."

Wolf made a second guess. "Linebacker?"

Parvin blushed at the attention. "Wide receiver, strong corner. Baseball, too. I moved around, infield. Played till I got hurt."

"A Two sport-man, huh?" Let me guess," said Wolf. "Football. Blown knee?"

Wincing at the telling, Parvin said, "Knee. Was doing basic training at Fort McClellan with the Guard between my junior and senior years, took a cheap shot in the pugil pit finals. Back at school that fall, one tackle too many finished the job."

"Too bad. Lot of members in that club. But you stayed in the Guard, huh?"

"Knee healed. Did four years, including Bosnia. When nine-eleven happened I went full time. Stayed in Special Forces. Got out four years ago."

"Miss it?" said McFadden.

"Can't lie. Miss the camaraderie. Made a lot of friends. Lost some. All good guys."

Wolf said, "Aren't they all? Care to join us for a round?"

"I'll stand, sir. Didn't mean to interrupt your business."

Wolf said, "You don't have to call us 'sir', Parvin. We're retired."

"You hold the rank, gentlemen. And the stories..."

McFadden chuckled. "Remember, don't believe everything you hear."

"Yes, sir."

Wolf shook his head, "We told you..."

The man flashed a nervous smile. "Hard habit once you have it."

"It is indeed," said Wolf. "Okay, well, stand at ease, Parvin. What can we do for you? You have our full attention."

Parvin's face thawed. "Actually, I was thinking maybe I could do something for you gentlemen."

"Really?" Intrigued, Wolf pushed his bottle aside. "Okay, what can you do for us?"

"Heard you were looking for some guys for a possible mission."

McFadden and Wolf exchanged wary glances. Wolf said, "What exactly have you heard...and from whom?"

Shifting his eyes at the ceiling, then his feet, Parvin said, "Word is you need some volunteers for a mission in Mexico. Some sort of recovery deal or rescue. Not sure. The skinny on this was sorta' vague according to Chief Hackett."

McFadden caught Wolf's eyes, said, "Ah, Preacher's been trolling."

"No doubt." Nodding, Wolf lowered his voice, pointed to an empty spot in the booth. "Better take a seat, Mr. Parvin. This might take a while."

Chapter 16

Parvin sat. The three talked. Wolf sketched bare bones of the Baja mission. He bought one round, McFadden another, Parvin a third. Wolf asked background questions.

"Family?"

"Wife and son."

"She know what you're thinking?"

"No sir."

"Not a good idea to disappear on the missus, Parvin."

"She's never limited me in anything."

"Job?"

"I drive for a freight company out of Reno. Eighteen-wheelers. Short runs. Got a great boss. Company has lots of ex-military. Can get a leave if I need it."

"Might have to." Wolf rubbed his chin, said, "We're aiming for a two-week mission, max. In and out. Not looking for trouble. But I have to warn you it's no cakewalk. One or more of us could come back hurt or not at all, understand?"

Wolf got a nod and continued. "We have a kitty to draw on. We pay your expenses out here and back, a bonus if all goes well. If our people get hurt we help with that up to a point."

Parvin said, "That I can live with."

"Okay, I think we've covered most of what you need to know at this stage. Sam will need two references. We're under a time crunch. If we get the green light you get a twenty-four hour notice as early as tomorrow. That enough?"

Stroking his goatee, Parvin said, "Hmm, yes sir. That's workable."

Wolf looked at McFadden, busy with notes. "Sam, anything to add?"

"Okay, if we go you'll need to make two phone calls, Parvin."

"Sir?"

"Your boss and your wife. Hell to pay if you skip the second one."

Parvin grinned. "Time comes, I'll run it by her."

"Good," said McFadden. "We need your room number and a mobile number. We'll be at the reunion this afternoon talking to other folks. Appreciate your coming forward, Parvin. Clock's ticking on this. We'll be in touch."

Parvin said, "Works for me." He slipped from the booth and snapped a salute. Wolf responded likewise and added a request. "Don't get a haircut or shave until you hear from us either way on this. You've got military or law enforcement written all over you. Won't help where we're going."

"Got it."

After Parvin was on his way, Wolf huddled with McFadden. "What's your take on the sergeant?"

"A gift. Dropped right in our laps. I'll check his references."

Wolf smiled across the table. "Good. He's interested. Guy looked like he could put his head through a brick wall if asked."

"Always a good quality to have for something like this," said McFadden. "We need two guys just like him as alternates to make this work."

"Shouldn't be a problem, Sam. Most of these guys would go halfway round the world for a good fight."

The boisterous group had deserted the bar, leaving the server alone with a forest of beer bottles and dirty glasses. She shot a look at Wolf but he waved off another round. He and McFadden rose from the booth and headed for the hotel's ballroom to find Preacher Hackett.

Chapter 17

San Diego, mid-morning

Sam McFadden rapped knuckles on a writing desk in Preacher's crowded hotel room. "Gentlemen, listen up. We need to get this show on the road. Appreciate your coming on such short notice. Wolfman and I didn't set out to crash your reunion this weekend. However, we figured this would be our best chance to collar some like-minded guys for our Baja mission." He cleared his throat. "The timing is perfect from our point of view since you are all proven spec ops guys. Each of you has the skill set needed. You were also picked because you're in good shape. We won't have to call anyone's cardiologist for a waiver." Soft laughter.

McFadden pointed to the close-cropped, poker-faced former SEAL on his left. "You already know Chief Dennis 'Preacher' Hackett. He shanghaied everyone in this room." More laughter.

Wolf jumped to his feet. "Just to let you know, Preacher and I served in the Philippines together. Good man in a fight. Loves to mix it up with the bad guys. A Bible-quoting Midwesterner. A little strange for a sailor but don't be fooled, saltwater runs in his veins."

A grinning Preacher acknowledged the introduction with a wave and stood. Nodding at a relaxed figure at his elbow, he gestured. "Mike Parvin. Twentieth Special Forces. Hails from Alabama. Good rep with peers. Dependable. I've checked."

A faint smile from Parvin and Wolf kept going, moving to the side of the table and placing a hand on the shoulder of a tall, goateed black man. "Maverick Gideon, Third Battalion, Fifth marines. Fallujah. And yes, that's his real name, not a *nom de guerre*. Skilled at unraveling a turban at six hundred meters...of course, using a 7.62 round will likely ruin anyone who's wearing the thing."

The group laughed, clapping to Gideon's embarrassment. Preacher yielded to McFadden, who said, "That's our team. You're it, gentlemen." He picked up a TV remote and aimed it at a flat screen on the wall to his left. "Preacher gave each of you a heads up on what we're trying to do. We're volunteers. We owe you for expressing enough interest to stay on after the reunion."

Parvin and Gideon stirred, uncomfortable with McFadden's praise.

"In case you missed it, I'm going to show you the latest news reports we have on the missing young men in the Baja. This will give you a general run down of what the public knows. After the clip, Wolfman will share what else we know as of today. Our solid intel is courtesy of anonymous connections with local law enforcement."

McFadden stabbed a finger at the polished tabletop. "Remember, everything we talk about, everything we plan, and everything we end up doing is strictly off the books. We're on our own, gentlemen."

"Wouldn't be the first time," growled Gideon, prompting laughter.

McFadden shrugged. "True. We've all been there. It is what it is, guys. We won't be going in completely blind, though. Our sources have been good enough to share whatever they have picked up so far."

McFadden played three news reports from different networks. When the screen went dark, he said, "If you're agreeable, we'll chow down together for lunch on our dime. We'll get to know each other a little better. As of this morning your rooms are comped as well. Wolfman and I have an off the books fund we tap from time to time. That's all you need to know about how we're paying for this. After lunch he and I will lay out the op plan for how we see this thing going down. Work for you?" His suggestion was a formality. He had expected a chorus of agreement and got it.

Chapter 18

At noon the five veterans ate together then commandeered a horseshoe-shaped booth in the hotel's bar and relaxed by trading stories. That afternoon, they carpooled to Sam McFadden's indoor range, where they loosened up with M4s and various handguns. Following that, they gathered in one of the classrooms where a table was covered in a 1:50,000 color map of the Baja peninsula.

"We're going as two teams initially," explained Wolf. "Preacher, Parvin, and I cross the border tomorrow at zero nine hundred. We'll travel in a van as surfers, carrying everything we need. Shouldn't be a problem going in."

"'Cept I don't surf," objected Preacher.

"Me neither," said Parvin. "Not about to learn either."

"Well, Sam and I do surf," said Wolf. "You don't have to. We just have to look the part to fit in. Baja's known for its surf. For Californians it's kinda like making the *hajj*."

McFadden frowned. "Bad analogy, Wolfman. Try again."

"Point taken, Mister Politically Correct." The remark prompted more laughter. "Okay, call it a rite of passage. That's what these college guys were doing when they disappeared. We're following in their footsteps."

Preacher said, "Didn't the FBI already do that?"

"Not exactly," said Wolf. "On our watch we're not holding hands with the *federales* or any of their state or local police. Same for their military. We have our own itinerary." Hovering over the map, he traced a route from San Diego to the port city of Ensenada. "We have phone records for all four of the missing. We also have a general idea of where they were going. And we have law enforcement notes about confirmed sightings picked up during the earlier investigation."

"We follow the money," said McFadden. "Credit cards, debit cards, gas stops, restaurants, hostels, and surf camps."

"What about you guys?" said Parvin, eyeballing McFadden and Gideon. "You taking another van at a different time?"

"Negative." McFadden tapped the map with a red marker. "Snuffy Larson, a civilian friend of ours, will show later today with a fishing yacht." He traced the coastline below San Diego. "Gideon will be with the boat's skipper and me. We'll meet Wolfman's team in Ensenada at the port's marina. By the time his van crosses the border we should be pulling into Checkpoint One—the harbor."

Squinting at the chart, he circled the coastal resort town. "From all appearances, we're just sport fishermen on a trip of our own."

"Maybe we can switch," said Parvin. "Fishing's second nature to me."

Wolf raised both hands. "Stow the fishing talk, gentlemen, we've already figured this out. This works for us." He put his finger on the map and followed the peninsula's west coast. "My crew will make the same stops these missing boys did once we leave Ensenada."

McFadden smoothed the map and pointed to Ensenada. "Next stop was here. That's where we're headed."

"Tell us again, why Ensenada?" said Preacher.

"Because that's a crucial stop for the group. They picked up some dirt bikes and a trailer there. That may have attracted more attention than they wanted."

Gideon pulled a chair close to the table and sat. "What did the feds say about that, Sam?"

"Just a theory they floated. Young, rich-looking Americans, all that nice gear. Bikes, trailer, boards, and vehicles. Not exactly low-key."

Silence, the caravan's image filling everyone's mind.

McFadden broke the quiet. "After Ensenada we'll head south, hit all the surf spots, talk to people, show pictures, stay where they did when possible, and visit restaurants and cafes where they likely ate."

"Bring plenty of gut medicine," groused Parvin.

Preacher elbowed the Alabaman. "Hey, the food's great, *gringo*."

"I don't have an iron stomach."

"You'll be okay, *amigo*. Trust me."

"You I trust," said Parvin. "It's the no-name chefs I don't trust."

"Mikey, have you ever actually been to Mexico?" said Preacher.

"Once. In Juarez. On government business. Didn't stay long."

"See, you missed the whole experience."

Parvin said, "Enough to satisfy me for a lifetime, thank you."

McFadden put an end to the chatter. "It's set. My team moves down the coast on the water. Between the two of us poking around we should pick up clues."

"A bit loosey-goosey for me," said Gideon. "Too many of us asking the same questions might arouse suspicion."

"You're right," said McFadden. "Too many *gringos* wandering about might bring us attention we don't need. So be low key, discreet."

Gideon leaned over the map. "Sam, you said the FBI's been down this rabbit trail, right?"

"Correct. I have a printout of all their stops. Why do you ask?"

Gideon scratched his whiskered chin. "Just wondering. What's the last reported phone call or credit card use for these guys?"

Wolf said, "You're getting ahead of the process, Marine."

McFadden waved away the objection. "It's okay. In that part of the Baja phone reception is lousy to non-existent until you reach Cabo San Lucas. They were supposed to do some R&R at one of the resorts, then start back, do some surfing, return the bikes, and after that, home."

The group fell silent again, waiting for McFadden to continue.

Gideon finally said, "So what happened? How far north did they get on the return?"

"It's assumed they made it to Cabo because their credit cards showed up. The feds speculate they were there, but after that the trail gets cold."

Preacher looked worried. "Well, what's the last known stop on the way to Cabo San Lucas?"

McFadden flipped through a set of index cards and planted a finger north of Cabo. "A Pemex station in this town—Los Colinas."

"Why not start there," said Gideon. "Save time."

"At that point in their travels we don't know for sure who was using the credit cards."

"But the FBI checked, right?" said Preacher. "Did an on-site visit?"

"That's a bit fuzzy. Mexican authorities claimed the boys stopped there, but it's unclear if that was coming or going."

"What's the timeline, Sam?" said Wolf.

McFadden checked the card against a calendar's spreadsheet. "Eight days from when they were supposed to be in Cabo."

Wolf said, "That could be coming or going, right?"

"Yeah, I suppose."

Gideon said, "Then what's the next stop along the way after their refueling? Without knowing that they actually stayed in Cabo we're kinda in the dark."

"End of the trail," said a grim McFadden. "No contact after that. Your guess is as good as mine whether they made it to Cabo. I'm going on the assumption they did. That's why we have to follow up on the card use."

Studying the map again, Wolf said, "They could have stopped anywhere along the coast to do some camping, surfing. We'll have to check out those spots as a precaution."

"I don't like it," murmured Preacher. "Too much time's gone by."

McFadden didn't disagree. "It's all we have at this point, guys."

Chapter 19

The mood in the conference room was subdued. McFadden searched for something to say but had nothing. To his relief, Parvin regained the focus. He crossed his arms, studying the Baja chart. "How long will it take us to trace their route down and back?"

Wolf said, "Straight through would be twenty hours."

"San Diego to Cabo?"

"Correct. One way. Little over one thousand miles."

"ETA by boat?" said Parvin.

Rapping knuckles on the map, McFadden said, "Seven hundred fifty-miles. Three days if weather holds."

Parvin asked, "And San Diego to Ensenada by van?"

Wolf said, "Two hours. Good road. Eighty-four miles. Less by sea."

"Better get moving then," said Gideon, "We're burning daylight."

"My crew leaves the harbor tomorrow at first light," said McFadden. "Snuffy's laying in supplies and fuel right now."

Wolf eyed Preacher. "I'll pick up you and Parvin tomorrow morning at zero nine hundred hours. I'll have all our food and gear and the boards packed tonight and ready to roll."

Preacher counted on his fingers. "Fuel?"

"Topped off, plus two five gallon cans, and siphon hoses."

"Spares? The Baja eats tires, you know."

"Two spares, patch kits, and inflator cans."

"First aid?"

"Enough kit to do minor surgery."

"Jumper cables?"

"Yep. Also spare hoses, belts, shovels and tools. Anything else?"

Preacher rubbed his jaw. "Duct tape?"

"I thought you'd never ask. Beaucoup rolls."

"Ah, a man after my own heart."

Parvin laughed. "Leave any room for us?"

"Barely," said Wolf. "You guys just worry about your own gear. If I haven't packed it, trust me, we don't need it."

McFadden and Gideon enjoyed the show, glad for the brief comic relief the banter between Wolf and Preacher provided.

Wolf shot a stern look at his team. "Just make sure you and Parvin are ready to depart at zero nine hundred. That gives Sam and his boat a head start."

"We'll be ready," said Preacher. "I like daylight. Heard bad tales about crossing in the wee hours. No use tripping wires before we have to."

McFadden rolled up the map. "We'll be in touch down and back, people. Satellite phones and cells. We'll support you all along the coast."

Returning to his favorite subject, Parvin brightened. "Think maybe we could switch off every so often? You know, get out on the water, and do a little fishing. For appearances sake, of course."

McFadden softened. "We could arrange that, I suppose."

Wolf held up his hands, a quizzical look on his face. "All this noise and not one of you has asked the one question Sam and I thought you would."

Gideon was puzzled. "Which is?"

Wolf said, "Weapons."

Parvin flashed a Bowie knife aloft. "I'm good."

Gideon scoffed, "Gonna bring a knife to a gun fight, huh?"

Parvin sheathed his blade. Wolf said, "We can carry spec op knives, but keep them out of sight, of course." Nodding at Parvin's Bowie knife, he said, "Mike can bring his sword along if he sits on it."

Gideon said, "Well, we sure as hell can't carry guns across the border. Remember what happened to that Marine with guns in his trunk couple of years ago?"

Wolf nodded. "Took a wrong turn, sat in jail a good while."

"Not going there," said Parvin. "No way."

"Not to worry, people," said McFadden. "We're bringing some hardware with us on the boat. And we'll have a secret weapon with us once we dock in Ensenada."

"Make and caliber," said Gideon, "and how many?"

"About five-nine, one hundred-sixty pounds," said McFadden. Enjoying the puzzled looks, he said, "Major Luis Lopez, Mexican Marines. Retired."

"A friend, I take it," said Gideon.

"He is."

"Incorruptible, I hope," said Preacher.

"Good as gold," said McFadden. "He knows what we want to do and he's agreed to help. To quote one of Preacher's favorite verses—'He'll smooth what's rough and straighten what's crooked.'"

"Then he's going to be busy," said Gideon. "I'm impressed."

"You should be. All of you will like this guy. Luis is the real deal. An original badass. We've worked together before. On the government's clock and doing something much different than what we're up to. But take it from me, this guy has his act together."

Gideon frowned. "What good will he do us on the boat?"

"He's only meeting us at the marina. Once we marry up he'll ride shotgun with Wolfman's crew. He'll handle any translation problems. That alone should make our job easier."

"Sure would be nice to fish at some point," said Parvin.

McFadden put an arm around the Alabaman's shoulders. "Mikey, don't worry. If there's a fish out there somewhere with your name on it we'll make sure you get a crack at it. Happy?"

"Hell yes. I'm ready to move."

"Get some quality rack time first. See you in Ensenada, gentlemen."

Chapter 20

To hear Wolf tell it, the border crossing next day was a piece of cake. Timing was everything, he said later. At the entry plaza lined with gates a pickup truck wearing a rusting camper top cut them off. For his move, the impatient driver was ordered aside to an inspection lane. Wolf and crew stopped, filled out their paperwork, and rolled past the checkpoint untouched, drawing only bored looks from customs officers who waved them through. Once across the border, Wolf took the Tijuana-Ensenada ramp to pick up the *cuota*—the toll road —good highway that would keep them close to the sea. Tijuana's ugly sprawl, held in place under a hovering cloud of polluted sky, dropped behind, replaced by a corridor of coastal development hugging both sides of the road.

"Plenty of good breaks along here," said Wolf, darting glances at the lines of shorebreak. "Our MIAs made two stops we know of that first day." He pointed to breaking waves. "That spot's called Baja Malibu. Connor phoned his mom from there to check in with her. Told her he stayed with the vehicles while the others went out. Smart move if you want your stuff to be there when you get back."

Preacher said, "We're not gonna make every stop they did are we?"

"Nope. Just orienting you. They were still on the radar for this first part of their trip."

The D-1 toll road unspooled past building blocks of apartments, high-rises, cafés, tourist traps, and repair shops hugging the shoulders. At times a serpentine line of bright yellow concrete divided north-south lanes through built-up areas. Relaxing, Wolf locked on cruise control just under the speed limit and shot longing looks at empty waves.

Parvin said, "Don't lie. You'd like to be out there wouldn't you?"

"There was a time," confessed Wolf. "Not today. Not now."

The toll road cut deep through a series of chiseled rocky escarpments crowned with houses. Skirting the ocean, Wolf and his team wound past parched brown hills where homes spilled down to the roadway. The highway unspooled to a city of walled seaside estates and a forest of hi-rise apartment buildings and hotels overlooking breaking surf—Rosarita.

"Lot of weekenders visit on holiday," Wolf said. "Good seafood."

Parvin turned to Wolf. "Safe?"

"Hmm, iffy. Depends on who you talk to. Lot of cartel violence in the early to middle 2000s. Still ugly stuff happening now and then. In my youth it used to be a big party town for *gringos* who avoided Tijuana. Not that far from the border but I'd stay away as a rule."

"I didn't expect it to look so modern," marveled Parvin.

"You were expecting strings of burros and rug sellers?" said Wolf.

"Nah, but this place is bustling. And the traffic..."

"Could be uglier parts of San Diego," said Preacher. "And the desert look kinda reminds me of Tucson. Gotta love the beach, though."

Wolf nodded, smiling at some memory. "The beach is the draw."

South of town Wolf pointed out a painted statue of Christ crowning a dusty hill dotted with mansions on the city's outskirts. He took his eyes off the road for a quick look. "The Sacred Heart of Jesus. Seventy-five feet tall."

"*Cristo del Sagrado Corazón*," sniffed Preacher. "Very Mexican. Way too gaudy for me. Like their churches."

"Yeah," said Wolf, "not exactly Rio's Christ of the Andes is it?"

Funneled to the first tollbooth, Wolf slowed, paid in pesos and kept going. Rejoining southbound traffic, he passed two tanker trucks laboring uphill, drifted to the right lane, and checked his watch. "Making good time. Should be in Ensenada by eleven thirty hours. Perfect."

He spoke without looking at his passengers. "Sam said our boys also got in the water at K-38. It's coming up. They spent about an hour-plus there."

"What's K-38?" said Parvin, clueless, his eyes on the turquoise sea.

"Kilometers in distance from the border," Wolf explained. "Surf spot about a third of the way to Ensenada. Sam's source told him one of the kids ended up with a palm full of sea urchin spines. Nasty things. Got himself doctored at a friend's condo just down the road. Feds confirmed it after talking to Connole's parents and the friend."

They drove in silence for thirty minutes. Parvin shot a glance Wolf's way. "Were you sweating the border crossing?"

"Nothing to it. Why do you ask?"

Parvin twisted in the passenger seat to eyeball Preacher. "Did you tell him?"

Wolf took his eyes off the road to glance at both men in turn. "Tell me what? You two up to no good? Hey, no surprises, guys. Give it up."

Preacher leaned forward, elbows on the backs of both front seats. "Nothing. Just some hardware."

"Hardware? What the hell you talking about, Preacher."

"Doesn't matter. Nothing to worry about. We're over the line now."

Wolf studied Preacher's widening grin in the rear view mirror. "I don't like the way you're smiling. You're both like cats with feathers on their faces. What did you do? Tell me or so help me I'll pull over and brace both of you on the side of the road."

Parvin chuckled. "Wouldn't pay to do that, sir. What's done is done. Let's just say Preacher and me have a little surprise in store."

"That's right," said Preacher. "After all, you did tell us to pack our own gear."

Passing a white jeep and a bus, Wolf's brow furrowed in a worried V. "Sam know what you're up to? He in on this?"

"Negative," said Preacher. "This is on us. We'll lay it out for you once we reach the boat. All in good time. Trust me."

"So help me, Preacher. You better not be blowing smoke up my ass. I hope you realize we're off the reservation here. I sure as hell don't need the agitation."

Preacher patted Wolf's shoulder. "You'll thank us for this later. Didn't mean to get you all worked up. Keep your eyes on the road. Let us worry about the rest."

Twenty minutes out of Ensenada and Wolf was steaming. Preacher sat back, smiling at his fellow conspirator in the passenger seat. Wolf caught Preacher's truant's grin in the van's mirror. Avoiding Wolf's stare, a beaming Parvin looked right, focusing on the waves. Hunched over the wheel, Wolf couldn't get to the city's marina fast enough.

Chapter 21

Ensenada

They went through a second toll and fought for position in the increasing traffic approaching the harbor city. In the distance, a bloated white leviathan nestled against the harbor's Cruiseport Village quay. Towering above its dockside mooring, the liner dwarfed a sea of ants heading for the shops and bars downtown. Small boats crisscrossed the harbor like water bugs avoiding a corpse. Slowing at the town's limits, Wolf swore under his breath at the stop-and-start dance through the carnival that was downtown Ensenada. By the time he hit another light the testy exchange with Preacher and Parvin was forgotten. Foot traffic clogged sidewalks and intersections with gawking tourists, a gaudy herd of snails shuffling en masse.

"The curse of a cruise ship in port," sighed Preacher. "Actually, that might be a good thing. Gives us cover of sorts."

Eyeing the endless stream, Wolf inched forward, nervous fingers drumming on the wheel. "Yeah, we'll fit right in. Based on how they're dressed, five dollars says they're all *gringos*."

"That's a sucker bet," said Preacher stretching across the middle seat. He stared as a wall of overweight fellow

Americans in matching tropical shirts and wraps flowed past, armed with cellphones and selfie sticks. "We could be in the middle of Epcot's Mexican plaza for all I know," he groused. "Get a life, people."

Wolf snorted. "How about I let you out to proselytize?"

Preacher shook his head. "I'll pass. By the time I cleared a corner to speak from they'd all be margarita-deaf and out of money."

Wolf told Parvin to call McFadden for directions to the boat. Snuffy answered. "Sam's already out working the streets with Major Lopez," he said. "Me and Gideon are staying with the boat. I'll get you here."

Relaying Snuffy's words, Parvin coaxed Wolf to a side canyon of small shops and fenced boatyards on the harbor's northeast corner. A forest of masts and hulls belonging to beached sailboats and trawlers on blocks poked above a walled-off repair compound. Wolf threaded the narrow street, found an open spot on a concrete pier, and parked at the rear of a hulking two-story building.

Wolf took the phone from Parvin and got out. "Snuffy, we're here. Got Sergio's Sport Fishing to port, boat ramp and a bunch of slips to starboard. Where are you? What's your status?"

"I got you, Wolfman. We're at the end of the dock, tied up astern of a dark green trawler. You parked behind the movie theater but not to worry. Should be a little guy in a shack the size of a phone booth. Name's Juan, no kidding. Give him five bucks US and tell him you're with us. That way your van won't be going anywhere without you."

Wolf scanned the harbor, spotted Snuffy waving at the end of the pier. "Got you. We'll stow the boards inside and cover everything with canvas. Once we get the van squared away and locked down we'll come your way."

Chapter 22

"Good to see you," said Snuffy. "Trip went well?"

"No problems," said Wolf. He followed Snuffy topside to *South Wind*'s flying bridge. They sat in captain's chairs, under a canvas top rippling in the breeze, the locked van in view. Preacher and Parvin, content to be out of the vehicle, joined Gideon in the boat's main cabin for a tour.

An hour later, McFadden and Major Luis Lopez showed, strolling the length of the dock. The two made an odd pair— McFadden, six-foot, an athlete's easy gait, unruly dark hair salted with gray, and Lopez, a compact muscled Mexican, whose broad face and high cheekbones hinted at Indian blood. Matching the taller McFadden's stride, the retired Mexican marine showed his military bearing. Snuffy welcomed them back, and the two climbed aboard and went to the main cabin.

Breaking into a huge grin, Wolf engulfed the stocky Lopez in a bear hug. "Hey, *amigo*," he said, "the last time I saw you, we were battling our way out of a bar in Juarez."

"Yes, I had to carry you on my back if I remember correctly, eh?"

Amid the laughter, Lopez offered his hand to each man as Wolf recited short bios for him. Shoehorned around the U-shaped table, the Americans waited for Lopez to speak.

The Mexican didn't waste words. "*Caballeros*, from what I know about you, and what you're trying to do, I applaud you for attempting this. I myself have been making this kind of fight for a long time. It is a good fight. The right thing to do."

Wolf threw an arm around his friend. "I can't think of a better addition to our team, Luis. With your help, how can we fail?"

"We can't afford to," said McFadden. "But before we get carried away with old home week, Wolfman, the major and I need to brief you guys on what we learned in your absence."

Wolf groused. "Can't it wait, Sam? Luis and I have a lot of catching up to do."

"This won't take long," scolded McFadden. "Listen up, everyone." He motioned to Lopez. "Major, tell them what we turned up today."

"Of course. We spent the better part of the day finding this Sebastian Saguaro, the man who rented motorcycles to your missing students."

Lopez took his listeners through the search he and McFadden had made. Unnerved by two strangers prowling his motorcycle shop, Saguaro had initially been reluctant to talk. Lopez bullied the mechanic into producing copies of the rental agreement and color copies of the missing bikes, serial numbers included. The information had been missing from notes furnished to Wolf and McFadden by their police contact in the States.

"According to Sebastian," added McFadden, "he admits stepping out when the feds and the *federales* came looking. He was a bit surprised to find us on his shop's doorstep today."

"Why the hell would he refuse to cooperate earlier?" said Wolf.

Lopez shrugged. "It's as you say, complicated. He did not actually lie. He just made himself unavailable until the authorities went away."

McFadden said, "When we promised to try and recover the bikes, he got real interested." He waved copies of the rental papers and the pictures of the bike and trailer. "Sebastian's small time. Losing the machines put a huge dent in his business."

Wolf tapped the table. "How do you know this guy didn't sell out Connor and his friends?"

"We don't," said McFadden. "Down here it wouldn't surprise me."

"Is possible," said Lopez. "I know this sometimes happens."

Parvin said, "But he wants the bikes back, right?"

"Affirmative. I doubt we'll see them again but it was worth getting this guy to cooperate. It confirms the Ensenada connection before they went south. We'll go with what we learned. Tomorrow we pick up the trail."

Snuffy dug into a cooler and produced chilled bottles of beer. Wolf offered a toast to the Mexican. "I know you as a man of honor, Luis. I know you have suffered grievous loss in your life, in your career. Yet you have fought the good fight. I salute you."

A chorus of "Hear, hear," rang out, drawing a pleased smile from Lopez. He offered a salute of his own. Lifting his bottle aloft, he said, "*Con la ayuda de Dios, vamos a tener un final exitoso. Que los hombres malos cumplan con un fin justo!*"

Parvin and Gideon shot puzzled looks at each other but joined with Lopez and the others as they tapped each other's bottles.

"What did the major say, Sam?" whispered Parvin in the midst of a cacophony of voices led by Wolf and Lopez.

McFadden leaned close to the Alabaman. "Something about God blessing what we're doing and to hell with evildoers. Not exact, but it's close enough for our purposes."

"I'll drink to that," said Parvin.

"Same for me," added Gideon.

The tall tales began, sprinkled with Spanish, occasional profanity, raucous laughter, and repetitive toasts to every branch of the service mentioned with each telling. A forest of beer bottles grew on the galley table as two hours passed. At one point, Lopez and Wolf, arm-in-arm, led the teams to a

dockside cafe for a late dinner. Afterwards, they retraced
their steps to the moored *South Wind*, where McFadden
finally restored the evening's sanity by reminding everyone
of tomorrow's mission. The men sprawled throughout the
boat on every horizontal space.

Wolf and Lopez staked claims on two forward berths with
their bedrolls and went topside in the cool air to share stories
about cross-border missions. They chatted for another hour
before going below to join the snoring chorus.

Chapter 23

In the pre-dawn darkness, Snuffy checked *South Wind's*
mooring lines, started the coffee, and bagged the previous
night's bottles. He carried the clinking cargo to the
nearest marina collection bin, and then strolled to the
local *panaderia*. Returning ten minutes later with a baker's
dozen of *conchas*, sugary rolls, he made enough noise in the
galley to wake the dead. Eager to shove off, he began
mopping morning dew from the deck. Wolf rose, poured
two mugs of fresh coffee, and carried one topside to
Snuffy. They sat on the fantail, watching the sky beyond
the hills cycle through dawn's pinks and golds.

Wolf said, "Talk to Connor's mom yesterday?"

"I did. She must sleep by the phone. Can't blame her."

Nodding, Wolf sipped his coffee. Gideon and Preacher
came on deck in sweats and T-shirts, despite the chill.
Mumbling their hellos, the two climbed to the pier. When
they reached shore, both broke into a jog down the alley,
vanishing at the mouth where the main street flowed with
early bird traffic.

Wolf snorted. "Crazy *gringos*. Who else runs in the
morning? There goes their anonymity."

Snuffy tossed the dregs of his coffee overboard and climbed the ladder to the flying bridge, where he busied himself wiping the seats and controls. The smell of more coffee and fresh rolls drifted from the galley. Nibbling a roll, McFadden showed, licking his lips. "Gotta get this show on the road, Wolfman. Where's your team?"

"Preacher and Gideon. Morning run," said Wolf, motioning to town with his mug. "Parvin and the major up?"

McFadden bit into his roll and laughed. "Parvin's AWOL. Slept in the van. Said something about keeping an eye on your gear. Frankly, I think it was your snoring that drove him out. Roust him, Wolfman. I'll wake Luis."

"Do that. He's riding with me today. And for the record, it was your snoring, not mine."

Mug in hand, Wolf strolled down the pier to the parked van and rapped knuckles on the passenger's window. A bleary-eyed Parvin shot up, blinking at the hour. He stumbled from the van, rubbing his eyes. "Zero six fifteen," he said, squinting at his wristwatch. "I musta overslept."

"Coffee's on, rolls on the table in the galley."

"No need to shave, right?"

"Correct. You're looking downright scruffy. Perfect."

His arms a slow-motion windmill, Parvin trotted across the parking lot to the pier, Wolf behind him. On deck, Lopez was shadow boxing. McFadden had traded his coffee for pull-ups in the passageway leading below deck. Snuffy was burrowing in the engine hatch among his beloved twin diesels. Gideon and Preacher showed, helped themselves to breakfast rolls, and finished the coffee. McFadden gave a quick briefing over the unfurled Baja map, took questions, and then sent Lopez and Wolf ashore with their team.

The comforting rumble of *South Wind*'s engines signaled the second day's start. Amid a blue cloud of diesel exhaust, Gideon cast loose the lines and leaped aboard. Piloting his boat from the flying bridge, Snuffy eased from the dock, slipping past sleeping trawlers and moored day-trippers. Few boats were about the harbor at this hour save fishing charters. *South Wind* fit right in. From the stern, McFadden raised a mug to a watching Wolf and Lopez, and then went below to stow his gear.

Chapter 24

Merging into one lane, traffic flowed, then slowed, and then crawled. Lopez behind the wheel, Wolf, in the front passenger's seat, both suddenly alert.

"What's happening?" said Preacher, next to Parvin in the middle seat. "Why the slowdown?"

"Army checkpoint," said Lopez. "They move around. Mostly stopping northbound traffic. This close to Ensenada is unusual."

"Like LA rush hour," griped Preacher.

Wolf peered through the windshield. "Negative on the rush hour. Looks like there's been an accident up ahead, a fender bender. Great. Traffic's backing up and the army is checking people."

Parvin sat up, gripping the Wolf's seatback. "Can't we pull over and grab a spot at one of these *cantinas* until they're done looking?"

"If you haven't noticed, Mikey, we're pretty much in the middle of nowhere. There ain't any cantinas, just a bunch of stalls, gawkers, and fruit stands. Not much cover for mingling."

Over his shoulder, Wolf said, "Our bad luck. They're checking southbound traffic as well. Now might be a good time to tell me what you and Preacher are hiding. Would it be too much to ask what it is I'm probably going to jail for."

"No problem," said Preacher. "We'll handle things if it comes to that. Besides, this way you can plead plausible deniability if we're caught."

Wolf fumed. "Yeah, like that's going to work in Mexico."

The line of cars and trucks inched forward, adding to the congestion. Horns blared. Voices rose. Tempers flared. All to no avail. The bottleneck thickened. Seeing an opportunity, a flock of street vendors selling cold drinks, sweets and roasted corn descended to work their way down the column of trapped vehicles. Six of them weaved overloaded carts along the crowded shoulder, hawking their wares in the chaos. Carrying trays piled high, more vendors came down the line on foot, their faces framed in every open window they passed.

Seizing the moment, Lopez glanced at Wolf. "Get out," he said. "I pick you up past the checkpoint."

"Not a good idea," said Wolf.

"Trust me," said Lopez. "Hurry before the line moves. All of you go."

Wolf slipped from his seat, his feet hitting the ground beside the slow-moving van. Parvin followed. Preacher shut the door behind them and wiggled into Wolf's vacant seat. "Hope you know what you're doing, Major."

"And I hope you know what you're doing," said Lopez. "You should have left with the others. Whatever you and Parvin have brought with you could be big trouble."

"Is that what's worrying you? Relax. I promised the Wolfman it wouldn't be a problem."

"Does he believe you?"

Preacher laughed. "Not a chance. He's a slow learner."

Lopez shook his head. "You are taking a dangerous chance."

"Trust me."

"So you say."

In the rear view mirror, Lopez spotted Wolf and Parvin strolling among the vendors, easily outpacing the line of cars.

Wolf bought two ears of roasted corn and began nibbling one. Parvin haggled over a bottle of water, ended up with that and two tacos wrapped in newspaper.

Army troops just ahead were giving the most cursory of looks into yawning trunks, and waving every third car on its way.

Voicing empathy for his thankless task, Lopez greeted the approaching private with a broad smile. His tactic failed. Noticing Preacher's white face, the soldier slapped the van's side. They were pulled out of line for inspection just short of the checkpoint. Temporarily marooned just beyond the highway circus, Wolf and Parvin were helpless witnesses to the unfolding drama.

Chapter 25

At the soldier's insistence, Lopez parked and got out. Preacher did the same. Both men gathered at the rear of the vehicle. Ordered to open the van's rear doors, Lopez shot a wary glance at Preacher, who was doing his best to appear unruffled.

A captain, curious, sent a loaded truck on its way and wandered over to investigate the van's contents along with the soldier. The officer watched his man root through the cargo section.

Jabbering excitedly, the private lifted two odd-shaped camouflage-patterned bags from beneath a jumbled pile of sleeping bags, camping gear, clothing and coolers. "*Capitán Huerta, qué es esto?*"

From the roadside, Parvin caught the discovery and took a step toward the van. Wolf caught his arm and pulled him back.

"Not yet. Let's see where this goes."

Turning the larger of the two bags in his hands, the captain frowned, and then turned on Lopez. *"De quién es esta bolsa?"*

Preacher caught the question. *"La mía, Capitán."*

Unsure he had been understood, Preacher tried English while gesturing to himself. "Mine, Captain. Both belong to me."

About to intervene, Lopez was waved aside by the officer, who broke into English. "So, yours, eh? What is inside?"

Preacher reached for the oval bag "May I?"

The captain surrendered it and snapped his fingers, demanding the second one as well, all without shifting his gaze from Preacher. Keeping one eye on the nervous private to his left, Preacher unzipped the bag. He held a compound bow with its attached quiver of arrows. He offered it to the officer.

Preacher tugged a picture from his shirt pocket, one of him kneeling beside a downed boar. The photo had been taken four years ago during an Arkansas trip. "We are hunting wild boar—*la caza del jabalí.*"

The captain ran his hands along the bow, saying, *"Ah, jabalí."*

"Sí, sí, jabalí."

Returning the bow and shafts to Preacher, he said, "And this other bag, another bow?"

Shaking his head, Preacher reached for the second bag, a zippered T-shape. "May I?" he said again.

"Of course. Open the bag."

Two more soldiers left their traffic duties and drifted to the show.

Ripping the zipper the length of the bag, Preacher withdrew Parvin's crossbow and handed it to the officer, prompting murmurs of admiration from the knot of soldiers.

"Jabalí?"

"Wild boar, yes," said Preacher. "A crossbow." He caught the major's eye. "How do you call it?"

"*Ballesta*," said the grinning soldier. Tucking the camouflaged fiberglass stock into his shoulder and squinting through the telescopic sight, he sighted over the crossbow's limbs. "Ah, beautiful."

Gambling on the officer's fascination with Parvin's weapon, Preacher showed him how the safety worked, the trigger's release, and the cocking of the bowstring, all the while hoping the demonstration would be enough to back his claim as a boar hunter en route.

Traffic came to his rescue. A chorus of horns erupted, shattering the show. Rattling off commands, the captain scattered his men. One last longing look at the weapon and he returned it to Preacher.

"*Buena caza*," he said with obvious envy.

Turning on his heel, he went about untangling the mess his traffic stop had become for more than one hundred cars and trucks and their smoldering drivers.

Lopez helped Preacher bag the hunting weapons. "Let's move before the man changes his mind and decides he wants what you have."

"Roger that."

Preacher stowed the zippered bags back in the van and locked the rear doors. Back behind the wheel, Lopez bulled his way into a line of freed cars angling into flowing traffic. Once past the last parked army Humvee, he slowed, allowing the jogging Wolf and Parvin to leap aboard before accelerating.

"Close call," Wolf said, taking a seat.

"Not even a first or second look," said Preacher. "Easy."

"Huh, so that was the big secret you and Parvin were carrying across the border? This whole thing coulda gone either way, you know."

Lopez said over his shoulder, "Admit it. He played it perfect, *amigo*."

"Luck of the Irish," grumbled Wolf, arms crossed.

"I'm not Irish," said Preacher, "and I don't believe in luck."

"Okay, have it your way," said Wolf. "Divine Providence then."

"You must be living right," said Parvin, brushing taco scraps from his shirt. "We watched you the entire time. You're one cool customer. Had me worried you were gonna give away my crossbow, though."

Grateful to be moving again, Preacher—eyes on the road—propped his arm in the open window. "Wasn't sure myself at first," he said. "That captain about wet himself when he held that baby."

Wolf said, "He practically drooled over it."

Mopping his brow, Parvin slumped back against his seat. "I know the feeling. That's one fine piece of work. Cost me an arm and a leg. Man, you had me holding my breath, Preacher."

Wolf said, "Whadaya know, you ran into an honest man. Thought for sure it was *la mordida* time."

His jaw thrust out in triumph, Preacher grinned. "Piece of cake."

Wolf slouched in his seat, his eyes boring into Preacher. "You keep saying that. Anyone ever tell you that you're insufferable at times like this?"

"You have. But it's part of my job description. You should thank me for my confidence. And we all owe the major a big thank you for thinking on his feet and dumping you guys upstream."

"Yeah, thanks, Luis," said Wolf. "Forgive me for doubting you."

"You are not the first one. I'm used to it by now."

"Well, consider me a believer from this point on."

Chapter 26

The sun had an hour of life left. Ankle high waves lapped at the cove's stony beach covered with rocks the size of small loaves. A handful of overturned skiffs were drying on driftwood chocks, keels to the sky. Eight worn-out fishing boats bobbed at anchor in the sheltered bay, their pilothouses dark like sightless eyes.

Only the *South Wind*'s salon glowed with light. McFadden and crew had arrived three hours ago, anchoring in the cove to give moral support to the land search. Wolf and the others called on the satellite phone to say they were fifteen minutes out. While waiting, Snuffy threw on a hooded sweatshirt, climbed topside, and called on the satellite phone to report their progress to Connor's mom.

Sam next spoke to Reggie, calming her concerns. "We're working our way down the coast," he told her. "Picking up the route tomorrow. Things are quiet. No trouble. Beautiful scenery."

As he finished his call, the van arrived with Preacher at the wheel. While Wolf and Lopez made arrangements with the site's manager, Snuffy came ashore in the rubber dinghy to fetch the two for a strategy session.

While waiting for their arrival, McFadden spread a map across the cabin table to address a promising lead. Earlier that day, Wolf and Lopez had stumbled on an intriguing clue during a break at a cantina forty miles up the coast. As he had done at previous stops, Wolf flashed pictures of the missing students. The restaurant's owner had recognized the four Americans. The woman's adolescent daughter confirmed her mother's story—a sighting of the missing students the FBI and their Mexican guides had apparently missed. As he smoothed the map, McFadden thought about Wolf's words.

"She said our boys asked about rumors of a surf spot some sixty kilometers south of her cantina. Two other Americans surfers eating there confirmed the camp's existence and sent them on their way with directions."

Scanning the chart, McFadden found the nameless cove where the *South Wind* now lay anchored at Wolf's suggestion. The purr of the dinghy's outboard broke his contemplation. Wolf and Lopez came aboard, followed by Snuffy.

McFadden waved them into the cabin. "Great job finding that woman today, Wolfman. That's a crucial clue."

Wolf shrugged. "Give Luis the credit, Sam. My Spanish is okay, but the woman was a talker. Mouth was going eighty miles an hour."

"Major, appreciate your being there to cover for the Wolfman."

"Ah, he does the right thing, showing the pictures. I was able to ask the right questions. It's important to know this, yes?"

"Hell yes. That puts us right behind our boys' footsteps. A good break for our side. Fills in where they were between here and Cabo." McFadden spread his hands across the familiar map, eager to compare notes with the two. "Here's our location," he said. "If your witness overheard those other surfers correctly about the distance, that puts that surfing beach roughly..."

He drew his finger along the coast and tapped a thin, hook-shaped spit of land. "*Punto Rocoso*—Rocky Point. That's about thirty klicks south of our present location. You agree?"

Wolf eyed the jagged coastline. "Might be a point break there." Chin in hand, a faint smile formed. "I could see a west swell wrapping around that point. Could be a sweet break if you were a surfer who knew what to look for."

McFadden said, "Or if someone put you on to it."

"Like another surfer who didn't mind sharing a secret spot," said Wolf. "Worth a looksee, Sam. I vote we check it out."

Glancing from the map to Lopez, McFadden said, "Major, what are your thoughts?"

Leaning over the table, the Mexican drummed fingers on the map. "This is all rugged country. Every kilometer of the coastline the same. Very little settlement along the coast until Cabo San Lucas. A few towns inland, okay? Maybe a few places like our current location. It would take time to find that particular surf break."

Wolf said, "You heard her story, Luis. Did she tell us the truth?"

"She had no reason to lie. She had spoken to no one about this before we showed. It's important that we posed no threat to her. So, yes, I think she tells the truth."

McFadden said, "Not like the FBI to miss this, though."

"Even the Bureau can make mistakes," said Wolf.

McFadden opened a laptop, called up a satellite image of Baja's coastline, enlarged it, and placed the computer on the map, screen toward the two. "Take a look at this. There's definitely surf there."

Snuffy came up from below. "Caught the last part of what you said, Sam." Joining the group, he shouldered his way between Wolf and McFadden. "We could take *South Wind* along the coast and check it out."

Wolf brightened. "Perfect. We'd get back on the main road headed south until you zero in on this spot."

"Sure, we stay in touch via satellite phone, steer you the right way."

The four studied the chart, planning the next day's land and sea search. "Okay, I think we've got our op order for tomorrow," said McFadden. He looked out the cabin's window filling with sunset's tints. "Good timing, too. Glad we're not at sea."

Wolf had made the same decision about further travel. "Nobody in their right mind drives the Baja at night," he said.

Leaving Snuffy and McFadden on board, Wolf and Lopez shuttled to shore in the rubber dinghy and relayed the news to Preacher, Parvin and Gideon.

"You guys head to chow," said Parvin. "I'll hold down the fort until you get back."

"Why not come with us," said Preacher. "Nobody's gonna walk off with our gear."

Tossing a piece of driftwood on the campfire, Parvin dropped into one of the ancient beach chairs and declined. "I'd just as soon stay. You know, keep an eye on things."

"I'll spell you when I'm done eating," said Preacher.

"Appreciate it."

Chapter 27

Dinner was served in a beachside *palapa*, a romantic thatched-roofed addition to the site manager's casa overlooking the sheltered cove. Covered with oilcloths and lighted by candles in hurricane lamps, rough-hewn picnic tables sat on a sand floor where campers ate in shifts. Bottled water or tequila, the only drinks offered, lined the middle of each table.

Wolf and the other two walked to the seaside shack and claimed two benches at a spot being cleared. They sat down to a feast prepared and served by local villagers. Without being asked, two stunted, silent round Indian women set heaping plates of lobster, fresh fish, rice, beans, and tortillas in front of Preacher and Gideon. They returned with two more for Wolf and Lopez. The four of them shared small talk about weather and the roads. Preacher and Gideon finished before Wolf, paid their tabs, and left, replaced by other overnight travelers drifting in for dinner.

Parvin arrived and ate alongside Wolf and Lopez, who lingered to keep him company. The three toasted other diners with tequila and were saluted in turn. Declining seconds, Parvin excused himself and headed back to the van while Wolf and Lopez stayed for the changing of the guard. The thinning dinner crowd listened to mediocre guitar played by an American duo staying the month. Dying light painted the clouds orange and the rippled bay a deep indigo.

Shattering the sunset, a pair of rattling pickups roared up as the sun dipped below the horizon. Wolf and Lopez eyed five rough men exiting the trucks. The five, stunted, bowlegged and round-faced, wore the usual *campesino* attire—straw cowboy hats, western-style shirts, big-buckled jeans, and boots. Strutting to the open-air café, the new arrivals claimed a table by themselves and demanded service. The obvious leader, thicker through the body than the others, his brown face scarred by pox, gave orders to the women at the brick oven, then swiveled on the bench, barking at the guitarists.

"*Segan tocando, mis amigos.*"

Interrupted mid-song, the musicians, two bearded students in their twenties, glanced at each other, wary of the strangers.

"*Tocar*—play," ordered the group's leader. Fluttering his stubby fingers as if strumming an imaginary instrument, the man flashed a malevolent gap-toothed grin. The nervous Americans resumed playing, dropping chords and missing notes to the strangers' amusement. Along with plates piled with the last of the tortillas, fish, rice, and beans, three new bottles of tequila arrived. Turning his back on the guitarists, the alpha male attacked his food, washing it down with tequila straight from a bottle. His *compañeros* did likewise. Wolf shot a glance at Lopez, who had not taken his eyes off the five.

"*Debemos ir?*" said Wolf.

Lopez straddled the wooden bench. "Yes, we should go."

Chapter 28

The two rose, pinning pesos under their empty plates. Wolf nodded to the two servers, mouthing his thanks. He and Lopez retreated out of earshot of the remaining diners in the thatched hut.

"Bad men, *amigo*," said Lopez. "I think they are here to make some trouble. The head man carries a gun."

Wolf looked back. "I agree. I'll tell the others. You'd better get back to the boat. Tell Sam to stay alert."

Lopez shook his head. "Maybe is better I stay with you and your friends."

"I'd feel better if you were on board, Luis. My men and I will be okay. Gideon will stay with us. We'll keep an eye on things."

He and Lopez strolled to the parked van where Preacher perched on a canvas campstool, feeding kindling to a flickering fire. Gideon showed with an armful of wood, Parvin on his heels, the two adding more driftwood to the pile. They dropped their bundles at Preacher's feet.

"That's it for the night," Parvin said. "Can't see much out there now."

"It'll do," said Preacher. "We should be good till morning."

Wolf gave the men a rundown on the strangers, then said, "Major Lopez is going to keep Sam and Snuffy company tonight. Gideon, you stay with us as backup."

"Roger that," said the big man.

Wolf walked Lopez to the dinghy. "Tell Sam about our visitors. If you hear all hell break loose, don't wait for an invitation. Come ashore."

"Keep an eye on those men, *amigo*," said Lopez, pushing the rubber boat into the shallows and climbing in. When the engine coughed to life, Lopez waved and was gone, his wake a trail of bubbles leading to the anchored *South Wind.*

Wolf returned, claimed his seat next to the fire and lowered his voice. "I think we have a situation here, boys. Those five yahoos showing up for a late dinner just about the time the place was done serving is no coincidence."

Seated on a smooth log, Gideon probed the embers with a stick. "Figured we might have to take them on sooner or later. What's your read?"

"Your run of the mill bad guys," said Wolf. "Up to no good."

"They're doing a little recon of a soft target, huh?"

Wolf eyed Gideon. "Exactly. I think they waltzed in here, saw the happy campers all lined up, and figured it might be easy pickings."

Gideon withdrew a glowing brand and blew on it to keep it alive. "How do you see it going down?"

"Don't know if you caught it," said Wolf, "but the big boy had a pistol underneath his shirt. Either that or he was happy to see the manager's daughter." A ripple of laughter circled the fire. "Probably dumb enough to shoot his balls off," he said. "But before he does that he'll make a lot of noise. Scare the shit out of most of the people. Might even hurt someone."

Preacher, eyes on the flames without looking at Wolf, added a stick to the fire. "His friends carrying?"

"Not sure," said Wolf. "They could have guns stashed in the trucks."

Preacher said, "Everybody in the Baja is armed except us."

"My guess is they'll probably leave and come back," said Gideon. "Can't see them trying this when everybody's awake."

Wolf nodded. "My take, too. Catch the camp asleep. Maybe midnight or later. That's what I'd do."

"Should we warn the others?" said Parvin.

"Good idea. Once these *bandidos* leave, you, Gideon, and Preacher make the rounds," said Wolf. "I'll talk to the campsite manager."

"Maybe he knows," said Preacher. "I don't like it. They probably did a head count while they were eating. Likely figured to hit us and then get back on the road."

Gideon laughed. "Not a good idea to be driving at night on these roads. Isn't that what you said, Wolfman?"

"True. You can never be sure what you'll run into out there."

"Like a bunch of badass former spec ops types," said Parvin.

"Something like that. It could be hazardous to their health."

"I certainly hope so," said Preacher. "I'm overdue for a good fight."

"We'll take turns on watch," said Wolf, reading his watch's luminous dial. "Twenty-one hundred hours now. We'll each do one hour. I'll take the first hour. Gideon, you relieve me. Then Parvin, followed by Preacher."

Preacher slapped Wolf on the back. "See now why Mikey and I came packing? Told you it would come in handy."

Wolf shook his head. "You two want to play Robin Hood, fine. Just make sure neither of you puts an arrow in my ass by mistake."

Chapter 29

Dying campfires dotted the beach. A quarter moon's reflection floated on the bay. Slivers of lunar light revealed shaggy *palapas*, domed nylon tents, pickup camper trucks, and three Airstream trailers parked among the lots in the brush. Flashlights bobbed like fireflies. Dinner had ended an hour ago, replaced by Tequila-fueled laughter and music spilling from the cantina. Eventually, the guitar duo begged off and returned to their tent. The five strangers finished an additional two bottles of tequila and showered greasy pesos on the servers before making a loud show of leaving. The pickups roared away south in clouds of dust, but Wolf and his team were not fooled.

Their warnings, delivered throughout the camping sites one hour earlier, had been courteously received by some and ignored by others who thought them overly dramatic. The manager, placid mask in place, listened to Wolf's concerns about the evening's five visitors but gave no indication he agreed. Gideon, Preacher, and Parvin reported similar responses.

"Denial," said Preacher. "'Not gonna happen to me,' they said."

Gideon said, "Some were worried. Said they'd probably stay up all night just to be sure."

"What can you do?" Parvin said. "Put your head in the sand, I guess."

Gideon dropped into a rickety chair next to Preacher and Parvin. He rubbed his hands and held them palms out to warm them. "Temp's gonna drop tonight," he said, eyeing the moon. "Wind off the ocean has bite."

Preacher, his voice low and menacing, poked at the embers and added a twisted log to the flames. "Not to disparage our host's hospitality, but so help me, if he's setting us up I'm going to have a problem."

"You got a feeling he's in on this?" said Parvin.

Staring into the fire, Preacher shrugged. "Possibly."

Wolf gestured to the *South Wind* tugging at its anchor. "Snuffy, Sam and Lopez have our backs. The major's armed and Snuffy's got a shotgun."

"Lot of good that'll do from offshore," said Preacher. "So, Gideon, I see you got the short straw on guard duty."

"Works for me."

"You're gonna be high and dry with the troops tonight."

"Fine by me," said the Marine. "I kinda like the feel of old *terra firma*."

Parvin cocked his head at Preacher. "I have an idea. What say you and I double up when it's our watch. Do a two-hour turn. Take our stringed instruments and set up in the brush about ten, twenty yards from the van."

"And see what happens?" said Preacher.

"Exactly."

Preacher smiled in Wolf's direction. "What's our CO think?"

Wolf broke some dried brush and fed it piecemeal to the fire. "Up to you guys."

"Roger that," said Preacher.

"What time you planning this Boy Scout action?" said Wolf.

Parvin rubbed the stubble on his chin and shot a grin at Preacher. "'Bout zero dark thirty to my way of thinking."

"Go for it," said Wolf. "Wake me when you head out."

Gideon stared at the flames. "Just remember, when you're lining up your targets, I'll be the tall one."

"Got you covered," said Preacher. "Think I'll turn in." He rose, tossed a branch on the fire, and said to Parvin, "Wake me when you're ready, pardner."

"Roger that, Chief."

"Good hunting," said Wolf.

Chapter 30

Wolf woke with a start. A metallic rattle. A muffler's cough. Tires on gravel. The yawn of a truck's door in need of oil.

They're back, he thought. Rolling from his sleeping bag, he dropped to his knees. Prodding Gideon, he woke him, whispering, "They're coming. South, on the road. On foot. One hundred yards. Moving fast."

Nodding, the black Marine sat up, knife in hand. He got up, kicked at the fire, scattering a handful of glowing embers, sending up a coil of smoke in the pale moonlight. Wolf cradled an oiled machete in the crook of his arm, his eyes searching the rutted dirt track leading to the campgrounds.

"Preacher, Parvin," hissed Gideon. "They out there?"

Nodding, Wolf backed from the smoking campfire. "This way."

The pair crept into thick brush at the rear of the van and went to ground, invisible in the shadows. A dog, the site manager's skinny mixed-breed, growled low and threatening in the distance.

A shot. Twenty yards away. The sound of ripping nylon mingling with hammering on aluminum.

Going for the tents and trailers, thought Wolf.

"They're hitting the campsites," hissed Gideon, his hot breath sour in Wolf's face. "Gotta stop 'em, Skipper."

Another shot, followed by a woman's scream, then pleading voices. Laughter. More shots, an AK-47 firing short bursts. A shotgun answered. Peering into the dark, Wolf raised himself on one knee; machete ready, Gideon's hurried breathing alongside.

Angry shouts in Spanish. A dog's barking challenge. Another shot and the canine howled in pain, then stopped. Footsteps pounded in Wolf's direction. Crouching, Gideon at his elbow, Wolf pushed through clinging brush, pointing to a fleeing figure. A naked woman, pale, blonde hair flying behind her, stumbled, rose, and hobbled toward them, her shadow distinct in the moonlight. Behind her jogged one of the *campesinos*, machete raised, his raspy drunken laughter ringing across the campground.

"Catch her," said Wolf. "I'll take him."

The two burst from their hiding place. Gideon went for the woman, Wolf for her pursuer. Leaping into the man's path, Wolf waved the flat blade to distract him. An arrow beat him to it, burying itself in the short man's shoulder. Howling in pain, the woman's attacker dropped his weapon and went down hard in a cloud of dust.

Preacher. Wolf picked up the second blade and circled the stunned man, ready to strike. Confused, the wounded *campesino* crabbed across the rocky ground. Wolf brought a boot down on the man's left leg, snapping it, ending his escape. Clawing at the embedded arrow, the little man screamed in agony.

A figure loped past Wolf—Preacher—fitting another shaft to his bow, yelling as he trotted past. "One down. Parvin ahead of me. Needs help."

Gideon emerged from the dark, carrying the unconscious woman in his arms. She was wrapped in his windbreaker. "Beat up pretty bad."

Wolf looped a machete's rawhide leash over Gideon's wrist. "Hold on to this blade and take her to the van. Stay with her until I get back."

"Where you going?"

"Following Preacher. Parvin's out there. It ain't over yet."

"Roger that." Then Gideon was gone.

Wolf used a belt to tie the wounded man's arms behind his back, prompting piercing cries of pain. He left the arrow where it was and dragged the trussed man along the ground behind him despite his pleading. People were gathering at the manager's casa where lanterns had appeared. Wolf dropped his burden there.

"*Uno de ellos*," he yelled. "One of them."

"*Hombre malo*. Watch him. *Mírenlo. Comprenden?*"

"*Sí*, we understand." The campsite's manager, heavy gnarled club in one hand, lantern in the other. Wolf kept going.

In the distance, somewhere on the main road, a single truck engine cranked into life and roared away, chased by two shotgun blasts. With one of Parvin's crossbow bolts in both front tires, the second pickup wasn't going anywhere. Neither were the driver and his passenger. The battle was over.

Chapter 31

Dawn took forever to arrive. Three of the *bandidos*, one of them Wolf's prisoner, had been captured during the raid. Surrounded by their angry victims, all three lay wounded —one by gunshot, one by arrows fired by Preacher, the third immobilized by a crossbow's bolt piercing his lower abdomen. Parvin showed and yanked the shaft from the man's body, adding to his agony.

McFadden and Lopez worked the crowd, calming the voices. The two had come ashore during the assault to hunt down the attackers. It was McFadden's shotgun Wolf had heard. Lopez had downed one of the *campesinos* with his handgun. McFadden's next volleys had driven off the leader, who fled empty-handed along with a fifth man. Six campers, men and women, had suffered beatings during the aborted raid. Despite the ferocity of the assault on the compound no lives were lost thanks to Wolf and company.

The woman rescued by Gideon and Wolf had been beaten in her tent by the *campesinos'* leader, who had been intent on raping her. Left in shock by her narrow escape, she was mute and inconsolable. Fighting to defend her, the boyfriend had been pistol-whipped during the attack and left for dead. He survived, bloodied and dazed.

McFadden and Wolf took charge. With the help of an American nurse from one of the trailers, who volunteered her skills, they turned the open-air cantina into a triage center. Using a kit from Wolf's van, Gideon, the nurse, and two volunteers treated the wounded on picnic tables by lantern light. Bow in hand, Preacher came in from sweeping the brush for stragglers and reported the property secure.

Dragged to a secluded edge of the campground, safe from their victims' wrath, the bandits were tied to trees and interrogated by Lopez. He was not gentle, but he was effective. The resistance by Wolf and the others had been a total surprise. There was no risk of a reprisal, he said.

Chapter 32

Later that morning, with order restored, Snuffy came ashore to be greeted with merciless ribbing about his absence during the fight.

McFadden led both teams away from the main body to brief them.

"The good news," he said, "if there is any to be found in this botched raid, is that Luis says this is not connected in any way to what we're here for. This was strictly a crime of opportunity by thugs who had no idea what they were getting into."

"Serves these assholes right," growled Gideon.

"The bad news?" said Preacher.

"Bad news is, this is a helluva mess," said Wolf. "We have to make a decision before the cavalry shows. Do we abort our mission and head for the border or do we carry on?"

Parvin said, "What happens if we continue on?"

"Couple things," said McFadden. "If the news of what happened here catches up with us while we're still in the Baja, we'll likely face some embarrassing questions asked by unpleasant people."

"For doing the right thing," snapped Gideon.

McFadden shrugged. "'Fraid so. We stepped up, stopped the raid. Two of the five bad guys got away, though."

He nodded to Lopez. "Major, what happens next?"

Hands on hips, his eyes flashing with anger, the Mexican said, "The two who got away will likely return to even the score. They will bring their friends. The ones left behind say they control this stretch of road from here until Cabo San Lucas. Their leader will be back. By the time they do that, we'll be long gone."

"But the people here will suffer, true?" said Wolf.

Lopez shook his head. "Of course. It is not fair but that is what will likely happen."

"If what they said about this road is true, we will probably run into these dogs again."

"Yes, this is possible," said Lopez. "We bloodied their noses."

"And made new enemies," said Wolf. "Just when we don't need them."

"Inevitable, *amigo*."

"What happens to the prisoners?" said Parvin.

Lopez shrugged. "There are three graves being dug in the hills as we speak, gentlemen."

"That makes us accomplices," said Snuffy. "I'm not cool with that. Can't we turn these assholes over to the *federales*?"

"Dunno," said Preacher, "I think the locals might have something to say about that."

"If we wait for the police to show," said Wolf, "we'll have to explain what the hell we were doing here. If we leave these three behind and they spill their guts, the *federales* will come looking for us."

Snuffy said, "And if we let the locals have their way, they'll butcher these guys."

"And the *bandidos* weren't intent on doing that to us?" said Preacher.

"It's a risk," said Wolf. "Look, either way we might have just a few days of grace left to continue our mission before word gets around."

McFadden held up a hand. "Wolfman and I are not going to make this decision on our own. We should vote on this. It's up to you guys. We're one hundred-fifty miles from Cabo San Lucas. That puts us close to where our MIAs were last seen. Even so, I'm willing to pack it in if that's what you decide to do."

Preacher fumed. "A vote? We just survived a firefight in the middle of nowhere and you want to take a vote? Make a decision. Simple as that. Go or stay."

Wolf said, "I'm with Sam, Preacher. I've got no problem with this."

"Secret ballot," McFadden added. "We'll tear up some paper. Mark an X if you want to turn back. A blank ballot means we keep going."

Snuffy again. "Either way, what happens to the prisoners?"

Wolf said, "They stay behind. They sealed their own fate as far as I'm concerned. Their kind wouldn't think twice about putting us in those graves had it gone their way. No one would ever find our bodies."

Lopez put a hand on Snuffy's arm. "He is right, *amigo*. I'm sorry, but these people give no thought to killing people like you...or that woman in the tent, or me. I can appreciate what you say, but the reality of this is not so black and white, you know? I lost my wife and child to animals like these."

The sun burned a hole through the shade in the grove as McFadden produced a notepad and two pens. He tore a single sheet into squares and handed one to each man. Despite his tirade, Preacher took a ballot like the others.

"Think this through carefully," McFadden said. "This is not a hasty decision to make." He tossed an upturned ball cap on the ground. "Drop your ballot in here when you're done."

Wolf took ten steps to a gnarled tree, then returned, dropping his folded ballot in the hat with others.

McFadden was the last to add his vote to the pile.

He unfolded the ballots, smoothing the paper slips in his hands, scanning each as he did so. Passing the votes to Wolf, he kept his face neutral as he faced the group to announce the decision.

Chapter 33

"Seven votes to keep going," McFadden said, crumpling the ballots. "That's settled. Let's get something to eat and break camp. We'll have to move fast to minimize our risk."

A whispered word from McFadden and Wolf herded the group back to their campsite, leaving Snuffy behind with him in the grove.

"I figured you would have voted to turn back," said McFadden. "Mind if I ask why you changed your mind?"

Eyes on the ground, Snuffy scuffed the dirt with his boots, then looked at McFadden. "I only raised the question about the prisoners because it needed to be said."

"You sounded reluctant to leave them to their fate."

Arms folded, Snuffy leaned against the tree's weathered trunk. "I could care less what happens to these guys, Sam. Like Preacher said, they would've killed us just as soon as look at us. But sometimes it's best to raise the point when folks are about to make a choice like this, one they might regret later on."

"You wanted to give our guys a way out of this situation?"

"Yeah."

"We're not a mob, Snuffy. These guys can think for themselves."

"I know that. I'm just saying that decisions have consequences. You guys are all trained in this kinda stuff, you know?"

"Killing people?"

"Killing the enemy. There's a difference."

McFadden said, "I'm glad you recognize the distinction."

Snuffy locked eyes with McFadden. "Whether you agree with me or not, I figure peer pressure plays a role in your line of work. I wanted to leave an out, you know?"

McFadden put a hand on Snuffy's shoulder. "I get it. And I appreciate what you're saying, what you did, okay?"

"Thought it was worth a shot."

"It was." Dropping his arm, McFadden said, "I'm saying thanks on behalf of the guys...even if they don't have a clue about your reasons for raising the issue."

Snuffy nodded.

"Now let's get this outfit moving," said McFadden. "We've got some ground to cover."

Heading back to the campground where their teams waited, the two walked into another crisis.

Chapter 34

"We got big problems," said Wolf, scratching his head. He took McFadden aside.

"Now what?"

Wolf motioned to the milling crowd at the outdoors cantina. "The girl Gideon saved. She's in no condition to be left behind, Sam."

"Agreed. She and her boyfriend are in bad shape. I suggest they double up with some of the other Americans and head north, ASAP."

Rubbing his hands together, Wolf glanced around to make sure he wasn't being overheard. "Uh, they want to come with us."

"What? No can do, Wolfman. How would that work? We're in harm's way as it is. Those two tagging along compromises our job. No way."

"Hear me out, Sam."

McFadden glowered, shaking his head at Wolf.

"We can put them on board Snuffy's boat with your team and..."

"No, that's..."

Ignoring the interruption, Wolf kept going, his hands in a pleading pose. "We keep them on board until we get to Cabo San Lucas."

McFadden scratched at his four-day beard "Crazy. Then what?"

"We get them to a clinic in Cabo. These two need follow-up medical care, Sam. We call their families on the sat phone and have them make arrangements to fly them out once we get there. End of story."

"What about their car?"

"Big deal," said Wolf, "it's a rental jeep. Leave it in Cabo. Let them handle the drop charges, if any."

"Why can't he drive it?"

"C'mon, you're kidding, right? He has no business behind a wheel. This kid needs some serious sick bay time. Gideon or Parvin can drive the jeep to Cabo. And the girl's a basket case. Think about it, Sam."

Scratching his forehead, McFadden stared at the ground. "I don't like it. It complicates things."

"Won't argue with that. But we can work around it. Fog of war. Hell, Sam, our whole plan went south when the *bandidos* showed up last night."

McFadden spotted Snuffy heading their way, about to interrupt. He waved him off. "I'm listening, Wolfman. Explain. But make it quick."

"You and your guys get to Cabo, square away the girl and friend, then follow what leads we have about our MIAs in Cabo. You know, see if they actually stayed there."

"And you?"

"Major Lopez comes with my team. We continue on to that surf camp to check out the rumor our boys may have been there. Meanwhile, once you learn the skinny on Connor and friends in Cabo, you either hunker down until we show, or top off on fuel and head north to rendezvous with us along the coast to tie up loose ends."

"Dammit, Wolfman. You're backing me against a wall."

"Say yes and we'll be on our way."

Reluctance etched on his face, a harried McFadden capitulated. "Okay, okay. Fine. Let's break the news to the teams and get moving."

Grinning, Wolf slapped McFadden's back. "I knew it! Hey, I love you for your compassion, Dawg."

McFadden let Wolf explain the change in plans. With no one objecting, he ordered both teams to pack up. Snuffy made two trips in the rubber dinghy, settling the wounded couple in the boat's one stateroom, then returning with the major's belongings.

Lopez and McFadden made the rounds, warning remaining campers and the site manager about possible retribution from the surviving *bandidos*. None of the raid's survivors needed encouragement to leave. With the *South Wind* weighing anchor, the remnant headed out—most Americans fleeing in a north-bound convoy of Airstreams and vans—the others aiming inland or south, toward Cabo ahead of Wolf.

Chapter 35

Preacher and Wolf stood on the shore, waving to the departing *South Wind* with its wounded cargo. As planned, the fishing boat turned north as it moved out to sea where a distant squall offered cover. Snuffy suggested the change of course to McFadden as a precaution against being trailed. "If the manager's asked, he'll say we went north. Might buy us some time."

"Worth a try. Do it."

Two miles up the coast, the *South Wind* would head out to sea, using the rain to screen the turn south toward Cabo.

Wolf had already planted numerous hints about returning to Ensenada. Once back on the main road and out of sight, the plan was to turn south as well.

Hands jammed in his pockets, Preacher watched the boat grow smaller. He turned to Wolf. "Did you tell Sam about letting those three surfers hitch their wagon to ours?"

"Nope. Didn't seem the right thing to do at the time."

Puzzled, Preacher said, "Why not? He was okay with taking that couple along."

"That took some convincing. Confronting him with these surfers woulda been the proverbial straw on the camel's back.

Trust me, Sam would have said 'no' to the surfers. The whole change of plans might have gone up in smoke."

"That would have been my call as well."

Wolf frowned. "Good thing I didn't ask for your input. Better to ask forgiveness instead of permission. I made a command decision, Preacher. These guys say they know the exact spot where our boys may have gone. As surfers they'll give us legitimate cover. Plus, they're scared as hell about traveling alone after what's happened. It's a win-win in my book."

"If you say so. What do they know about us?"

"Not much. Really, what do they need to know? We saved their asses, along with everyone else's. I told 'em we were ex-military, guys who like to surf."

"And they bought it?"

"Enough to want to stick with us."

"More mouths to feed. More butts to cover."

Wolf threw an arm around Preacher. "Shouldn't be a problem. They'll carry their own weight. What's not to like? Strength in numbers. Plus, I'm heading south with my own two heroic Merry Men."

Preacher surveyed the landscape with disdain. "You looked around lately? This ain't exactly Sherwood Forest."

"Which means we don't have to worry about the Sheriff of Nottingham."

"Don't count on it. I'm sure he's got an evil Mexican twin somewhere hereabouts."

Chapter 36

At the sound of a laboring engine, Preacher and Wolf turned from the sea to witness the camp manager at the wheel of a rusting flatbed pickup turned tumbril for the occasion. Shifting gears, the swaying vehicle inched by at a funereal pace; its bed loaded with the three bound and bloodied prisoners. Four stoic Indians, wearing traditional peasant cotton shirts and trousers, and armed with machetes and shovels, rode as guards. Carrying the captured AK-47, a village elder leaned against the cab's roof, a large sheathed knife at his belt. Behind the truck marched three serving women from the beachside cantina. Each carried a knife in one hand and a sharpened hoe balanced on shawled-covered shoulders.

Preacher said, "*Their violence will come down on their own heads.*"

"Another one of your Bible verses?"

"Psalm seven, verse sixteen."

"You speaking about the locals?"

"No, the condemned."

Wolf let out his breath. "How appropriate."

The grim procession wound past Wolf and Preacher before disappearing in a grove of trees crowning a low stony hill where waiting graves yawned.

After the truck passed, a subdued Wolf and Preacher walked to their waiting convoy. A dusty red pickup camper belonging to three tagalong California surfers, idled in the lead spot, surfboards strapped to the roof.

As Wolf approached, the stunned driver leaned out the window. "Dude, did you just see..."

"Shhh," Wolf said, a finger to his lips. "Don't ruin the moment."

He said, "You lead. We'll stay close."

Anxious to leave the carnage behind, Wolf got in the van next to Lopez, Gideon behind him on a bench seat, and started the engine. At the end of the line, Preacher slipped into the jeep's passenger seat next to Parvin.

Second in the caravan, Wolf tied a bandana over his nose and mouth against the dust, and then impatiently tapped his

horn, a signal to move. He shadowed the Californians' red
camper from the sheltered bay, following the twisting, rutted
track leading to another spur—a pounded gravel route baking
in the sun. Wolf followed in a cloud of spiraling dust. Parvin
and Preacher stayed glued to his tail, right where he wanted
them. At the junction, the Californians turned southeast,
aiming toward Federal Highway One.

Two hours later, the Californians left the desert's paved
road and headed almost due west, searching for a promised
secondary road paralleling the sea. They found it and
followed it for a punishing twenty minutes before making
a wrong turn down what looked to be a cattle path.
Testing Wolf's patience, the leader traded drivers and
retraced their tracks to a turnoff passed earlier. Given the
condition of the side roads, Wolf couldn't fault them.

This time the three-vehicle caravan halted at a T-junction
amidst cactus and skeletal brush. A weathered post wreathed
in rusting barbed wire leaned drunkenly to the left. A yellow,
bullet-riddled metal sign with a faded surfer's silhouette on a
wave was bolted to the top of the post.

The red pickup's driver, a tousled blond, barefooted and
bare-chested, got out and walked to the van behind. Wolf
rolled down the window.

"Quarter mile down this path. Hope you have four-
wheel drive."

Wolf nodded. "I do. Lead on."

The blond returned to the truck and led Wolf and
Parvin down an eroded switchback trail cut through
more cactus and mesquite. A challenging passage, at
turns steep and unforgiving, the road eventually broke
from the brush at a level bald spot offering a sweeping
horizon where the sea met the sky.

Chapter 37

Another conference, this one overlooking a collection of
shingled houses nestled against a cliff. Below the cottages,
a pebbled beach two hundred yards from where Wolf and
his caravan had halted in the open flat space. Wolf got out
of the van and scanned the beach below. Two surfers sat
in long blue swells wrapping around a rocky point. He
grabbed a pair of binoculars and focused on the people in
the water. The pickup's three surfers used the stop to get
out and stretch their legs, along with Parvin and Gideon.
Surveying the precarious descent before them, Preacher
and Lopez stood apart from Wolf and the others.

"Your opinion, Major," said Preacher.

"No opinion," said Lopez. "I'm only here to support
your mission."

"You familiar with this place?"

Lopez shook his head. "I am not. I know there are many
places like this along the coast. Only Americans can afford
to make these trips to ride the waves." He nodded at the
Californians standing by their pickup.

"Like those three," he said. "People like them have been
coming here for fifty years. They bring money. And money
attracts people. As you saw, money sometimes brings out
the worst in my countrymen."

Preacher said, "The love of money, Major. Jesus got
that right."

"True. Let us hope we find your missing friends and
avoid more of what we experienced last night."

The camper's driver wandered to where Wolf stood.

Wolf lowered the binoculars. "This place is kinda
isolated," he said. "Does it get much traffic?"

The blond shook his head. "It's a primo spot but not everyone knows about it. Can count on one hand how many people want to come down this far."

"I can see why," said Wolf. "Piss-poor roads."

"Worse when it rains," said the surfer. "And *bandidos*."

"Fact of life. Always prowling around the sheepfold."

The surfer said, "The owner keeps it private. He likes it that way."

Wolf said, "Not exactly Conrad Hilton, huh?"

"Who?"

"Huh, forget it."

The blond focused on incoming swells. "Decent break. It can hold eight feet at the point before it gets dicey. The bay stays calm regardless."

Eyes back on the glasses, Wolf said, "You know this spot, huh?"

"Three years in row."

"Could've fooled me."

"Dude, I wasn't driving at first."

Wolf held the binoculars against his hip. "Ever had problems like last night?"

"Never. Shakedowns on the road with hungry cops, of course."

"Typical," said Wolf. "You're welcome to stay with us. Safer."

Head down, the man shuffled his sandaled feet in the dust. "Look, we appreciate what you did. You guys kicked some serious ass, but if it's just the same to you, me and my boys will keep going. Like to get to Cabo before dark."

Calling over Preacher, Wolf passed the glasses to him and faced the surfer. "Long drive. Your call. Safety in numbers, you know."

The blond ran both hands through his hair, shook his head. "Yeah, but we'd like to keep moving."

"Okay. Before you go, tell me about the people who run this outfit."

"Owner's name is Max Parrish."

"Doesn't sound Mexican," said Wolf.

"He's not. Old American dude. Surfer. Mellow, but loves to talk if you're American. Got out of the Army after Vietnam and moved here to surf. Stayed. Married some Mexican whose family owned the land."

He turned away from Wolf, eyeing the hills above the beach. "Goes way back to Spanish days, I guess. They had a litter of kids, all ages."

The surfer was apologetic. "You know, I'd stay if it was just me."

Wolf didn't believe him. He glanced at his watch. "We'll take it from here. Appreciate your getting us here. By the way, I'll be sending one of my guys along with you. Not negotiable. Have one of your boys ride with him in the jeep to Cabo."

"Uh, what if we decide to stop along the way?"

Wolf frowned. "Don't." Silence followed.

"Okay, sure." He went back to the truck to pass the word.

Lopez came up and Preacher passed the binoculars to him.

Wolf ambled to Preacher's side. "These guys aren't gonna stick around. They want to keep going all the way to Cabo. I don't have a problem with it, but I want one of our guys along. What do you think?"

Preacher glanced over Wolf's shoulder at the three in question. "Let 'em go. They got us here, that's the main point. How about the major and I keep you company? Gideon or Parvin can follow them to Cabo in the jeep. They can help Sam check out Cabo and then come back on the boat."

Wolf looked at Lopez. "Luis, you think that's a good idea?"

"No problem. They go, we stay."

"Preacher agrees," said Wolf. "We'll send one of our guys with them to hook up with Sam. Gideon and Parvin can flip a coin."

"I'll go," said Gideon, waving the coin toss. He volunteered to drive with the Californians to Cabo if Parvin agreed.

"Go for it," said Parvin. "Just don't stop till you get there."

"Okay, Gideon," said Wolf, "you're up." He handed the big Marine one of the spare satellite phones. "When you arrive, call Sam. He has a checklist of what credit cards belonging to our boys showed up in Cabo. Stay together. Watch your backs. Keep in touch. Sam will tell you where to dump the rental when you're done."

"Roger that."

Locking eyes with Gideon, Wolf said, "Do not hang around longer than you need to. You find nothing, get back on the boat and head up here ASAP."

"What will you be doing?"

Wolf lowered his voice, "Checking out this place to see if we find any clues to our missing kids. If this place is a dry hole we'll come your way. If not, you come here."

"Got it."

Wolf slapped him on the back. "Stay in one piece. Watch Sam."

"Understood." Gideon grabbed his gear, walked to the jeep, and got in next to his new passenger. The two vehicles retraced their tracks along the tortured trail to the main road and from there, the highway. When they were gone, Wolf trained the binoculars on the surfing camp below.

"Smoke from a stack," he said. "A crew working on one of the roofs. No other signs of life that I can see."

"Two more people in the water," said Preacher, pointing.

Wolf took the glasses and focused on the breaking waves. "You're right. Three in the lineup. One paddling out. Guess we might as well go down there and see if Max Parrish knows where Connor and his friends might be."

"Be careful," said Lopez. "Things are not always what they seem. You must not be too obvious, eh."

Wolf nodded. "Good advice, *amigo*. First things first. Let's just hope there's room at the inn." The three went back to the van.

"I drive," said Lopez, sliding behind the wheel ahead of Wolf.

"Because?"

"It's better that I appear to be someone you hire to drive you and your two friends in the Baja."

"You think this is really necessary?"

Lopez shrugged. "We won't know that at first. Maybe later we will discover if we were right to do this."

"I'm not going to argue," said Wolf.

"Good. Because I am rarely wrong about such things."

Preacher leaned from the backseat. "*Un gato sabio.*"

Lopez grinned. "*Sí. Con seis vidas.*"

"Care to translate," groused Parvin.

"I told him he was one smart cat," said Preacher.

Lopez shot a quick glance at Wolf. "But one with only six lives."

Chapter 38

Cocooned in a shaded rope hammock between two gnarled trees, Max Parrish kept an eye on the swaying white van gingerly working its way down the rutted track to his compound. A black cat curled on his bare chest lifted its head, yellow eyes wide in alarm at the sound of the approaching vehicle. Leaping to the paving stones, the cat vanished in clustered aloe plants lining the shaded patio's beach side.

Parrish was seventy-two but looked older due to a lifetime in the Mexican sun. He pivoted in the sagging hammock, his splayed feet searching for sandals. Stretching to his full six-foot height, he added a faded T-shirt to frayed denim shorts. He ran both hands through thick graying hair, and smoothed his unkempt beard—his only concessions to formality when greeting visitors, expected or otherwise.

Lanky, with scarce meat on his bones, Parrish moved with measured grace despite two bad knees a lifetime of hard work had left him with. Creating his refuge—a hideaway surf camp chiseled from the cliffs by hand—had taken a toll. Each nail and scrap of lumber had been carried down the cliffs by hand and it showed in his once broad shoulders now slightly stooped with age.

Parrish waited on the patio's top step, arms folded, his frame leaning against one of the smooth white plastered pillars supporting an arbor thick with vines. The van stopped at the bottom of the rocky slope in a gravel car lot. Three Anglos and a Mexican got out. Theirs was the only other vehicle besides a parked pickup truck with California license plates.

The four newcomers surveyed the main house, the modest decked cottages, and the cavernous boat shed at water's edge.

"*Bienvenido,*" Parrish called in a raspy voice from the shaded patio.

Lopez returned the greeting. "*Bienvenido, señor. Mi nombre es Luis López.*"

Parrish offered his hand. "*Mucho gusto, amigo.* Your friends Americans by any chance?"

Lopez laughed. "Of course." He gestured to the three. "Tom Wolf, Mike Parvin and Preacher Hackett."

"I'm Max Parrish." The men shook hands in turn.

Parrish said, "Preacher, huh? You out harvesting souls in the Baja by any chance?"

"Just a nickname," said Hackett.

"Good. Don't need religion raising its ugly head in my world."

Eying Parrish, Preacher didn't flinch. "To each his own."

"Amen to that," Parrish snapped. He kept to the shade while questioning them. "What brings you this far south?"

"Surf," said Wolf, gesturing to the ocean. "Heard this is a sweet spot."

Parrish followed Wolf's eyes. "It is indeed. We're off the beaten track and that's the way I like it. And you're in luck. The swell's running."

"We'd like to do an overnight," said Wolf. "Maybe get in a session while it's still light."

"Help yourself. The waves are free."

"Nice place," said Parvin, gesturing to the buildings.

"We're not four-star," said Parrish. "Hell, we're not even two-star. But you get clean sheets and towels. Forty bucks a man, per day. A bargain when you figure that you get bottled water and three squares. Breakfast nine to ten, lunch at noon, and supper at sunset. Tequila, rum or beer is extra. Run a tab. Pay when you leave."

Parrish shot a stern look at his guests. "And don't even think about shorting me. Did I mention no drugs, including weed?"

Wolf smiled. "Neither one of those crossed our minds."

"You have good timing. Only have two other guests. They're out in the lineup with my daughters. Your choice, bunk together or split it any way you like. We have three vacant cottages. Compost toilets out back. Surfboards or kayaks for rent if you want."

"We brought boards," said Wolf. "And we'll bunk together."

Parrish cocked an eyebrow at Lopez. "That go for your driver too?"

A polite smile. Wolf said, "Like family by now."

Parrish snorted. "If you say so." Fumbling with a ring of keys dangling on a belt loop, he removed one and tossed it to Lopez.

"*Flor, número tres.*"

"Thanks, we'll make ourselves at home," said Wolf.

Parrish returned to his hammock. "No cable," he said over his shoulder. "If my girls and cat like you, we'll invite you to the main house to watch satellite TV. Real *fútbol*, not that other crap. We don't roll up the sidewalks early. Don't have any." He lay back, laughing at the old joke.

Chapter 39

Cabo San Lucas Marina

About to lose his wheels without a fight, Gideon sat in the captain's chair on the *South Wind*'s enclosed bridge. Staring through a pair of marine binoculars, he felt helpless as he watched four policemen swarm the rental jeep. He had parked it on a side street on the north side of the marina where he could keep an eye on it. The jeep had been left untouched until now. Scheduled to call Wolf in one hour, Gideon knew the loss of the wheels would be a footnote to his more unwelcome news.

He had arrived several hours late to find *South Wind* moored but deserted. Gideon's first thought had been that McFadden and Snuffy had likely taken the wounded couple to a hospital for care. A search of the main cabin had turned up the missing men's luggage and a hidden satellite phone McFadden had been using. Nothing else looked to have been disturbed.

But something not quite right, he thought.

Gideon's arrival had not gone unnoticed.

Neighbors aboard a larger yacht in the adjacent slip had been watching Gideon's every move. Despite his best efforts to remain low-key, his presence aboard the *South Wind* had attracted unwanted attention. Prodded by his wife, the yacht's reluctant owner crossed the dock and hailed Gideon at the fishing boat's starboard rail.

"Hello, Anybody home?" He called again. "Hello!"

Wary, Gideon poked his head from the main cabin's hatch. A balding, porcine figure wearing a floral shirt, shorts, and deck shoes sans socks, stared back at him.

"Are you Gideon?" said the stranger.

"Who's asking?"

"I'm William Porter. Sam McFadden said to expect you."

Relieved, Gideon came up on deck. "Where is Sam?"

Glancing over his shoulder, Porter said, "Perhaps it's better we talk aboard my boat. They may be watching."

"They?"

Porter shrugged. "Maybe the police. I'm not sure." Gesturing to his moored yacht, Porter lowered his voice. "My boat, please."

Gideon did his best to act nonchalant. "Sam and I were to meet when he docked but I was running several hours late."

"Afraid I've got bad news."

"What is it?"

Porter inclined his head to his yacht, his eyes pleading.

Sizing up the beefy American, Gideon felt no threat. He followed the yacht's owner across the pier to the bigger boat's fantail. Porter entered the main salon, Gideon behind him.

Once inside, the man, extended a hand. "William Porter," he said.

The Marine took it. A short, tanned, apple-shaped woman in pink sweats waved from behind an upholstered bar.

"My wife, Val," said Porter.

"Drink?" said the silver-haired woman, hoisting one of her own.

Gideon declined. "No thanks. Okay, what's your bad news?"

Chapter 40

Porter settled on a stool at the galley's padded bar and took a generous tumbler of scotch from his wife. "Two hours ago we were on the top deck, tidying up. Your friends arrived. As soon as they tied up, the police appeared. A young couple was taken off first. They looked to be in bad shape. Next, off went your friends with the cops."

"I certainly hope drugs weren't involved," interrupted Val Porter.

"Not a chance," said Gideon. The Porters, he learned, were a retired couple in their late sixties, from Huntington Beach. Eager to tell him what they had seen, the pair interrupted each other.

"Your friends were outnumbered," said Porter. "As he was being hustled away, McFadden yelled for me to keep an eye out for you."

His wife chirped, "Who were those young folks?"

Sketching the barest of details about the rescue of the battered couple, Gideon pressed the Porters for more details.

Both described behavior of the police with righteous indignation.

"Obviously looking for a handout," steamed William Porter. "We've seen this before. One my business associates was bullied by these cops last year. They claimed he was buying drugs at some nightclub."

Porter's wife had clucked sympathetically at the tale. "Can you imagine that? Theo was quite shaken."

"Shaken down is what you mean," growled Porter. "He got off cheap, but it's crap like this that leaves such a bad taste in your mouth about the whole Mexican experience. They've had a chip on their shoulders ever since the election."

A third cocktail and Porter was soon pacing the salon, egged on by his wife's tales of other slights she and friends had suffered at the hands of rude taxi drivers and cops seeking bribes during her times ashore.

"You could check the hospitals for that young couple your friends brought here," said Porter's wife. "They didn't look like they were going to be getting out that day or the next."

"Any idea which hospital they may have taken them to?"

Porter thought for a moment. Turning to his wife, he said, "Where did Dottie go last year when she had those stitches put in?"

Her brow furrowed, Val Porter, stared out the salon's windows. "Ah, I remember. *Americamed*, or *Amerimed*. 'First-rate care,'" Dottie said.

Porter beamed. "Of course. Start there, Mister Gideon."

"Thanks. You've both been very helpful. I'll make a call to my other friends to tell them what's happened. Then, I'll check that hospital."

"And then, you must come back for dinner," said Porter.

His wife, face flushed, waddled from behind the bar, pointing at Gideon. "I insist. It's the least we can do."

Gideon rose. "I'll run my errands first. Dinner sounds good."

"It's no problem," said Porter, following him to the stern deck. "We'll hold off until you show."

"If I'm not back by twenty-hundred hours, go ahead without me."

Porter raised his glass as Gideon returned to the *South Wind*.

Aware he was Wolf's only set of eyes and ears in the port city, Gideon would begin with the battered couple.

Contacting them would be part of the puzzle. Finding out where McFadden and Snuffy had been taken would be a challenge. As for roaming the city asking after the missing college students based on credit card use—too risky. And the idea of showing the pictures of the four lost Americans was out. To add to his precarious situation, he was without transportation and facing the next day hiding in the *South Wind*. Gideon was following Wolf's advice to stay invisible —though hiding in plain sight aboard a forty-foot sport fishing boat moored in a crowded marina was not exactly a guarantee of invisibility.

Chapter 41

Wolf and his crew unloaded the van, claimed bunks, and settled in.

"I'm going to get in the water," Wolf told them. "I'll talk to the people out there, see if I can find out anything useful."

Preacher smiled. "Not wasting any time, are you?"

"Gotta make it look authentic."

"Yeah, right," Preacher said. "What do you want us to do while you're out enjoying yourself?"

Wolf ignored the dig. "Do some recon on the property. Be casual. Poke around. Get the lay of the land. Walk the roads. We'll compare notes when I come in. I'll call Sam later tonight for an update."

Worming into his wetsuit, Wolf took a nine-foot board from the van and headed to the beach with a broad smile. Parvin and Preacher followed to watch him paddle out. The four surfers Wolf had spotted earlier, two men and a pair of women, were still out. The waves were six-foot rights, bluish-green walls wrapping around the rocky point for long rides into the bay. Wolf stroked to the takeoff point and sat watching, content to wait his turn.

His patience was rewarded. He caught and returned a loose board to one of the women after a spill. Surfacing, she introduced herself as Maria, Parrish's daughter. The other woman, a sister named Elizabeth, paddled over between sets to meet Wolf. Stunning beauties with long black hair tied in ponytails and wetsuits molded to shapely bodies, both caught Wolf's eye. In their late-twenties, the sisters were at home in the water, taking wave after wave, carving radical turns on their short boards. Wolf was impressed and told them so.

While waiting for incoming waves, Wolf met the two journeymen surfers from California. They told him they were working their way north along the coast. Both thirty-something, and less flamboyant than the Parrish sisters, they were nonetheless capable watermen and welcomed Wolf. With only four surfers plus Wolf at the break, there was none of the usual scrapping for waves that characterized California's selfish beach culture.

In between sets, Wolf chatted with Parrish's daughters, learning a brief story of the tiny resort and the family's routine. He gave away nothing of his own history to the women. As far as they knew, he was what he appeared to be— an older American male on a personal surfing safari with friends. After two hours in the water, Wolf paddled in. He rinsed off, hung his wetsuit to dry in the remaining sunlight, and took a short siesta until called by Lopez to dinner.

Chapter 42

That evening, the patio table was set for six guests. Parrish's daughters served the meal. Having delegated the care of the resort's guests to his offspring, Parrish was nowhere to be seen. A fireplace set in the patio's adobe wall kept the night's chill at bay while the six guests ate.

Afterwards, with dishes cleared and coffee served, Wolf regaled the group with stories about his college years and close calls with marriage. Parvin talked about Southern football. Preacher and Lopez listened. Trading tales about their years of surfing the Baja, the Californians admitted this trip to be their last. Family and work demands interfered more these days, according to the two. Wolf probed about the level of crime along the highway and rumors of cartel killings but got little. Sports talk, then a debate on politics took over but ended without rancor.

The two surfers eventually begged off, leaving Wolf, Lopez, Parvin and Preacher to themselves. Reviewing again what they had learned that day, the four huddled by the fire comparing notes, the sound of surf masking their voices.

"I talked with some of the locals doing roof work," said Lopez. "They live in Las Colinas, a small town two miles inland. They say it's just a few homes, some trailers, a general store, a Pemex station, a cafe and one bar."

"And a police station," added Preacher. "They mentioned police."

"How many police?" said Wolf.

Parvin rubbed his chin. "We'd have to go to town to find out."

Wolf said, "Could that be a problem, Luis?"

A shrug. "Hard to tell. The police in towns like this are always a risk."

"Always with their hand out," groused Parvin.

"I'll ask Parrish about the place," said Wolf. "My gut feeling is that we shouldn't take chances. You think it's risky to ask about these missing kids, Luis?"

Lopez hesitated. "I think I should go myself to ask these questions. Tomorrow I will take the van to Los Colinas to get fuel."

"One of us will go with you," said Wolf. "Those wheels are our only transportation. If something happened to you or the van we'd be in a helluva fix." He glanced at his watch. "Hold that thought. I promised Sam I'd talk with him tonight."

He excused himself and climbed the road to the top of the bluff to make the satellite call. In fifteen minutes, he returned with sobering news.

Chapter 43

Wolf pulled a chair close to his team. "The police in Cabo San Lucas picked up Sam and Snuffy for questioning."

Preacher and Parvin sat in shocked silence. Lopez said, "On what charge?"

"When they got to the marina, Snuffy asked the harbormaster to recommend a clinic where they could take Kelsey Magano and her boyfriend. Next thing they knew, police showed and hustled everyone off the boat."

Wolf got up to pace, tapping the satellite phone against his leg.

Lopez said, "But he had time to call you?"

"No." Wolf shook his head. "I couldn't raise Sam. That was Gideon. He was calling from the marina where *South Wind*'s docked. He got there late but met an American couple who saw the whole thing go down."

Preacher said, "What about Kelsey and her boyfriend?"

"Gideon says this couple saw another police truck take them away. He's going to try and find what hospital they're in."

"And Snuffy and Sam?"

"As far as he knows, they might be sitting in police headquarters."

The news hit hard. Only the hissing surf and the occasional pop of a dying ember in the fireplace broke the silence blanketing Wolf and his team. Twice, Preacher started to say something but couldn't find the words. Lopez hunched forward on the edge of his chair, elbows resting on his knees, eyes on Wolf.

Thinking aloud, Wolf said, "We need that boat. That's our ticket out."

Preacher shook his head. "Reggie's gonna fall apart when she hears."

"I'm not telling her," said Wolf, "at least not yet."

Parvin fed the last of the wood to the fire. "Call the girl's parents."

"What?"

Looking up at Wolf, Parvin said, "Call the girl's father, see if he can help Sam clear up this mess with the police."

Throwing up his hands, Wolf said, "I have no idea who her father is or how to contact him. Sam was supposed to do that when they docked."

"But you saved his daughter. This guy owes you."

"Even if I knew how to contact her parents what makes you think they have that kind of clout?"

Parvin was insistent. "For starters, they're back home and we're here. They can probably pull strings from there. Call Gideon and tell him to get the girl to make that connection. Find out if her parents can do something to get our guys out of jail. And you're right about our needing that boat."

Preacher said, "We could pack up first thing in the morning and head to Cabo, see what we can do to spring Sam and Snuffy."

Wolf stared at Lopez. "Luis, do you have any contacts with the military or police? Might be time to call in the chits."

Lopez said, "I can make some calls tomorrow."

"Good. We'll try that. Meanwhile, we can't do anything tonight," said Wolf. "I'll call Gideon at first light to get a fix on what's happening. If he says he needs us, we'll get on the road."

Parvin got to his feet. "That's it? That's all we're gonna do?"

Wolf said, "Yeah, it's the only option for now."

Pleading, Parvin turned to Preacher. "Say something."

"Like what? I'm willing to wait. Wolfman's right. Can't do anything from this far away, at this time of night. Don't know about you guys, but I'm gonna hit the sack."

Lopez put a hand on Parvin's arm. "*Amigo*, he is right. There is nothing to be done at this hour. In the morning, we will think clearly about what to do." He turned, following Wolf and Preacher to their rented cabin.

Abandoned on the patio, with Wolf's words little comfort, Parvin sat in front of the fireplace, watching the glowing embers die, willing dawn to arrive early.

Chapter 44

The angry snarl of dirt bikes sent Wolf bolting from his bunk. Wrapped in a blanket, he crept barefooted to the door and stepped outside, keeping to the shadows. Lopez followed, then a rousted Parvin, all drawn by shouts and screaming engines.

Preacher grabbed his bow and fitted four arrows to the quiver. He slipped out the back door, creeping behind the parked van where he crouched, hidden. He nocked a razor-sharp broadhead arrow and waited.

Four motorcycles crested the road leading down to the seaside hostel and went airborne over the ruts, slamming down hard. They ran the length of the property and returned. Doing wheelies, the riders, anonymous in black, skidded to a stop in front of the main house. Firing raised pistols in the air, the quartet executed a series of tight rodeo turns, spitting dirt and rock in their wakes.

From his vantage point, Wolf spotted Max Parrish exiting his doorway. Wearing a loose, knee-length nightshirt, the hostel's owner, glowing lantern in hand, left the safety of his threshold to stand on his front steps, confronting the bikers. Rapid-fire words, loud, profane and unintelligible, flew between the riders and Parrish. More gunshots and the motorbikes screamed up the hill, disappearing in the dark.

The acrid stench of gunpowder hung in the drifting dust. Wolf retreated back inside and latched the door.

"What the hell was that all about?" said Parvin.

Wolf shook his head. "Not a clue." He grasped Lopez's shoulder in the darkened room. "Did you catch any of what they were saying?"

"Threats, challenges, insults to ancestors."

"But who were these people, Luis?"

Wolf felt the Mexican's shoulders shrug. "Whoever they were, *Señor* Parrish seemed to know them, I think. Perhaps they are drunken fools from the village."

"Where's Preacher? Anybody seen Preacher?"

"He was right behind us," said Parvin.

A figure slipped in the back door—Preacher holding his bow.

"What were you thinking?" said Wolf.

Slipping the bow into its case, Preacher ran the zipper and stood up.

"Wasn't sure what these guys were up to. Thought I should be ready just in case."

"Tell us next time," said Wolf. "You might have got yourself killed out there."

"I doubt it." Reclining on his bunk, he said, "This Parrish guy has guts. If these yahoos were trying to scare him, they failed. Did you see him out there? Never flinched."

"Major *cojones* if you ask me," said an admiring Parvin. "And by the way, Preacher, I should have had your back." He pointed a finger at the former SEAL. "Next time, don't leave without me."

"You're on, *hermano*."

"I'll talk to Parrish in the morning," said Wolf. "Find out what the hell that was all about."

Quiet descended. The hypnotic rhythm of the waves resumed, providing a sense of peace again. Wolf lay awake for another hour, expecting the sound of the bikes to split the night. But they didn't return. He eventually fell asleep, his mind replaying the image of a defiant Parrish holding his lantern in the midst of the uproar.

Chapter 45

After breakfast, Wolf sent Lopez and Parvin in the van to *Las Colinas* to refuel and sniff about. He and Preacher climbed the bluff and called Gideon. Nothing had changed. Snuffy and McFadden were still in custody as far as he knew. He was off to visit a local hospital favored by ex-pats in hopes of finding the wounded couple. Still reporting from *South Wind* where he had spent the night without being discovered, Gideon wasn't idle. The American couple moored in an adjacent slip had offered whatever help they could. He was weighing their offer he said and promised to call that evening with news before signing off.

"We ought to head down there to back him up," said Preacher.

"Not yet," said Wolf, putting away the sat phone. "Let's see if Lopez and Parvin turn up anything. If it's a dry hole here we'll head to Cabo."

The two retraced their steps down the road.

Preacher said, "You should talk to Parrish in the meantime."

"I'll feel him out to see if he's a friendly."

"And if he is?"

"Then I'll show him the pictures of our MIAs and see what he knows."

Wolf and Preacher returned to find Parrish on a ladder giving orders to a worker repairing a section of the boathouse roof. Wolf sent Preacher to quiz the two Californians about their reaction to the previous night's circus. The two were busy packing their truck for what looked like an early departure. Wolf headed for Parrish.

"Morning," he sang out. "Another day in paradise, eh?"

"*Hola*," said Parrish from the top of the ladder. "Sorry about the disturbance last night."

"Had a hard time getting back to sleep. What was that all about?"

"Give me five minutes," said Parrish. "We'll talk on the patio."

"I'll wait," said Wolf. He walked to the vine-covered arbor and settled in a chair facing the ocean. The waves had dropped in size, still tempting, however. He pictured the Parrish girls and thought about going out later.

Parrish rattled off more instructions to his man aloft and then came down the ladder. He ambled to the patio and took a chair opposite Wolf.

"Appears most of my crew got the word," he said. "Only Jorge Ruiz showed this morning."

"Something to do with last night?"

"Unfortunately, yes. On the bright side, you'll have the place to yourselves," he said. "The other gentlemen are clearing out, heading back north a couple days early."

Wolf followed Parrish's eyes to the Californians' truck where Preacher was chatting with the pair.

"Another casualty of last night?"

"Yeah," said Parrish. "Can't blame 'em."

"What was going on? And by the way, you impressed the hell out of us with the way you stood your ground."

Parrish shrugged at the compliment. "Typical behavior from Garcia's boys."

"You know those guys?"

"I do. They've been showing up with some regularity these last few months. At first, it was frightening. Scares the hell out of the guests. But I'm used to it now. It's irritating. They don't give up easily. But then, neither do I."

Wolf held up his hands. "If you don't mind telling me, what was it about?"

"Intimidation. A campaign to get me to quit this spot."

"What's the reason?"

"Let's talk over coffee, eh?" He waved to Maria, who was wiping down the breakfast table. "*Café, por favor, Cariño.*"

In minutes, she arrived with a tray and two steaming cups of fresh coffee. "Maybe you like to go out later," she cooed to Wolf. "The waves are smaller than yesterday, but just as much fun, eh?"

"Maria, dearest, the man is resting. Don't bother our guests."

Wolf hoisted his cup, smiling. "Not a bother. Actually, I'd like that. Perhaps after I've had time to talk with your father."

A wink and a curtsy and Maria retreated, despite her father's feigned scowl. "Hard to get the work done when the ocean calls," he said.

"A no-brainer when you're young, Max."

Wolf sipped his coffee and leaned forward, cup and saucer balanced on a knee. "Somebody wants you out of here? Why? We were told you've been here since the early Seventies." The black cat circled behind Wolf, leapt into Parrish's lap, and settled, its eyes fixed on Wolf. Parrish stroked the cat, producing a slow purring. "True. Ended up here in late sixty-nine."

"Vietnam along the way?"

A nod. "Yep. Got out in Oakland and headed south. Bought an old Ford panel truck and two used boards. Just like Steinbeck, except no dog. Hit the border and just kept going. Found this spot and camped for two months straight."

"What'd you do for money?"

"Separation pay. Down here you can nurse it a long ways."

"Came to surf. Your own *Endless Summer*, huh?"

"True. But also came to clear my head. Get it on straight, you know."

"I know the feeling."

Parrish smiled. "Do you now?"

"Indeed I do."

An arched eyebrow at Wolf. "Military in your background?"

"In another lifetime," he said. "Another story for another time. I'd rather hear yours."

A sip and a sly Cheshire cat grin from Parrish. "I'll bore you."

"Given the surroundings, I doubt that. You were saying you came to the Baja to surf."

"Two months straight. The swell was running twenty-four seven."

"A fantasy of mine as well. Whose land was it where you squatted?"

Parrish smiled at some memory. "Ah, that was the beauty of the thing. This was all part of a ranch. Belonged to Don

Pablo Diego Alvarez." He spread his arms, taking in the beach and cliffs behind him.

"Almost eight thousand hectares. Old crown land deeded to his great grandfather before the revolution. Don Pablo ran cattle and horses. He took what was marginal land and made something of it. This far from the capital nobody bothered with Baja's coast. Las Colinas was just huts. No roads to speak of. If a guy was looking for isolation, this was it."

"Fast forward," said Wolf.

Chapter 46

The fickle feline fled from Parrish's grasp and vanished. "One day I came in from a session and found a beautiful woman on horseback at my campsite. Took my breath away, she did."

He pointed over Wolf's shoulder where the rutted road rose to meet the bluffs. "Just beyond that spot up there. She asked me what I was doing on her father's land. I said I was surfing, of course."

"She run you off?"

"On the contrary, *amigo*. She invited herself to coffee and came back the next day, and the day after that."

Wolf grinned. "I can see where this is going."

"You got it. Never left. Her father warmed to me eventually. I worked on the ranch for two years. Rosa and I married. Had a brood of kids..."

Interrupting, Wolf said, "I met Maria and Elizabeth in the water."

"So my girls said. Those two were already part mermaid by age ten."

Wolf sipped his coffee. "Top notch surfers, both."

"Don't I know it. They love it here. Couldn't run the place without 'em. All my kids helped out in turn. Maria and Elizabeth are the only ones still with us. We're the Mexican Von Trapps, you might say."

Wolf laughed. "Not easy to find you, though."

Parrish tugged at his beard. "I know. At first I wanted to keep it off the grid. But word got out. This point break is a classic shape. Takes a mushy west swell of any size and cleans it up."

"I agree. Nice shape. Clean. Long paper-thin walls."

"*Surfer Magazine* did a three-page spread fifteen years ago."

"That must have brought you some business."

"It did." A shrug. "I was ambivalent. But Rosa insisted we expand. The ranch was dying in a drought. Couldn't do both. We got rid of the cattle and horses. Sold off some parcels north of here and went on a building spree. Things were good. The town grew. The oil boom came. The roads improved, of course."

"Heard there's a Pemex station in town."

"Another sign of progress, I guess."

"Besides your kids, you have local help for the grounds?"

Parrish nodded at his man crabbing across the roof. "Jorge Ruiz and his cousins. Pays to put money back in the local economy."

Their conversation broken by the sound of a truck engine's rumble, Wolf and Parrish shifted in their chairs to watch the Californians grind up the furrowed road to the top of the bluff. Preacher waved to Wolf and hiked up the road, following their dust to the bluffs.

"Always this slow?" said Wolf turning back to Parrish.

"Been this way for the past three years."

"People reluctant to come this far south?"

Parrish scowled, waved his hand. "Between bad press about cartel violence, and highway shakedowns the trip is less appealing these days."

"But the waves," said Wolf, gesturing to the ocean.

Sighing, Parrish said, "All those waves going to waste, I know."

"Still get out?"

"Less and less. Knees give me trouble. Back's not much better."

"And the water temperature."

"There is that. It's not as much fun for me anymore."

Wolf got up to stretch. "Be like heaven to have a break like this in your front yard. And no crowds."

"Other than the hard core, where are the crowds when you need them?" said Parrish. "Can't make a living on fanatics alone."

Taking his seat again, Wolf said, "I'll tell you where the masses are. Scrapping over ankle-high mush, risking hepatitis in sewage run-off, sharing every wave with a dozen riders in *El Norte*. They don't know what they're missing down here."

"And so, that brings us to that shoot 'em up last night," said Parrish.

"Is that connected to what's driving your vacancy rate?"

"Unfortunately."

"You said they were Garcia's boys. What does that mean?"

Parrish stared past Wolf at the waves. "Miguel Garcia. *El Jefe*. He owns most of Las Colinas and the surrounding land. Rosa and I made a mistake. We sold him some acreage years ago so we could expand this place and pay off some debt. Garcia wanted to buy us out but we turned him down. Been turning him down every year since."

"Let me guess," interrupted Wolf. "Things got ugly when you wouldn't sell."

Parrish nodded. "Garcia's a rancher but he has bigger goals. There was a master plan years ago to build a string of marinas along the coast. Promises of jobs, tourism, the whole nine yards. Then the global economy tanked. The cartels got up on their hind legs. The government changed hands and the plan got sidetracked. Garcia had bet big. He owns the only general store between La Paz and Cabo. Sonofabitch raised prices, played around with my water access, and cut my power from time to time."

"I don't see any utility lines," said Wolf, glancing around.

"And you won't," Parrish said. "We're off the grid. Solar, some generator use, lamps, windmill up top, and other basics."

"What about food and fuel?"

Grinning, Parrish said, "I make a run to La Paz or Cabo every ninety days to stock up on what we need. Garcia won't sell to me anyway and damned if I'm gonna give him the satisfaction of spending my money with him."

"How long can you survive under these conditions?"

Parrish scowled. "As long as it takes."

"You worried about this guy?"

"He's your typical bully. Has a bunch of *matones* to do his bidding."

Wolf seized on the word. "Ah, bully boys," he said. "Classic case of *El Jefe* and his hired hands, huh?"

"It's an old scenario being played out all over this country."

Wolf leaned forward. "You mentioned something about highway shakedowns. What about the police in town? What about army patrols to keep the highways open. Explain that to me."

The cat chose the silence following the question to reappear, leaping into Parrish's lap to beg for attention. The big yellow eyes stared at Wolf.

"The local cops are a creation of Garcia's. They're in his pocket," said Parrish. "The army is hit and miss. Most of their officers and sergeants can be bought. Same with the *federales*. I call the stretch fifty kilometers north and south of us 'Garcia-land' for lack of a better description."

He held the cat aloft as if speaking to it. "Anyone is fair game, right, Paco? Police, cartel caravans, and military patrols excepted, of course."

"How does your wife feel about this?"

Parrish stroked the cat, calming it. "She's worried. That's why she's in the capitol as we speak. Gone to work her magic on a relative who's a senator. We can't get our own officials to pay attention to what's happening. Garcia keeps some of locals on his payroll."

Wolf frowned. "Easy way for the locals to make a few bucks."

"True. An old habit but it's getting out of hand. Bad for business."

"Thought of hiring some home-grown security?"

Parrish returned the cat to the paving. "And where would that put me? I'd have to hire someone who doesn't live in Las Colinas. It would start a war. Garcia would bring in his own *sicarios*."

"Hired guns, sure. But it sounds like you're already in a war."

Gripping both arms of his chair, Parrish squinted at Wolf. "Which brings up an interesting question I'd like to ask you."

"Fair enough."

Parrish laced fingers together under his chin. "What's the story behind that business at the beach campsite north of here the other night?"

"What business are you referring to?"

"Don't play games, *amigo*. Word travels fast. I'm talking about a botched raid some *campensinos* tried to pull off. Seems there were certain *gringos* who put up a helluva fight. My sources tell me only two out of five attackers got away."

"Really? Interesting tale," said Wolf, his face neutral. "Sounds like the good guys won that round. I'd like to know how news of this alleged firefight travelled this far, that fast."

"I'll make you a deal. I'll tell you what I know if you level with me about why you showed up on my doorstep and what it is you're after."

Chapter 47

Parrish studied Wolf without speaking, waiting for him to go first.

"Okay, I'll level with you, Max. My friends and I are looking for four missing college kids. Surfers. Post-school holiday. It's been ninety days since they crossed the border. We tracked them to Ensenada. We know they picked up some dirt bikes and a trailer there and headed south."

"Who you working for?"

"*Pro bono*. The mom of one of the kids asked for our help."

"Noble cause."

Wolf bristled. "It's the truth."

Parrish said, "Easy, cowboy. I don't doubt you."

Leaning back in his chair, Wolf locked his hands behind his head, wondering how much to give away. "We heard about your place from some cantina owner up north. She said our boys were headed this way."

"How did she know they were your guys?"

"Showed her some pictures."

Parrish shifted in his chair. "Gonna make me ask for them?"

"I wasn't sure at first." Embarrassed at his initial reluctance, Wolf pulled a folded sheet from his pocket and passed it to Parrish.

"Ah, yes. These guys. Shoulda showed this to me earlier."

Wolf brightened. "You recognize them?"

"I do." He reeled off the names. "Morton, Farrel, Connole and Connor. Two vehicles." Parrish nodded at the bluffs above. "Had a trailer with dirt bikes. Had to park it up there."

Wolf let out a low whistle. "How long did they stay?"

Handing back the color copy of the missing, Parrish said, "Four days. Took two cabins. Paid cash. Stayed until the swell gave out. They each had two boards with them. That's how I knew they were for real." He paused, letting his point sink in. "You, on the other hand—" Parrish hinted at a smile.

"Shoulda known something was up when you showed. Three *Anglos*, a Mexican, two boards among them, and one wetsuit. It didn't add up. Didn't make sense."

Wolf shrugged. "Pretty thin cover, I know."

"My daughters picked up on that right away, but I doubt any locals did," said Parrish. "Just some *gringos locos* with money to burn. Go on."

"These missing students were supposed to go on to Cabo."

"Supposed to? Didn't they show?"

Wolf shook his head. "Not sure. Some of our guys are down there now checking credit card records to see if they made it."

"Quite the operation you're running. Should be easy enough to run that down. Show those pictures in town. Stop at bars. Talk to people."

"It's complicated," said Wolf.

"Something to do with that little run-in north of here?"

"You're right, that was us. For the record, we stumbled into that."

Parrish toyed with his beard, his eyes on the ocean. "I believe you. I told you that word travels fast. My guess is you ran into some of Garcia's *matones*. He lets them freelance along the highway, north and south."

"That making it worse for you?"

A casual shrug. "More of the same. Actually, it's potentially a bigger problem for you."

"How so?"

"You took care of three out of five. The two who got away are probably looking for you now."

Wolf said, "If they connect us to you it might become your problem as well."

Parrish stood. "Garcia already has my number. My guess is that you and your friends are in his crosshairs now."

Chapter 48

Determined to be resourceful, if not truthful, Gideon headed for the Amerimed Hospital, where he hoped to find Kelsey Magano and her boyfriend, Philip. First, he stopped at the Porters' yacht to say hello, telling them only that he was doing a reconnaissance of the city on foot. He made no mention of visiting the hospital.

Avoiding the temptation to take a taxi, Gideon followed the tiled walkway bordering the north end of the marina. He crossed the public boat ramp and headed to the commercial heart of the city, *Puerto Paraiso*. Jammed with shoppers and tourists, Cabo's premier shopping center offered him the anonymity he needed. If Porter's warning about being watched were to be believed, the mall—a bloated Mexican version of Rodeo Drive boutiques meets garish Las Vegas chic—would cover his tracks. Gideon exited the shopping center onto *Boulevard Lazaro Cardenas* and turned right, certain he wasn't being followed.

As an afterthought, he stopped at a street vendor's stand to buy a prop—flowers wrapped in cellophane. Blending in with the crowds, he covered the four blocks to the hospital without once being stopped by police or hustlers.

Inside the hospital's entry he identified himself as Kelsey Magano's uncle and asked for her room. Gideon's luck held. Yes, said the lobby's receptionist, there was such a patient. Gideon signed in and was escorted by a nursing aide down a corridor and around a corner. There, Gideon ran into an unexpected hurdle.

A bored policeman sat next to the room's doorway, his eyes focused on a tabloid paper. To turn back now would arouse suspicion.

Gideon gambled, the flowers held chest-high.

The aide stopped in the room's doorway and knocked.

Lifting his eyes from the paper, the policeman eyed them both.

"*Quien es este?*" he said to Gideon's escort.

"*Es de la familia,*" she answered.

Gideon tensed as the officer began to rise. "*Familia?*"

"*Su tio.*"

Cradling the flowers, Gideon risked a smile. Shrugging, the policeman slouched in his chair and resumed reading.

"*Muchos gracias,*" whispered Gideon to the aide as he crossed the threshold. She left him with a shy smile and a puzzled Kelsey Magano, who lay on her back, eyes fastened on her visitor. Both arms wore scratches and purple bruises, her nose was swollen and her bottom lip puffy.

"Who are—?"

Gideon crossed the floor, finger to his lips, tilting his head toward the policeman in the corridor.

"I know you," she said. "That night—"

"Maverick Gideon," he said, offering the bouquet. "My friends and I were there when it happened. How much do you remember?"

She turned away. "Enough," she said. "How did you find me?"

"Educated guess." He placed the flowers on a bedside table and stood at the foot of the bed. "My friend, Sam McFadden, brought you here on the boat."

"Yes, I know. There was a mix-up when we got here. Police. No one would listen to us. They drove Philip and me here."

"You're in a good place," he said. "You're looking better." She turned back to him. "Philip was hurt. Have you seen him?"

Gideon shook his head. "Can't risk it yet. Took a chance you might be here. Any idea where they took Sam and Snuffy?"

A slight shake of her head. "No. The police were there when we docked, I remember. Philip and I went one way, your friends went another way."

"I'm trying to find them, Kelsey."

"What can I do? I don't even know where Philip is."

Gideon glanced at the guard over his shoulder. "Maybe you can help me. Do your parents know where you are, what's happened?"

Tears pooled in her eyes. She shook her head. Gideon said, "I have a satellite phone. You want to call your family?"

She shook her head. "Not yet."

"I can call them for you if you'd like."

"Wouldn't do any good."

"But wouldn't they want to know?"

She shrugged. Gideon said, "Could they help my friends?"

"What do you mean?"

Now at the bed's raised side rail, Gideon said, "I think the cops have thrown my friends in jail, Kelsey. If there's any way you think your parents could be of help, please tell me."

"We're better off talking to my mom. My dad might listen to her."

"Let me guess, this have something to do with your boyfriend?"

She bit her lower lip and nodded.

"Give me a number. I can call her."

Eyes squeezed tight, she recited a number. Gideon used a marker to write on the back of his hand. "Thanks," he said, "I'll give her a try."

She reached for him. "Will you find Philip for me? They didn't tell me anything when they brought us here."

"I'll see what I can find out. How long you going to be here?"

"Another day at least the doctor said."

"I'll call your mother," Gideon said. "Best thing for you to do is fly home as soon as you can. Look, if you need a place to stay when you get out, come to the marina. Dock F is where *South Wind* is moored. Next slip over is a yacht named *One More Sunset*. Go there first and ask for William or Val Porter. You get all that?"

She nodded. "Repeat it to me," he said.

"Porters. Dock F. *One More Sunset*."

Gideon took her hand. "Good. I'll try to get back to you, Kelsey."

"Tell my mother I'm sorry."

"It'd be better coming from you," he said. She turned her head.

The policeman outside had abandoned his post for the nurses' station to flirt. Slipping from the room without being noticed, Gideon took the stairs. Back on the street, he returned to the harbor determined to call Kelsey Magano's parents from the *South Wind*. After that, he'd call Wolf. The original mission of finding the missing college students was taking second place to this Cabo sideshow.

Chapter 49

Anticipating Gideon's afternoon call, Wolf climbed to the top of the bluff above the beach and found what shade he could under a skeletal olive tree ringed by an army of encroaching cactus. From the heights above the bay, he watched the incoming waves. Two tiny figures, the Parrish sisters, bobbed in the swells at the point. Wolf envied them.

Movement in the thick brush to his left drew his attention. Preacher, compound bow in hand, stepped from behind the olive tree and ducked a low branch. "Catch you off guard?" he said.

"Never," lied Wolf. "Been listening to you stepping on every dry branch you could find for the last fifteen minutes. You losing your touch?"

"I seriously doubt that," huffed Preacher, joining Wolf in the shade.

Wolf nodded at the bow. "You catch anything with that?"

"Saw some coyotes and two guys on dirt bikes."

"They spot you?"

"Blind as bats," said Preacher. "Coulda dropped both of them."

Wolf held up the satellite phone. "Waiting for Gideon's call."

"Hope he's got better news," said Preacher.

Wolf got to his feet. "Speaking of news—I got a hit from Parrish on Connor and the others."

Preacher interrupted. "You showed him the pictures?"

"I did. He IDed them. Said they stayed a week and left, headed for Cabo. Guess that'll be our final stop after all. When Parvin and the major get back we'll head out. Still plenty of daylight to make it to Cabo."

"Outstanding," said Preacher. "We're making progress."

"Still don't have word of Sam and Snuffy. I'm hoping Gideon's got some good news for us on this next call."

"Roger that. But at least we're gonna stop in Cabo. Be a lot easier in town than stuck here in the middle of nowhere. Because right now I'm not liking this, Wolfman. Kinda like having both flanks up in the air. You know what I mean?"

Wolf wiped his brow with a bandana. "I hear you. I promise we'll have a sit down to weigh our options as soon as Parvin and Lopez return."

The satellite phone beeped in Wolf's hand. "Yeah, Wolf here." Motioning to Preacher, he mouthed 'Gideon' and covered one ear to hear better. Minutes passed, a series of grunts and short bursts of, "Uh, huh. Right. Good. Yep."

A final nod and then, the question Preacher wanted to hear. "Okay, that's good news. What's the skinny on Sam and Snuffy?"

Preacher closed with Wolf, straining to listen, his head down.

"Understood. Yes, go ahead and make the contact," said Wolf. "Pressure the parents to give us a hand. Roger that. And good news from this end. Turns out our boys spent seven days here, then left for Cabo. I figure we'll close up shop here and head your way ASAP." Wolf caught Preacher's eye and held up a hand, stopping his pacing. "Call us with more information when you get it. Out."

Nervous, Preacher backed off. "Sounds like Gideon had something positive to say, right?"

"Good news, bad news. He found the girl, Kelsey Magano, in a local hospital. No sign of the boyfriend. She gave him her parents' number and Gideon contacted the mother. She's going to talk to Kelsey's father. Then she'll scramble to arrange an airline ticket home. Kelsey's parents are divorced. But her mom told Gideon she'd get her ex to pull some strings."

"He a big shot lawyer or politician?"

Wolf shrugged. "Didn't say. Did say the mom was grateful for the news about her daughter. We'll wait and see if something breaks loose."

Preacher smiled. "Nice touch. Maybe she can book a group ticket as well. What about Sam and Snuffy?"

"Nothing yet. Gideon will nose around."

Preacher glanced at his watch. "You know, Parvin and the major have been gone most of the morning. Should we be worried?"

"They're big boys. They can take care of themselves. I think we should tell Parrish we're gonna pack it in and head for Cabo."

A horn blared. Bumping along the hardened track, the team's van showed, chased by a tail of choking ochre dust. Waving at the driver, Wolf and Preacher stepped into the road. The van rattled to a stop in the ruts, a battered, bloodied Lopez at the wheel.

Chapter 50

Wolf hurried to the driver's side and yanked open the door. "What the hell happened?"

Lopez eased himself into the front passenger seat. "You drive, *amigo*," he mumbled.

Climbing behind the wheel, Wolf shut the door. He glanced at a disheveled, bleeding Lopez. "What the—?"

"We'll...talk. Just drive, eh."

Preacher crawled in the back and leaned between the front seats. "No Parvin," he said. "Where's Mikey?"

Waving a hand, Lopez mumbled, "Los Colinas."

Wolf steadied the wheel for the descent to Parrish's camp. "Don't talk, Luis. We'll get you cleaned up. Then you can tell us what happened."

A weak nod. Lopez's head fell forward on his chest, his breathing ragged. At the bottom of the hill, Wolf parked in the gravel lot and came around the passenger side to help Preacher carry Lopez into their cabin. They laid him on a bottom bunk and stripped off his shirt and boots.

Preacher broke out the medic's kit and waited as Wolf toweled blood and dirt from the marine's head and torso. Soaking a clean gauze square with disinfectant, Preacher dabbed at cuts and raw bruises on Lopez's face, hands, and chest. The Mexican's left eye was swollen, nearly closed.

"Get him something to drink," said Wolf.

A bottle of chilled water revived Lopez. Propped on pillows, he told them what he remembered. "We topped off at the Pemex station, and then drove around Los Colinas. Checking things, you know?"

"And Parvin?" said Wolf.

"I drove," said Lopez. "Parvin warned me we had picked up some motorcycles on our tail. Maybe two at first, then three, then suddenly six."

Wolf frowned. "The same ones who dropped by our first night?"

Nodding, Lopez added, "I'm sure of it. We pass the store, the jail, then we head back here."

"Then what?" said Wolf.

"Couldn't lose them." Lopez groaned, touching his sides with both hands. "I think my ribs may be broken, *amigo*. Sorry."

"Parvin," said Preacher. "What about Parvin?"

Attempting to rise on his elbows, Lopez fell back against the pillows. "The police come alongside in a truck. They pull us over. Not a good sign in my world, you know?"

"Did you stop?" said Wolf.

A weak smile. Lopez nodded. "Big mistake."

"We talked. The chief looked at my papers. They pull me from the van; start to push me around, you know? Big mistake. Parvin gets out, pushes back. He took down two of them. I fought back too. More *hombres* show. More bikers stopped to help the police, of course."

"So, where is Parvin?" said Wolf.

"They took him to jail. Me, they beat and sent away."

At the sound of footsteps behind him, Wolf turned in a crouch.

Parrish's lanky frame filled the doorway. "To bring a message," he said. "I should have known this would happen."

Wolf stood, facing Parrish. "Can't say you didn't warn us. Garcia's doing?"

Parrish nodded. "His style. The police are all his boys."

"We have to get Parvin back."

"Garcia will be expecting that," said Parrish.

Wolf knelt next to Lopez. "Were you given a message?"

"He is the message," said Parrish.

"We'll get Parvin back," vowed Wolf.

Parrish propped an elbow against the top bunk, looked down at Lopez. "How about I make a trip to town to sort this out?"

Glaring, Wolf said, "What's to sort out? I'm not gonna leave Parvin overnight in that asshole's jail."

"I agree," said Parrish, "but let me do a little snooping around before you start knocking down doors."

Preacher put away the medic kit. "He's right. Let's see what we're facing before we charge in there."

Lopez shook a finger at Wolf. "It's true, *amigo*. Parvin's tough. He knows we will not leave him."

Wolf backed off to cool. To Parrish he said, "Okay. Do it your way for now. We didn't come here to begin a war."

"This war's been building," sighed Parrish. "You didn't start it, Garcia did. I've been putting this off for a long time."

"If you can work out something to your satisfaction, great," said Wolf. "Just make sure it includes a get-out-of-jail card for Parvin."

"I'll try," said a grim Parrish. "Keep an eye on my place while I'm gone."

"Will do," said Wolf.

Parrish headed for the door, stopped and added, "And my family."

Preacher nodded, "You're covered."

"I'll be back," said Parrish.

Wolf locked eyes with the resort owner. "If you don't return, we're coming to get you...and Parvin."

Chapter 51

Beneath a single bare bulb, Sam McFadden paced in a twelve-foot square windowless concrete room. The room's only furniture, a wooden table with two chairs and a wooden bench, took up most of one wall. Slouching in one of the chairs, a bored Snuffy Larson stared at their cell door, a gray, rust-flecked steel slab set in the middle of the opposite wall. Cockroaches scurried through a food slot at the bottom of the door—the more brazen of the insects climbing the table, only to be flicked into oblivion by Snuffy.

"I hope they don't seize my boat," he said.

Ten steps up, ten steps back, McFadden, head down in thought, was trying to unravel this latest turn of events. He interrupted his circuit. "Tell me about it. Your boat's key—our only way out."

Disconsolate, Snuffy propped chin in hand. "Shouldn't have come, Sam."

Stopping at the table, McFadden claimed the empty chair. "Don't give up yet. If they were planning to kill us they would have shot us and dumped us in the desert by now."

"Comforting thought."

"It's their way of doing things."

"More comforting thoughts."

McFadden glanced at Snuffy. "Seriously. These cops are sweating us for a bribe. *La mordida*, you know?"

"I thought that was done by the side of the road after a traffic stop."

McFadden shrugged and resumed pacing.

"Besides, they haven't said anything. We've been here almost two days, Sam. One candy bar between us. No visitors. No contact."

"We've got water." McFadden handed his cellmate a half-full bottle. "We'll survive."

"Always the optimist, huh?"

McFadden said, "Hope. Good thing to have, Snuffy. We—"

The muffled sound of footsteps outside the steel door caught their attention. Two loud raps echoed on the metal, sending both to their feet.

The door creaked opened, scattering the roaches. The steel frame filled with the same four khaki-clad policemen and balding plainclothes detective who had met the *South Wind*.

"*Visitante*," the detective barked. "*Su abogado.*"

Visitor, our lawyer? McFadden started to answer, then thought better of it. The bald man retreated from the cell, replaced by a short, corpulent, mustachioed Mexican wearing a soiled lined jacket over white dress shirt open at the collar. He carried a bulging, worn leather briefcase in his right hand.

"Ah, gentlemen," he said, "I apologize for the delay."

Scraping across the cement floor, the steel door locked shut.

"I am *Señor* Alfonso Brada, counselor at law."

McFadden stepped forward. "Who sent you?"

"Ah, you must be Samuel McFadden, yes?"

"I am. Who sent you?"

Ignoring the question, the lawyer flashed a smile at Snuffy Larson. "And you, of course, are *Señor* Larson, eh?"

Snuffy nodded. "Answer Sam. Who sent you?"

"Details, *señors*. I am here because I heard of your detention. A matter of some concern to me."

McFadden crowded the visitor. "Are we under arrest? The police have told us nothing. We've been held for two days. Not acceptable."

The fat man backed away and took out a handkerchief to mop his brow. "I must agree. Most unacceptable. However, it's merely a precaution for your own safety, gentlemen."

"We've done nothing to deserve this," said McFadden.

Pulling out one of the chairs, the portly Brada sat at the table. Sweeping a cockroach to the floor, he placed the briefcase in front of him.

"Shall we talk, my friends?"

Chapter 52

McFadden took the bench. Snuffy took a chair opposite their visitor.

"Answer my question," said McFadden. "Who hired you?"

Brada flashed a quick smile full of bad teeth beneath his moustache. "I come of my own accord. Once I heard of your circumstances I arranged this meeting."

"Okay, how soon can you get us released?"

Snuffy added, "And what about my boat?"

The repulsive smile again and the lawyer held up both hands. "One thing at a time, please. First, my goal is to facilitate your release."

"Good start," said McFadden. "How do you intend to do that?"

Brada folded his hands on top of the briefcase. "Ah, that will not be easy. It will be expensive, I can assure you."

"I'm not giving up my boat," growled Snuffy.

Waving away the comment, a scowling Brada said, "Of course not. That would be foolish. You need it to return home, do you not?"

The two exchanged wary glances at the remark. Changing subjects, McFadden challenged, "Why were we arrested?"

"Not arrested, detained. And it was for your well-being."

"Bullshit."

The smile disappeared, replaced with a stern look. "Word travels, even here in the Baja. Your part in that little business north of here is cause for concern by certain parties. Such things do not go unnoticed despite what the media in your country chooses to ignore."

McFadden said, "To what exactly are you referring?"

Brada tapped his fingers against the briefcase. "We have no time for gamesmanship, *Señor* McFadden. Three men are missing...men I assume are dead. Two others fled for their lives after an attack by unknown Americans at a coastal resort."

McFadden stayed neutral. "And how does that concern us?"

"Very well. If you insist, I will humor you. Let us say that the men involved are still being sought to answer questions about this tragic event. Did you know that two Americans were brought to a hospital here for treatment of wounds suffered in this affair?"

Snuffy said, "Then why not ask them?"

Slamming his fist, Brada yelled across the table. "You think of me someone you can insult? You think the police have not talked to these two? They have!" Smoothing his lapels, the lawyer struggled to regain his composure. "I was told these two traveled here on your boat."

Ignoring the theatrics, McFadden said, "Speak plainly, *Señor* Brada. What do you want with us? Why did you come here?"

Brada brightened, his outburst forgotten. "Good. We understand each other. You want to go back to your boat and leave. I want to send you on your way. But first, I show you something I think is relevant to the reason you have come here."

More posturing, thought McFadden.

Pushing from the table, the lawyer stood and unbuckled the briefcase. He reached inside the worn leather flap and pulled out two water bottles, a package of crackers and a red, long-sleeved athletic jersey. Unfolding the shirt, he passed it across the table to McFadden, who held it aloft for Snuffy's inspection.

A quick sober nod. "It's Connor's," he whispered.

"How did this come into your possession?" said McFadden.

Brada sat. "A man I did not know called me two months ago."

"Of course," said McFadden.

Talking with his hands, Brada said, "This man tells me he and his friends are holding a young American."

"Kidnapped, you mean," shot Snuffy.

The lawyer shrugged. "If you wish to call it so, *Señor* Larson. They tell me this boy's name. I said, 'Let me talk to him.' He tells me his name is Connor. He says he is from *El Norte*. San Diego."

McFadden leaned in. "What did these men want?"

"Ah, what do men like that always want? Money. They give me a number to call. The mother. So I call. She cries for her son, of course."

"Of course," said McFadden. "What mother wouldn't? What did you tell her?"

Avoiding Snuffy's accusing eyes, Brada focused on McFadden. "I tell her what these men want. I tell her these people are desperate men. She asks me for time to raise this money. I promise to talk to the people who have her son and tell them this."

Worried about Snuffy's reaction, McFadden shifted, glancing at him as a precaution. He needn't have worried. Leaving the negotiating to McFadden, Snuffy was content to hold the jersey in his lap.

"Did you contact these people again?" said McFadden.

"They are the ones who call when they want, not me."

"And Connor," said McFadden. "Is he well?"

Brada shrugged. "As well as can be expected, I assume."

Not what I wanted to hear, thought McFadden. "What is our connection to this situation? Why do you come to us?"

"The last time I call the boy's mother she tells me men have come to find him. Is this not true? Perhaps I have confused you with others?"

McFadden stiffened. *So much for our cover. Stall for time.*

Snuffy derailed the conversation. Glancing up from the jersey, he said, "How much do they want?"

Brada brightened. "Fifty thousand American. A bargain when you consider what my fellow countrymen have to pay to get their loved ones back."

"That's a lot of money," said McFadden.

"I'd need two weeks to raise it," said Snuffy. "And I need my boat."

McFadden jumped back in, sweeping his arm around the room. "Of course we want the boy back, but it's obvious we can't do anything from here."

"I will do what I can," said Brada. "I warn you...do not underestimate these men, gentlemen. They are not to be taken lightly. If you come between them and the money they want for this boy, he will die."

"Understood," said McFadden. "You must make them see that we need two weeks to make this work."

A huge sigh and more of Brada's drama. "I will try. These are hard men, used to getting what they want. They will certainly contact me once I return to my office."

Snuffy got to his feet, the jersey in his hands. "Is Connor being held here in Cabo San Lucas?"

Brada picked up his briefcase. "I have no idea where the boy is, *Señor* Larson. But I know these people have eyes in this city. Why they pick me as the go-between, I have no idea. What I do is a service to the families. I am only a lowly lawyer who normally deals in property."

Snuffy reached for Brada's hand. "I will make sure you are compensated for your help, Counselor."

The lawyer wiped a stage tear from his eye and gripped Snuffy's outstretched hand. "Perhaps just a small token."

"But a well-earned one," said Snuffy.

What the hell, thought McFadden. *If Snuffy can do it, so can I.*

"You have my appreciation, too. Let's pray this all ends well."

Brada shook McFadden's hand and shuffled to the steel door. He pounded his fist and shouted, "*Abrir. Hemos terminado aquí!*"

The big door swung open, the same policemen at their post. A stage whisper to the officers and Brada beckoned Snuffy.

"*Señor* Larson, a word with you, *por favor.*"

"Go ahead," said McFadden, "I'm right behind you."

Snuffy joined Brada on the threshold, exchanged a few words, then was gone. McFadden paused in the door, his way blocked by the cops.

Brada, visible behind the police, looked back at McFadden. "Do not worry, *Señor* McFadden. Once arrangements are made I will return for you. Until then—"

"Sam—" Snuffy's voice came from behind the policemen.
McFadden shouted, "Gideon! Give him a sitrep!"
The steel door slammed shut.

Chapter 53

Gideon pried apart the blinds in the yacht's port window.
William Porter crowded his elbow. "What's happening?"
he said.

Staring across the dock to the moored *South Wind*,
Gideon whispered, "Police. Two of 'em just showed.
They're standing around."

"Are they going on board your boat?"

"Can't say. It's like they're waiting for someone."

Porter said, "Want me to go on deck and ask what
they want?"

"Not a good idea," said Gideon. "You wouldn't do me
any good sitting in jail."

"Or me," hissed Val Porter from the galley. "Either
of you want a drink?"

"Not me," said Gideon.

"Better make mine a double,'" said her husband.

Gideon ignored the sound of ice rattling against glass and
the sound of bourbon being poured. Only two days with his
impromptu hosts and he knew what both Porters favored.

"What are they doing now?"

Gideon backed from the blinds. "A yellow Mercedes just
pulled up on the promenade. I can't believe this."

"What? Tell me what's going on," insisted Porter.

Gideon hadn't heard. He was halfway out the salon's door,
headed to the fantail. Porter peered through the blinds. The
policemen were gone and Snuffy Larson was embracing
Maverick Gideon on the pier.

Porter turned to his wife. "The police have left, Val."

She rose from the cabin's love seat and followed her husband out on deck. The couple stepped to the pier to join Gideon and Snuffy.

Snuffy held out a hand to Porter. "I see you connected with Gideon. We owe you."

Porter and wife crowded around the newly freed Snuffy Larson. "What happened?" Porter said. "How did you get back here? And where did the police go?"

"Hopefully, back in the hole they climbed out of," said his wife.

Porter winced. "Val, please."

Glancing around, Snuffy said, "Don't have a clue. Forty minutes ago Sam and I were sitting in some holding cell. Next thing we know, the detective who picked us up when we docked says there's a lawyer come to visit us. Guy's name is Brada. We talked, I walked."

"Where's McFadden?" said Porter.

Gideon frowned. "There's been a hitch. Sam's still being held. Snuffy thinks the cops are sniffing around for a bribe."

Arm around his wife, Porter turned glum. "What can we do?"

His wife snarled, "These police, they're all a bunch of crooks."

"Not too loud, sweetheart."

"She's right," said Snuffy. "And I have no idea where we were being held. Maybe somewhere in town. I don't think it's an official jail. More like some jury-rigged holding cell. Hell, I don't even know if the cops were real."

"But they took that couple with them," said Porter. "We saw it."

Vera Porter raised her voice. "Coulda been cops moon-lighting and using real vehicles. I've heard about that."

Porter turned to Snuffy. "She might be on to something."

"Could be," said Snuffy. "They put blindfolds on us after they put us in their truck. Did the same thing when they brought me back here."

"But you got out of a yellow Mercedes," said Gideon.

"That was our so-called lawyer. I was between two cops on the ride back. They took off the blindfold when we reached the marina."

Gideon said, "So you've got no idea where Sam is?"

His eyes sweeping the marina, Snuffy shook his head.

Ignoring the gravity of the situation, Vera Porter shifted into high gear as if the homecoming had been normal. "Hungry? I've got some pizzas I can throw in the oven. You fellas like deep dish?"

His voice hollow, Snuffy said, "Sounds like a taste of heaven to me. Sam and I had one stale candy bar between us these last forty-eight hours."

"I'll get them started," she said. "I'll send Bill over when they're ready." She shuffled to her boat drink in hand.

Porter followed his wife, saying over his shoulder, "Give us twenty minutes."

Gideon called after Porter. "We're going to check over the boat. Give us a yell when you're ready."

"Will do." The yachtsman waved and returned to the *Two Sunsets*.

Snuffy said, "We need to call Wolf."

Gideon said, "We will. But first, let's talk on board. Check over your baby to make sure nothing's missing. We may have to make a break."

Snuffy turned on him. "Not without Sam."

"Roger that," said Gideon. "Don't worry, we're not going anywhere without him." He followed Snuffy across the pier. "I got here two hours after you docked. No sign of the police. The Porters spotted me and passed on your message."

Snuffy paused at *South Wind's* rail. "Glad you had the presence of mind to ask them. What about the girl and her boyfriend?"

"Found them—or at least Kelsey Magano," said Gideon. "She's recovering in a local hospital not far from here. Might be out tomorrow. I told her to come here for shelter."

"And the boyfriend?"

"No sign of him. I haven't looked too hard to tell you the truth. I did get hold of Kelsey's mother. She's agreed to talk to her ex-husband about our situation. I suggested she make arrangements to fly her home."

"I've got hopeful news about Connor."

Dropping his voice, Gideon said, "Let's talk on board."

They went below, Gideon following Snuffy and filling him in as the boat owner checked *South Winds* vitals—gauges, fuel lines, and electrical systems.

Snuffy said, "Sam and I think this lawyer is in deep with the whole kidnapping thing." He showed Gideon the jersey Connor had worn. "He said the kidnappers turned it over to prove they had him."

Turning the shirt in his hands, Gideon said, "And the others?"

Snuffy shook his head. "Didn't say a word." He inspected the engines and gave them his okay.

"What's your gut feeling about this lawyer?" said Gideon.

Leaning on one of the twin diesels, Snuffy said, "He's part of it. He admitted talking to Sara about a ransom."

Gideon tossed a rag to Snuffy. "You positive this is the same guy who's been calling her?"

Snuffy wiped his hands on the oily towel and stared at Gideon. "It's him."

"Where is the sonofabitch?"

Shrugging, Snuffy said, "Somewhere in Cabo. Might not even be a lawyer for all we know."

"Should be easy to find out."

Snuffy went topside and dropped on a sofa in the main cabin. "One other thing, Gideon. This lawyer, or whatever he is, connected us to that fight at the campground along the coast."

"Well, shit, that can only complicate things."

Staring at the bulkhead, Snuffy sat opposite Gideon. "I don't know about you, but I sure as hell didn't sign on for this."

"None of us did," said Gideon. "But let's put it behind us for now and think about how we're gonna get Sam back."

"Agreed. Any suggestions?"

"We need to coordinate with Wolf and his guys first thing."

"And I need to call Sara," said Snuffy. "She hasn't heard from me for two days. McFadden's Reggie has got to be worried, too. You have the sat phone? The cops took ours."

"Right here," he said. "But I'll call Wolf first. He has to know you're back and what's happened to Sam. And we need to know where we go from here."

"Agreed," Snuffy said. "And what's the Porters' story? They seem a little weird. I mean, pizza? Like this is some kinda misunderstanding with these cops."

Smiling despite the situation, Gideon said, "They mean well. They've offered to help, but there's no reason to repeat what we've talked about. Understood?"

"Got it," said Snuffy. "Okay, call Wolf. Tell about Connor's shirt. I'll call Sara."

"Roger that. Then we go next door for pizza."

Chapter 54

Silver Stardust Casino, Reno, Nevada

Posing between a pale, overweight couple from Michigan, Casino owner Salvatore Magano flashed a million dollar smile for the camera. Tanned, tuxedoed and bull-necked, gray hair slicked back, Magano was a charismatic showman. The crowd was eating out of his hand.

"Take one more for the family back home," he ordered. Magano chided the plump matron hanging on his arm. "Your boss know you're here?" Snapping a selfie, Beth Northrup erupted in nervous giggles. The audience loved it. Hovering off to one side, two long-legged blonde amazons held a giant casino check between them. Dressed in skimpy silver costumes and feathered rhinestone headdresses, the two played eye candy to the delighted crowd. Beckoning to the women, Magano snapped his fingers, anxious to present the dummy check and bolt the scene.

"Ten thousand dollars is a nice nest egg," he said. "Couldn't happen to two more deserving people. Folks, give it up for Vern and Beth Northrup, all the way from Michigan." The ring of gawkers erupted in jealous applause.

"Now get back out there and double down," crowed Magano. "When you're riding a hot streak you can't lose." The Northrups beamed at the outsized check, the glitzy showgirls, Magano, and the casino crowd.

Magano hushed his audience. "At least give the house a chance to win some of that cash back, Vern."

The onlookers roared. Confident the house would get their money back; Magano threw an arm around Vern Northrup, pecked at Beth's rubbery cheek, and then headed for the elevators. An aide caught up with him halfway across the casino's floor.

"Boss, check with Sylvia. You got an emergency call."

"About what?" said Magano.

The elevator doors opened, disgorging eager players, who brushed past the two men. Magano's aide punched the top floor button and held the door for him.

"Dunno. She's been paging you. Couldn't get you. Texted me."

"In case you hadn't noticed, I was busy with the winner's circle."

The aide released the car. "Check in with her."

Magano reached for his phone as the doors closed.

"Hey, Sylvia, it's Sal. What's up?"

The elevator car shot to the top floor, the lights of Reno a blur beyond the glass shaft. Magano's brow furrowed in a scowl.

"She said what? Okay, I'll call her. Yeah, I promise. Send Mario up to the Hermans' suite. Tell him they've got comp seats at tonight's fight. They're high rollers. Make sure he follows up. Yes, I'll call Barbara."

Magano cursed under his breath at the thought of phoning his ex-wife. *Emergency my ass. Probably spilled Merlot on her carpet.*

He got off at the top floor and marched to one of the casino's tenth floor honeymoon suites. The double doors were open, two maid's carts parked in the entry, a crew putting the finishing touches on a welcome package for incoming newlyweds. A vacuum was busy in the bedroom, another maid polishing bathroom fittings, and a florist flitting about, adding more roses to an oversized silver vase.

Magano did a quick walk-through, checked his watch, and then found a quiet spot in the suite's theater room. He closed etched French doors behind him and drew back silk drapes at a picture window overlooking Reno's glittering downtown.

Taking a deep breath, Magano tapped his cellphone screen. He imagined Barbara, lonely, bored, wineglass in hand, pacing the plush bedroom carpet in her Tahoe condo.

This better be good, he thought.

Barbara Magano's smoker's voice filled his ear. This time he heard panic, not her usual accusatory kvetching.

"Sal, something terrible has happened. It's Kelsey."

Not good. His stomach tightened. "Calm down. What's happened?"

"I had a call from some guy in Mexico. Kelsey is in the hospital down there. Cabo San Lucas."

"Gimme details, Barb. Some guy? Cabo? What? How bad is it?"

"This guy said she's recovering."

"Who is this guy? Tell me it's not that little prick, Philip."

"No. This was some American who took Kelsey on a boat to Cabo."

"Boat?" Magano fumed. "I didn't even know she was in Mexico. What the hell was she doing there? Or is this one of those phone scams? You know, 'Send money.'"

"It's not. She was down there with friends. They were camping in the Baja."

"You let her go camping? What the hell is wrong with you?"

His ex-wife snapped back. "She's an adult, Sal. I don't keep her under lock and key. She's your daughter too."

"She lives with you, Barb. Did you forget that?"

"I didn't call to fight. I want to get her out of there, get her home."

Magano lowered his volume. "What hospital is she in? What's her condition? And just who is this American you're talking to?"

"She's in the *Amerimed* Hospital."

"I know it. Decent place to be if I remember right."

"So he said."

"The American with the boat?"

"Yes. His name is Gideon, a former Marine. Apparently, he and his friends rescued Kelsey from some campground along the coast. There was a fight. Guns. Some bad element came to the—"

Magano laughed, incredulous at his ex-wife's description.

"Bad element? Are you fucking kidding me, Barbara? Do you know what that means in the Baja? Hell, you have no idea what you're saying." Silence. "Are you still there?"

"It's our daughter, Sal. This is no time for you to bully me."

He glanced behind him. The maids were following the florist out the suite's door. The newlyweds were due in the morning. Magano rubbed his eyes, trying to bank his anger, to think.

"Have you talked to Kelsey?" he said. "Was Philip involved?"

"No, I haven't spoken to her yet. I don't know what Philip has to do with this. He was apparently hurt as well. I told you, this Marine, the man who called, said he visited her in the hospital. He said she's safe for now. But he wants our help, needs your help, really."

"You better not be playing me."

"It's Kelsey, our daughter, you sonofabitch. I know you have friends down there. You know people. This Marine needs your help."

"My help? What the—? This guy says our daughter's in the hospital and he wants my help? Is this some kind of scam? You don't even know if he's telling the truth?"

"It's complicated, Sal."

It's always complicated with you, Barbara.

Hand to forehead, Magano sank into the sofa facing the room's wide-screen television. "Well, try and simplify it for me, dammit. Start from the beginning and tell me everything this guy said. Don't leave anything out."

Chapter 55

Two hours passed with no sign of Parrish. Lopez recovered sufficiently enough to sit up without hurting but was still feeling sub-par. The three team members held an impromptu war council at his bunk. Wolf's blood was up. "Time to go and get our guys," he said.

"Never should have let Parrish go into town," Preacher said. "Leaves us a man short. Wish we had a better idea of what kind of odds we're facing."

"Does it matter?" said Wolf. "It's obvious Parrish is probably sitting in the same jail cell as Parvin."

"I agree," said Lopez. "But now we find ourselves without transportation, a disadvantage."

Preacher said, "What about Parrish's family?"

"I'll check on them," said Wolf. "Given the way things have been happening he must have some sort of plan in place."

Lopez sat on the edge of the bunk. "I should go with you."

Wolf put a gentle hand on the marine's shoulder. "Luis, stand down until we can figure this out."

"You need my help," he rasped. "We must act now. Parvin and Parrish are in trouble."

"The major's right," said Preacher. "Every minute that goes by puts us more on the defensive."

"I agree," said Wolf, standing alongside the bunk. "But first, I'm going to check on Parrish's daughters. Be right back." He went out the door, leaving Preacher and Lopez to brainstorm about a rescue plan.

Fifteen minutes later, Wolf was back with Maria and her sister. Wearing jeans and a dark sweatshirt, Maria had draped a bandoleer over one shoulder. She carried a vintage rifle, her sister, Elizabeth, a pistol.

Grinning, Lopez hailed her. "Ah, *adelitas!*"

Both women blushed. Gesturing to Parrish's daughters, Lopez said to Wolf, "*Las soldaderas están entre nosotros.*"

Both Americans were clueless. Seeing their bewilderment, Lopez rose to his feet and saluted the sisters. "*Adelitas*—the women of the revolution," said Lopez. "They rode with Zapata and Villa and became a legend. We just increased our odds, gentlemen."

He lowered himself in agony.

"You're hurting," said Wolf.

"*No es nada.*"

Wolf knelt beside the bunk. "If you say so, Luis."

"I do," said the marine, with a faint smile, his eyes closed.

Intrigued, Preacher asked to inspect the long gun. Maria handed it to him. He hefted the weapon, sighting at the ceiling. Caressing the oiled wooden stock, Preacher said, "Springfield '03. Good weapon in its day. But they're more of a collector's piece." He handed it back. "Where did you get this?"

She worked the bolt. "My great, great grandfather," she said. "It has always been in our family."

"Mint condition," said an admiring Wolf. "A souvenir from Pancho Villa's day no doubt."

Preacher raised an eyebrow. "Know how to use it?"

Maria nodded, her face a determined stoic mask.

"We also have this," Elizabeth said, holding a pistol. Wolf held out his hand and she gave him the handgun. Wolf examined the weapon and then passed a loaded .22 Ruger pistol and two full magazines to Lopez.

Elizabeth said, "Father keeps it to shoot *serpientes*—snakes."

Lopez smiled. "Then we will do the same."

"Hollow point rounds," said Wolf. "Could do some serious damage."

"Huh, one rifle and a handgun," Preacher said.

He opened the door. "Will you excuse us?" He drew Wolf outside and closed the door behind him. "Lopez and Parrish's daughters," he whispered, "what are you thinking? You can't seriously expect them to go up against Garcia's people."

"Of course not. We leave them behind with Luis to hold the fort. Parrish was thinking ahead. He built a concrete-lined vault in the cliff behind the main house. It's hidden behind the stairs and equipped with a steel door. An escape tunnel runs uphill to an abandoned olive grove topside."

"You've actually seen it?"

Wolf nodded. "Can't even tell it's there. They'll be safe enough in the short run."

"So that takes care of the home front? This is still crazy. What about Parrish and Parvin?"

Wolf's eyes narrowed. "The only way to get them back is for us to go get them."

"With what?"

"Your bow and Parvin's crossbow."

"You ever shoot a crossbow?"

Wolf nodded. "I have. Can't compete with either of you when it comes to nailing a target, but the scope will give me an advantage."

Preacher rubbed the stubble on his head, his eyes on the ground. "I like a good fight as well as anyone, but I've got twelve broadhead arrows and you have ten bolts. Maybe we should think about trading for the Springfield and the Ruger."

Wolf shook his head. "No can do. They'll need the firepower if some of Garcia's people come calling." He gripped Preacher's shoulder, locking eyes with him. "And I can guarantee they will come calling."

"And what are we supposed to do in the meantime?"

"Play Robin Hood like you and Parvin did."

"Against automatic weapons?"

Wolf smiled. "We're going to take them from the bad guys."

"Up against AKs and who knows what else? Tell me you've got a plan. Because if we do this there's going to be no turning back once it starts. I have no idea how this is gonna end and neither do you."

"But I do have a plan," said Wolf. "Let's go back inside. I'll tell you and the others what I'm thinking."

Chapter 56

Paseo de la Reforma, Mexico City

Caught in a clogged river of cars and vans, a taxi carrying a single fare muscled its way into the far lane and turned at the corner. Joining a single lane that paralleled the main boulevard, the taxi slowed to a snail's pace at the rear of the line. In the back seat, Amada Parrish, handsome and raven-haired, with high cheekbones and green feline eyes, drummed her fingers on the armrest. City buses lined up nose to tail beneath the boulevard's shade trees, taking on passengers as three lanes of traffic flowed by. On her right, low cement blocks marked an empty narrow bike lane, beyond that a wide sidewalk hemmed in by a security fence of twelve-foot black iron spears. Her goal—*Senado de la Republica*—the Mexican Senate. Mid-block behind the forbidding palisade sat a massive concrete cylinder, home to the government's upper chamber. An example of modern Mexico's public works building spree, it was bookended by two soaring glass and stone office towers. The complex's massive footprint wore a skirt of plantings that seemed an afterthought, as did the sidewalk's trees and planters.

Waiting until the taxi slowed in the shadow of the towers, Amada Parrish rapped on the back of the driver's seat to get his attention. She pointed at the tree-lined sidewalk.

"*Aquí*," she ordered when traffic stalled. She handed him a one hundred peso note and got out. A cyclist flew past, and Amada crossed to the sidewalk, grateful to be out of the cab's confines despite the diesel fumes and cacophony of impatient horns. She tapped a number on her cellphone and held it to her ear while staring at a giant bas-relief of the senate's seal on the tower. Pedestrians hurried by, like her, cellphones glued to their ears, oblivious of their surroundings.

A clipped voice answered. "Senator Navarro's office."

"*Señora* Amada Estela Parrish for the senator, please."

"Is he expecting your call, *señora*?"

"Yes."

"One moment, please."

"Of course," said Amada Parrish.

One moment turned into two, then three. Ricardo Navarro's familiar baritone finally filled her ear. "Amada, my favorite niece, so good to speak with you. Where are you calling from, my dear?"

She glanced upwards at the senate building. "I've just arrived, *Tio*. I'm on the sidewalk looking at your senate chambers as we speak."

"Excellent. I have cleared my schedule to talk as you asked."

"I'm grateful. Shall I come up?"

A hesitation in Navarro's voice. "No. I will come to you."

"Is there a problem that we cannot meet in your office?"

"Of course not. But I need to get some fresh air."

She laughed. "You forget the traffic in the streets below?"

"True. But there is a small plaza at the end of the block that will provide some privacy. I'll meet you there. Look for a statue of Louis Pasteur in the center of a long pool. Wait for me in front of the statue, eh?"

"As you wish, *Tio*. Are you ashamed of your colleagues seeing you with family from the countryside?"

"Don't be silly, Amada. If anything, they would ask who is the beautiful woman I am meeting. No, dear, the park is more private."

"Very well, I will see you there." She ended the call and headed for a cordon of trees flanking walkways leading to an open plaza. Pocketing her phone, Amada Parrish joined a parade of pedestrians.

She found a bronze Pasteur, chin in hand, his meditative gaze fixed on passersby from his granite perch. Amada paced by the sculpture, her eyes searching the sidewalk for her uncle. As promised, Navarro arrived moments later.

A handsome man in his middle sixties, Navarro, a cosmopolitan city dweller, looked every inch the polished politician in a dark gray custom-tailored suit. One of his party's rising stars, he had parlayed movie star looks into a senator's seat and a stunning wife, a telenovela star twenty years his junior.

Striding across the pavement in hurried steps, Navarro spotted his niece and kissed her cheek. Holding her hands, he stepped back, smiling. "Ah, Amada, you don't age, my dear. Not one day. I don't know how you do it living in the wild Baja as you do."

She blushed at his stock compliment. "Still the same Ricardo."

Smiling, Navarro linked arms and ushered her to a shaded bench opposite Pasteur. "Your girls, are they still infatuated with the sea?"

"Yes, they love it there. Maria dreams of someday going on the professional women's surfing tour. And Elizabeth is her equal."

"Ah, such foolishness," he said patting her knee. "They should move here and find successful husbands. By now they should be making babies and letting them sit on your lap for family portraits."

Amada shook her head. "Some day, perhaps. They are strong women, both of them. Who's to say?"

"It's the American in them," sniffed Navarro. "Send them to us. The opportunities are here. This is where things happen."

She locked eyes with Navarro. "Things happen in Baja, too. Bad things, *Tio*. That's why I've come to talk with you. To ask your help."

"Something to do with that *gringo* husband of yours, dear niece?"

Dismissing a comment she had heard since her wedding day, Amada arched an eyebrow. "Max is in trouble. He is unable to send his greetings because he has been falsely accused and arrested. Maria called me to tell me this just yesterday."

They settled on the bench. Navarro unbuttoned his coat.

"I'm sorry to hear that. What has he done?"

"Nothing. He intervened on behalf of a stranger and was thrown in jail. It is Miguel Garcia's doing."

"Always Garcia's doing, eh? You should have abandoned that place years ago, Amada. A man like Garcia was bound to make trouble for you. And Max is his own worst enemy when it comes to dealing with the likes of someone such as Miguel Garcia."

"You make it sound as if it is my husband's fault that he has been imprisoned."

"Surely it's not as dramatic as you make it sound, niece. Remember, even I once found myself before the court."

"That was a political matter. And you were exonerated with the help of powerful friends. This is much more dangerous."

Navarro looked away. "What do you want me to do, Amada? I said to you and Max many times, 'Leave all that behind. Sell the property. Move here. Start over. It's not worth the trouble to keep it going.'"

"He loves the sea. And my daughters love where they live."

"What about you, Amada? Do you love it there?"

Eyes downcast, she said, "My husband poured his heart into our home. There is no way he will leave the ocean, *Tio*. You know this."

"So, tell me. Is Miguel Garcia still offering to buy your place?"

She nodded.

"Sell him the land, Amada. Make a profit. Be done with it. How long can this go on? I know you don't have such business as you had before. What will the land be worth next year? In five years, ten?"

Her eyes flashed. "We made a mistake by selling Garcia two parcels of land. He keeps asking for more. He won't be satisfied until he owns every inch of our property. Max thinks Garcia has darker purposes in mind for our property."

"Rumors. Talk some sense into your husband, Amada. I have contacts in a dozen cities who would be willing to help you find a new home to make you happy."

A couple strolled past and Navarro fell silent until they were out of earshot. "Just say the word, dear niece, and I will make introductions to those friends for you."

Grasping his arm, Amada pleaded. "What I want, *Tio*, is for you to send the army to put an end to Garcia's nest of vipers. Do you know he has taken over Los Colinas? A year ago, when I first called you, he had just named his man as police chief. A thief appointing another thief. Do you know the highway is not as safe as it used to be?"

"I've been told by others that this is an exaggeration."

"You're not listening to the right sources." Shaking her head, she said, "It's true. Our people have been abandoned

by their government. Written off. Each day that goes by with
Garcia's *sicarios* in place is one more day without justice."

"You say this because you face his pressure to sell."

"Not just his demands, *Tio*. His men control the highway
for fifty kilometers in each direction from Los Colinas. They
stop travelers at will and take what they want. Even the
gringos coming to surf tell us this."

"I've heard these stories before. Most of them likely rumors."

"Not rumors. It's true. There are people who have
disappeared on that stretch of road."

"I've seen no such reports."

"Because you are busy with your own concerns."

Navarro winced. "Appeal to your state senators."

"They dismiss our concerns. Use your influence on
our behalf."

"How am I to interfere outside my responsibilities? Such
a breach of courtesy is not done. Go to La Paz. Speak to the
governor of your state."

"We have tried," she hissed, "twice before. Both times
he makes such a serious face, listens to our concerns, then
promises to take action."

"Well?"

"Nothing happens. It is all political pretense."

"The federal police—"

Interrupting, she spat her words. "The *federales* made a
sweep for show and did nothing. They are corrupt. The
state police are just as bad."

"Then the army—"

Twisting hands in her lap, she said, "Ah, the army. Even
worse. They followed in the *federales*' footsteps. They took
what they wanted, bothered the women, devoured what little
the village had set aside, and then left. Nothing changed."

His expression hardened. "What are you saying? First, you ask me to send the army and now you say they are even worse?"

"Use the power you wield, *Tio*. Give us an honest soldier."

"How do you expect me to do this, Amada? I am only one of one hundred twenty-eight senators. I have enough problems of my own to address."

"Speak to your friends in the military. Send some of your special troops to clean out Garcia and his *sicarios*. Appoint some trustworthy men to restore our town."

"It's not that simple, Amada."

"Max says that if the government does nothing the problem will get worse until something terrible happens. Only then would the president act. But even so, it could be too late. Surely you must know people who would take this seriously."

Standing to face her, Navarro said, "I'll ask my seniors for advice."

She ceased pacing. "I will speak to the press if I have to."

"Why make this unnecessary threat. It does not become you."

She frowned. "I will if I am ignored. They might listen."

Waving her back to the bench, Navarro said, "Not yet. Let me speak to those in power."

"*El presidente?*"

"I think not. I will talk to his ministers who have jurisdiction."

"When?"

He temporized. "Within the next few days."

"Sooner," she said.

"If I'm able."

"What am I to tell Max in the meantime?"

Navarro rolled his eyes. "Tell him we've spoken and that I was sympathetic to your concerns. Tell him to be patient, Amada."

"If you send the army or police, *Tio*, send someone to help us."

He nodded while looking at his watch. "I will try."

She leaned close to him, her hand like a vise on his arm. "And when you send them make sure you put an honest man in command."

"You ask the impossible."

"I know you mean to make a joke, *Tio*. But I am not amused."

"Perhaps I am not joking. No matter. I must return to my office, Amada. I have meetings to attend."

"And calls to make to ministers, yes?"

He bussed her cheek in parting. "Yes, many calls to make. Will you be returning home?"

She let him go. "Not yet. I told Max I would stay until things change. Besides, most of the press is here in the capital if I need them."

"You're impossible, Amada. Where are you staying?"

"With friends."

Sighing, Navarro waved goodbye and retreated to his ivory tower without looking back.

Chapter 57

The angry buzz of motorcycles cut the afternoon air. In their second hour of hiding in thick brush, Wolf and Preacher lay still, watching a pair of riders pass and descend the road to Parrish's hostel. It was up to Lopez and Maria to make a stand.

As soon as the bikes dropped from sight Wolf sprinted across the road, dragging a length of barbed wire behind him. He had earlier twisted the rusty wire around a thick sun-bleached log and now knelt next to a tree where he had propped the loaded crossbow. Wolf jammed the wire-bound log crossways in the tree's crotch. Opposite him,

Preacher pulled the wire taut, winding his end around an olive tree's stunted trunk. Nearly invisible against a brush and cactus background, the wire now barred the road. Preacher waved to Wolf. Three shots rang out from below, followed by yelling and accelerating motorbikes.

"The Ruger and the Springfield," hissed Wolf. "Ready?" Preacher, silent, nodded and scuttled into the dry brush.

Heading back their way, the snarl of motocross engines grew louder. Wolf shouldered the crossbow, his eyes fixed on the crest in the road where the bikes would come. Across the road, Preacher knelt in chest-high grass, an arrow nocked and ready.

The roar grew. Louder. The first bike flew over the top of the hill, the fleeing rider crouching over the handlebars. Accelerating, he skidded sideways, one leg planted in the dirt for balance. The second bike showed, racing to overtake the lead. Both riders opened their throttles, weaving toward the curve where Wolf and Preacher waited.

The barbed wire garrote ripped the first rider's neck, decapitating him. With no time to stop, the second rider slammed into the lead motorcycle. Flipped upside down, his bike cartwheeled across a stand of cactus. Head over heels, he hit the rutted trail head first. Dazed, the biker rose on hands and knees in the dust, then staggered upright. Preacher sent an arrow into the man's chest, dropping him for good.

Wolf ran to the lead bike to untangle the rider's headless corpse from the twisted machine. He switched off the key to stop the spinning rear wheel and righted the motorcycle. Without saying a word, he and Preacher took the loaded pistols both men carried, and dragged the bodies from the road.

Preacher returned, found the severed head at the side of the road and booted it into the brush. He and Wolf turned their attention to the mangled bikes snared by barbed wire. It took the two of them to manhandle the ruined machines off the trail where they couldn't be seen.

Wolf uncapped a bottle of water, drank half of it, and tossed it to Preacher. "Worked like a charm," he said. "Shit. Lost the bikes, though."

"There'll be more," said Preacher. "The old barbed wire trick, gets 'em every time. Did you mean to set it that high?"

Shaking his head, Wolf said, "Nah, I misjudged. Thought we'd just hang up the bikes and get some prisoners."

"In case you didn't notice, they're not in any shape to talk," said Preacher.

Wolf nodded. "Don't know if we can play that hand again."

"I doubt it," Preacher said, "It was a good start. Reminds me of that movie where Steve McQueen steals the German motorcycle."

Wolf chuckled. "*The Great Escape.* I loved that movie as a kid."

"Can't believe we're talking about a movie after what we just did," said a grinning Preacher.

"Yeah, sick isn't it?" said Wolf.

He and Preacher looked at each other, saying in unison. "Just like old times."

"'Cept we're not on the government's dime. We're nuts to be doing this, Wolfman."

"Yeah, I know." Wolf dragged a branch across the road, erasing most of the signs of the ambush. "Lucky for us they weren't wearing helmets."

"A shame," said Preacher. "We could have done some recon wearing their clothes. Maybe the next crew."

Wolf held up a Glock, as did a frowning Preacher, who said, "Was hoping they would've been carrying AKs."

"Next time," said Wolf. "My guess is these two were sent to scout out Parrish's place."

"I agree," said Preacher. "When they don't report back someone's gonna come looking for them."

"That's what I'm thinking," said Wolf.

Preacher stuffed the pistol at the small of his back. "We might pull this off a second time."

Wolf shook his head. "Fool me once, shame on you. Fool me twice, shame on me. I don't think we—"

Waving Wolf into silence, Preacher cocked his head toward the road. A faint engine's coughing, joined by two others, was coming their way. "Two, maybe three. We got trouble, Wolfman!"

Chapter 58

Reloading the crossbow, Wolf next checked the pistol and said. "I'll set up at the crest of the hill by the trees. Let 'em pass and then come in behind! Keep to the right, out of my line of fire."

"Roger that!" Preacher went into the brush, far enough off the trail not to be seen by anyone on wheels. He had five arrows in his bow's attached quiver, and the pistol.

Dropping behind a mound of cactus, he fit a fresh arrow to his bowstring. *Quieter than the pistol*, he thought. *More sporting*. He squinted to spot Wolf, couldn't find him. *Good cover. They won't see him either.* Surprise was still their best weapon. The sun threw shadows across the road, adding to their cover.

Engines popped and snarled, closing with Preacher's hiding place.

Trailing blue exhaust, three riders passed, two in front, one trailing, their wingman with an AK-47 slung over his shoulder.

I want that, amigo, thought Preacher.

The trio was alone. He crept into the road behind them, keeping to the right, out of the riders' line of sight, bow drawn back, the Glock within reach.

The bikes paused at the top of the hill where the road dropped to the resort. Revving their engines, the three prepared to attack. Wolf heard gears shift. Then two shots.

The lead bike fell sideways, its rider down in the dust. The second in line raised his weapon but never got off a shot. He fell backwards, pistol in hand.

Leaping off his bike to crouch behind his sputtering motorcycle, the AK's owner unslung his weapon. He never heard Preacher.

Thok! A feathered shaft buried itself in the man's back. Surprise on his face, Garcia's thug turned, clawing at the arrow. Preacher put another arrow in the gunman's right side, and he folded across the AK-47.

Wolf appeared, prodding the fallen with a boot to make sure they were dead. He looked up at the approaching Preacher and smiled.

"Nice shooting, Robin."

"Not so bad yourself, Batman."

Glancing at the bodies, Wolf said, "Hard to miss at this range."

"Just like old times," said Preacher. "You good?"

"I'm good," Wolf said. "So far, five to zip. This won't last."

Preacher put down his bow and collected the AK-47. "Yeah, but I'm liking our chances better now."

Wolf picked up the pistols and ammo belonging to the dead. "Let's plant these assholes in the weeds with their buddies. This time we're taking their jackets and hats. Time to do a little recon."

The two dragged the bodies far from the road where they would not be seen. After stripping the corpses of useable clothing, they rode the bikes downhill and parked them in

Parrish's boatshed, away from prying eyes. Preacher jogged back for the third bike while Wolf replayed both ambushes for Lopez and the daughters.

Five down. Preacher was right—There was no going back.

Chapter 59

Two hours passed without a sound. McFadden lay on the floor, his eyes peering through the steel door's food slot at the bottom. Nothing moved on the other side. No sounds. No footfalls. No cops.

He got to his feet and worked one of the table legs loose, exposing the nail that had held it in place. Using his crude tool, he began chipping at the cement where he judged the bolted latch to be. The concrete wall was thick but old. Working steadily, he widened a small hole with the nail. Brushing away debris from the cavity, he ate away at the wall. Stopping every so often to make sure his efforts were not being heard, he lowered himself to the floor and checked the slot. Hearing and seeing nothing, he rose, brushed himself off, and resumed his efforts.

Twenty minutes into his attempt the nail broke.

Undaunted, McFadden upended the table and removed a second leg. In minutes, he was back at the wall. After three hours and a fourth table leg, he finally reached bare steel. The work paid off. He was able to loosen a large chunk of concrete. About to chisel an even larger piece, he paused. Voices on the other side. Loud Spanish. Exhausted and dehydrated, McFadden backed from the locked door and crept to one side, the table leg raised like a club to defend himself.

Shadows flitted in the slot. A sudden banging on the steel door. A bolt rattling. Crouching, McFadden tensed, certain he had been discovered.

I'm not going down without a fight, you bastards.

"Sam! Can you hear me?" The voice, not Snuffy's, but familiar.

McFadden cried out. "I can hear you! Who—"

"It's Gideon! Back away from the door, Sam."

Tossing the club, McFadden flattened himself against the wall.

Hammering, steel on steel. And then, the door creaked open. Light flooded the makeshift cell. Gideon stepped across the threshold, scattering concrete scraps with his boots.

On wobbly legs, McFadden staggered to Gideon's arms.

Two other strong arms supported McFadden, ushering him into the outer room. A chair appeared and he dropped into it. Someone passed him a bottle of water. He downed half of it, then doused his head and bearded face with cool water. Watching the ritual, four large Mexican men in suits formed a semi-circle around him, arms folded, faces passive.

Glancing at Gideon beside him, McFadden whispered, "Cops?"

"Uh, friends."

"What about Snuffy? The cops took him," said McFadden.

"Already back on the boat. It's a long story, Sam."

McFadden said, "The lawyer. Brada."

A fifth Mexican, slender and brooding, wearing a dark suit and gold spectacles with rose-tinted lenses, stood in the doorway. Hearing the question, he nodded to the big men, who retreated. The impeccably dressed newcomer stepped in front of the rumpled McFadden. "Ah, you ask about *Señor* Alfonso Brada, yes?"

"He spoke about Connor's kidnappers."

"Ah, *Señor* McFadden," said the man. "Unfortunately, *Señor* Brada is not only unavailable; he is unable to speak at the moment. Furthermore, I am not familiar with this kidnapping, the situation of which you speak."

Gideon put a hand on McFadden's shoulder. "Sam, this is Hector Carrera. He and his associates contacted me and assisted in locating you."

"At your service," soothed McFadden's liberator. A slight bow and he said, "The policemen who imprisoned you and *Señor* Larson will pay for the inconvenience they caused you. On behalf of the people of my city, and the people of Mexico, please accept my sincere apologies for your ordeal."

McFadden smiled. "Apology accepted. Don't know how you did it but I'm grateful, *Señor* Carrera."

"It was a favor to an old friend who knew of your dilemma."

"Who is this angel? I'd like to thank him."

A shrug and a coy deflection. "As I said, an old friend."

Gideon helped McFadden stand.

Gesturing to the open door, Carrera said, "My men will escort you to your friend's boat. You are free to go. My word is that no one will bother you. My men will see to it. Might I suggest you return home."

Another quick bow and Carrera was gone, leaving two of his sentinels behind. Gideon leaned close to McFadden's ear. "I think it would be a good thing if we take Carrera at his word, Sam. We don't want to overstay our welcome. The longer we hang around, the less chance there is of solving Connor's kidnapping."

In the doorway, McFadden squinted against the sunlight. "What about checking the credit card list against the Cabo hotels and bars?"

"All done. Carrera did our homework for us. We're clear here. Our boys never made it this far."

Another question. "And the girl, Kelsey?"

"On her way home."

"What about Philip, her boyfriend?"

"No clue."

"But—"

Gripping McFadden's right arm, Gideon urged him to the waiting van. "Let's get back to the boat. Snuffy and I can fill you in, okay?"

McFadden shuffled forward, regaining his balance with each step. "We'll have to top off the fuel, get supplies and—"

The two climbed in the idling van. "All done," whispered Gideon. "Courtesy of Carrera. Quite the character. I've said enough, okay?"

Nodding, McFadden caught the urgency in Gideon's voice. "Sure, I get it. But I still want a briefing."

"You'll have it. Let's move before our ride turns into a pumpkin."

Followed by two unsmiling escorts, McFadden and Gideon settled in the back seat and were driven to the marina. As security promised by Carrera, the watchdogs stayed until the dockside reunion with Snuffy and the Porters was complete. Carrera's men retreated to their parked van to keep watch. Persuaded by Snuffy and Gideon that their Cabo San Lucas stay was at an end, McFadden called Wolf to report his good news, only to get a disturbing update that spurred his resolve to head north.

Sent on its way with a cake from Val Porter's oven, *South Wind* cleared the harbor a few minutes after noon. McFadden shared Wolf's situation, prompting Snuffy to push his diesels to fifteen knots. Hiding his anxiety about what awaited them, McFadden made a long overdue satellite call to reassure Reggie. He said nothing about his two plus days in a make-shift jail or Wolf's dilemma. "On the way home with maybe one more stop," he said.

That out of the way, he went below to sleep.

Chapter 60

Wolf, meanwhile, passed the word about McFadden's ordeal and sudden release to Preacher and Lopez. Then he dropped the other shoe. Even if the weather held, *South Wind* wasn't due to show for eight hours.

"That puts Sam and his team in the bay around twenty hundred hours. Still some light, but who knows what we'll be into by then."

Lopez said, "I'm not sure we have the luxury of waiting, *amigos*."

Wolf paced. "We can't put this off," he said. "We have to make a recon of the town to at least find out the conditions under which Parrish and Parvin are being held."

"Sooner the better," said Preacher.

"Okay, Preacher and I will take two of the bikes. I'll lead while he plays wingman for me. We'll go in shooting if that's what it takes."

Lopez demurred. "Caution, *amigos*. By now Garcia knows you have taken five of his men. He may already have reinforcements. They will be expecting you. And they will return here at some point, you know." He tapped his forehead. "You must outthink them."

"What kind of shape are you in?" said Wolf. "Can you hold?"

Laboring to his feet, the marine said, "It is nothing. We are ready."

"Good. You and the ladies hunker down until we return."

Lopez nodded. He returned the .22 Ruger to Elizabeth and took the captured handgun Wolf offered.

"Don't engage them head on, Luis," warned Wolf. "Just delay them if possible."

"We will do better than that." He glanced at Parrish's daughters.

"*De acuerdo, mis adelitas?*" Maria and Elizabeth raised their weapons.

"See, they are committed. Now go. Our enemy is blind. Strike while Garcia is still confused about who you are and why you make this fight."

Preacher nudged Wolf's elbow. "We need to move."

The pair jogged to the boat shed where they had hidden the bikes and donned hats and jackets taken from the dead. They both knew their disguises were likely to get them into town, but any second looks and the game was up.

"Haven't ridden since the Philippines," confessed Preacher.

Wolf kicked his motorcycle into life. "Like riding a bike," he yelled.

"It *IS* riding a bike," said Preacher.

"Follow me!"

Chapter 61

Riding like their lives depended on it, Wolf and Preacher roared up the incline. Following the rutted track through brittle brush, towering cardon cactus, and orphaned olive trees, the two stayed alert, expecting an ambush at every turn. They crossed the main road, continuing to the outskirts of Los Colinas and wisely abandoned the road to avoid being spotted by Garcia's pickets. Seeking cover, they killed their bike engines and glided behind an overgrown elephant tree, its twisted, swollen branches offering perfect cover. Clustered palms added to their hiding place. Two hundred feet from their vantage point sat the town's Pemex station with its single row of pumps on a slab of concrete. One attendant lounged in a lawn chair beneath the overhanging canopy.

A pickup with a saddled horse tied in the truck's fenced bed was taking on fuel while the driver talked to his animal. A second station worker washed the pickup's windshield in slow motion. Save for the gas station and a handful of people on foot, the town appeared mostly deserted. Across a strip of aging blacktop running in front of the Pemex stop, a row of six, one-story, sagging storefronts sandwiched a newer adobe building. A dusty police pickup truck blocked the only door, a recessed entry.

"Bingo," whispered Preacher. "Hello, Mister Jailer Man."

Wolf nodded. "Has to be the place. Only one way in. Let's check around back to make sure our guys are there."

"Sit on this for a while," said Preacher. "Might get a head count."

"Roger that."

Twenty minutes passed, a lifetime. Their patience was rewarded. Two dirt bikes showed and parked in front of the truck. "Garcia's outriders," said Wolf. "They missed us on the way in. Wonder how many are still out there?"

"I know five who won't be part of the meeting," said Preacher.

The booted riders, swaggering in tight jeans and matching gray hoodies, pistols tucked in belts, pounded on the building's door. It opened and the men went inside. Before the door shut, Preacher glimpsed a tan uniform.

"I count three," he said. "Not bad odds."

Wolf shot a scolding look at Preacher. "We don't know how many other tangos are inside. Don't even know if Parvin and Parrish are with them."

"You kidding, Wolfman? Place is like the Alamo. Why else park the truck like that? They have to be inside. I say we ride up, knock, and rush 'em when they open."

Wolf smiled. "Hey, I like to break doors and make people fall down as much as anybody, but it's too risky, Preacher. We wait."

Preacher removed his borrowed straw hat, wiped his forehead, all while studying the door. "Easy shot with my bow. Nice and quiet."

A dusty SUV rounded a corner where the storefronts ended and double-parked next to the police truck. Two men wearing jeans and light jackets got out, pounded on the door, and went inside.

"Huh, two to five," said Preacher. "Still workable odds."

Wolf stared at the bikes and trucks. "We ought to take away their wheels while we're here."

Preacher nodded. "That would help. Wish I had my bow, though."

"I think we're past that," said Wolf, wiping his brow.

"Not necessarily." Preacher pointed at the jail. "I'd be able to take him down without a lot of noise."

"Who?"

Wolf followed Preacher's outstretched arm. On the jail's roof a cowboy-hatted guard cradling an AK-47 leaned over a corner parapet, studying the town's main street. "Damn. How'd I miss him?"

"Two against six now," said Preacher. "On second thought, I shoulda brought the crossbow. You know, with that baby's scope..."

"Hey, that gives me an idea. It's risky, but if you're willing—"

Preacher smiled. "I'm always willing, Skipper. What's the plan?"

Chapter 62

Wolf checked his watch. Preacher had been gone forty minutes. He finished the last of his water and buried the bottle in dead leaves. Still on duty, the jail's rooftop sentinel showed at the corner every ten minutes.

Predictable, he thought. *An amateur. You'll be sorry.*

Movement behind him. Wolf froze. Nearly invisible in the cactus surrounding the elephant tree's ground-hugging limbs, he readied his pistol. Preacher showed, pushing his silenced bike, Parvin's crossbow slung across his back. He leaned the motorcycle against one of the massive branches and crept to Wolf's hide, crossbow in one hand, water bottle in the other.

Wolf welcomed the water. He uncapped it and drank. "You had me worried," he whispered. "Trouble?"

"Nah. Had to dodge one of Garcia's foot patrols before I checked in with the major and the girls."

Wolf said, "They doing okay?"

Smiling, Preacher nodded. "Roger that. More than okay. Scratch one more biker."

"What?" Wolf's eyebrows shot up, his eyes questioning.

Stepping into the crossbow's stirrup, Preacher pulled back the bowstring with the loading cord, cocking the weapon. He set the safety and loaded a razor sharp broadhead bolt in the slot. The mounted quiver held six more. "Musta been another of Garcia's boys who didn't get the memo. He was nosing around. The major said the guy came alone, circled, and then headed for the boatshed. He found the bike we left behind and panicked. Lopez said Maria dropped the guy on his way out. One shot, one kill. One extra bike if we need it."

"Good news," said Wolf. "Garcia has to be running out of men."

"Don't know if you've been keeping score but that's six dirt bikes," said Preacher. "We oughta check their serial numbers against that list you have."

"Good idea. That slipped my mind."

"Understandable given the circumstances."

Preacher said, "Though serial numbers at this stage are probably a moot point."

Wolf sighed. "Yeah, besides, we've gone from a recovery exercise to survival mode in one week."

Tucking the crossbow under his right arm, his hand on the weapon's pistol grip, Preacher said, "I'm ready when you are. What's the sitrep?"

"Thought of two options."

"Okay. Run Plan A past me."

Wolf rose to one knee. "Nobody's gone in or come out since you left. I timed the guy on the roof. He makes a circuit every ten minutes. Shows up at the corner opposite our location and checks the street. You take him out for starters."

"Roger that. How much time will I have?" said Preacher.

"About ten seconds."

"I can work with that."

Wolf sketched with his hands. "Once you drop him, I'll circle the block to check out the rear of the jail before I hit the front."

"I'll cover you once you get back."

"My plan is to shoot the tires on the trucks. Next are the bikes. If I move fast enough I can put a round in their gas tanks. If anybody comes out that door while I'm doing that I'm in big trouble, Preacher."

"Negative. If anybody comes out that door, they're the ones in trouble. I'll be ready. With two pistols apiece we've got plenty of firepower to pin them down long enough to spring Parrish and Parvin. Let's do it."

Holding up a hand, Wolf paused. "Plan B. We wait until nightfall. Sam and his team would be here by then as backup."

Preacher crouched under an overhanging tree limb. "That's a big *IF*."

"Too risky for you?"

"I'm not one to question you, Skipper. It's just that we should use what little surprise we have left. Garcia doesn't have a clue what we're capable of. Plus, he doesn't know where we are at this moment."

"He's got to know there are just three of us," said Wolf. "He knows Luis is hurt bad. He also has to know we won't abandon Parrish and Parvin."

"What if we offered to trade his six for our guys?"

Wolf said, "You think he cares about his dead?"

"He doesn't know they're dead. All he knows is that six of his are missing. We don't fess up that they're dead. We propose a trade."

"Can't see him going for it."

"Take out some more of his goons," said Preacher, "and he'll see the light."

Wolf lowered his head, smiling despite their predicament. "I knew you'd go for Plan A." He looked at Preacher. "Not one to pass up the chance for a fight are you?"

"Garcia and his *sicarios* are evil, Skipper. They don't know anything but killing. But in the end they're still amateurs." Preacher thumped his chest. "We have the training. We know how to make this fight ours. Don't forget, we're the good guys here. "

Wolf shook his head, still smiling. "Okay, Chief Hackett —Preacher. Let's get this show on the road then. Stand by to put Plan A into action."

"I knew you'd see it my way." Preacher held the crossbow against his chest. "I'll wait until you bring the bike around. Don't start it until I take out my tango."

Wolf nodded and pushed the dirt bike as close to the edge of cover as he dared. Straddling the machine, he propped his boot on the kick-starter and eyed Preacher.

Crabbing to an open spot in the foliage offering a clear shot at the jail's rooftop, Preacher settled, his right leg curled beneath him, his left elbow resting on his raised left knee.

Peering through the scope, he found the corner of the adobe building and focused on the spot where the sentry would appear.

Glancing at his watch, Wolf hissed, "Twenty seconds."

With his index finger resting feather-light against the crossbow's trigger, Preacher eased his right thumb, releasing the safety. *Going hot.*

Preacher breathed in, held his breath until the guard's head filled the lens. He exhaled, stopped mid-release, and squeezed the trigger.

Chapter 63

Hit just above the sternum, the gunman staggered back, the arrowhead ripping through his back, emerging at the top of his spine. His last conscious act was to reach for the parapet's lip before crumpling from sight.

Wolf kicked his bike into life and headed across the blacktop strip to check the back of the jail. Preacher had already reloaded the crossbow and centered the scope's crosshairs on the front door. He heard Wolf's motorcycle circle, buzzing behind the adobe building. A lone figure, one of Garcia's *sicarios*, emerged, pistol in hand. Head thrown back, the hired gun yelled to the man on duty above. Getting no answer, he backed into the street to get a better look at the roof—a fatal mistake.

Preacher fired a bolt. Hit between his shoulder blades, the man dropped face first at the foot of the SUV's bumper. Preacher slung the crossbow over his shoulder and leaped on his dirt bike, just as Wolf roared around the corner.

Sliding to a stop, Wolf shot the rear tires of the pickup and SUV. Preacher flew across the street, screeching to a halt opposite the jail door. While Wolf shot out the SUV's front tires, Preacher trained his pistol on the door. It opened, spilling two armed men responding to the gunfire. Preacher hit one in the shoulder, driving both back inside. *Hurry up, Wolfman!*

Making a tight turn to gain some room, Wolf fired at the tanks of the parked bikes. Both exploded in balls of flame. Turning to Preacher, he waved his handgun, signaling a retreat. As Wolf roared away, a *sicario* bolted from the doorway, spraying the street with an AK-47. Preacher shot him in the forehead, stuck his pistol in his belt and accelerated after Wolf.

Not sure if Preacher had followed, Wolf pulled his bike into a tight U-turn to escort his friend, only to catch sight of another of Garcia's bikers on Preacher's tail, and gaining. Wolf gambled, aiming his bike at the weaving enemy who was firing left-handed. Braking mid-block, Wolf jumped, abandoning his bike. Blocking the middle of the street, he knelt in the dirt on one knee as Preacher screamed past.

Steadying his weapon with both hands, Wolf emptied his pistol at the approaching biker. Two of his shots hit Preacher's pursuer center mass. The dead man cartwheeled off the seat, sending the bike out of control. The machine bounced, skidding sideways at the kneeling SEAL. Wolf leaped out of the way as the bike slammed into his motorcycle, leaving him afoot. He reloaded and ran.

Preacher had seen the duel and made a wide turn, determined to rescue Wolf. The two met in front of the Pemex station. Preacher slowed, allowing Wolf to leap aboard. The pair raced away, leaving three dead and broken machines in their wake.

Chapter 64

Praying that Garcia had not sent his killers after Lopez and the Parrish daughters in their absence, Wolf told Preacher to bypass the main road and go overland until closer to the shore. They rode a punishing quarter-mile before Preacher stopped among stunted olive trees.

"Take over," he said. "Don't want to put the bike down with us on it."

Wolf drew back a hand covered with Preacher's blood. "You're hit."

"Forgot to duck back there."

Climbing from the idling bike, Wolf ran a hand over Preacher's blood-soaked shirt, Wolf said, "Where?"

Preacher grimaced. "Left side. Got winged coming out."

"Wolf tore off his shirt and fashioned a makeshift compress. He steadied Preacher and pressed the bandage against the wound. "I'll drive."

"That would be helpful, Skipper."

Wolf straddled the dirt bike, his hands on the bars. "Hang on. It'll be rough. Can you hold a weapon?"

Gripping his handgun, Preacher wheezed, "Piece of cake."

Easing into gear, Wolf found the dirt track to Parrish's beachside hostel. They bumped along, each jolt sending shockwaves through Preacher's body. Wolf got them back without coming across Garcia's men.

Lopez welcomed them and sent Maria to the top of the hill with the Springfield to provide warning. Despite his own wounds, he and Wolf dragged Preacher to a bunk at the rear of the main house. Working quickly, the two staunched the flow of blood and patched Preacher as best they could. He gobbled pain pills and slept sitting up. Elizabeth was sent to fetch her sister. Parrish's daughters came back via the tunnel.

While Preacher slept, Wolf recited the day's battle to Lopez and the women. Sam McFadden, he reminded them, was still six hours away.

"Might have to use that tunnel after all," warned Wolf.

"Garcia will make an offer," predicted Lopez. "But it will not be genuine and it will not end well for us if he gets his way."

"He will not get his way," said Maria. "My father will see to that."

Lopez smiled at Wolf. "You see, *amigo*. These two sisters are tough. I think Garcia has underestimated them."

Maria stroked the Springfield. "Just as he underestimated my mother and father before."

Wolf downed a bottle of water. "We need to prepare for Garcia's next move. Preacher's hurt and we returned empty-handed today. I'm open to suggestions, Luis. And that includes your *adelitas*."

Maria leaned her rifle against the doorframe and pulled a stool in front of Lopez and Wolf. "Elizabeth and I have an idea about your proposal to Garcia."

"I'm all ears," said an exhausted Wolf.

Chapter 65

Refreshed after four hours of sleep, Sam McFadden stopped in *South Wind's* galley to make fresh coffee before heading topside. The deck beneath his feet hummed from the laboring diesels. They were one mile offshore, plowing north through dark green swells along Baja's rocky coast. He poured mugs for Gideon and Snuffy, and climbed topside to the open bridge.

"Look who's up," said Gideon. "Sleeping Beauty."

"Beware of Green Berets bearing coffee," said Snuffy.

"I'm back to battery," said McFadden, offering a mug to Gideon. "Thought you guys might want some relief." He handed a second mug to Snuffy. "This a good time to brief me?"

"Be my guest," said Snuffy, taking the coffee. He stepped from the wheel, yielding his place to McFadden. "Where do you want to start?"

Hands on the wheel, McFadden flexed his legs against the rise and fall of the deck. He said, "Take me back to when *Señor* Brada pulled you out of our cell."

Bracing himself alongside McFadden at the control console. Snuffy sipped the hot coffee. "It was a setup, Sam. Brada was desperate to get his hands on some ransom money."

McFadden said, "He must have known early on the four families didn't have that kind of cash."

Snuffy said, "Whoever he was working for was getting impatient. His letting me go was a gamble. I thought they were gonna kill you, Sam."

"So what happened?"

"Brada and his four dirty cops hustled me to a police van. Took me to an ATM. Can you believe it? My limit was two hundred dollars. Chump change this late in the game. That told me these guys were running out of time."

McFadden kept his footing despite a series of waves pummeling *South Wind*'s hull. Snuffy dropped the speed again to lessen the pounding.

"Gonna add another hour doing that," said McFadden.

"I'd like to get us there in one piece, Sam."

McFadden shrugged. It was Snuffy's boat, after all.

"So, you're in the police van, on the way to a cash machine. What then?"

Snuffy warmed to the tale. "We get out of the van at a machine and the next thing I know, BOOM! Three black

Escalades come up on the sidewalk on all three sides. Six guys pile out, armed to the teeth. The cops folded. I got hustled into one of the cars."

Gideon laughed. "Tell Sam what was going through your mind."

Snuffy scowled. "Wasn't funny at the time. I thought for sure I was a dead man walking. Off we go to some warehouse. Hell, I didn't know where I was. Didn't know who these guys were. We end up in a big room. Brada's sitting there in the middle, tied to a chair with the shit beat out of him, blood everywhere. It didn't look good for either of us."

Snuffy described Carrea's sudden appearance.

"This guy in a suit comes in and everybody's falling all over themselves. I'm thinking, 'Who is this guy, why am I here, and what's going to happen to me?'

"He introduces himself, Hector Carrea. Somehow, he knows who I am, takes me back to *South Wind*, and lets me go in exchange for Gideon here. Leaving me in the dark they drive off together, on their way to pick you up, Sam. Crazy, huh?"

"Yeah, wild."

"I wasn't sure it was a good idea," said Gideon. "Not like I had a choice, though."

McFadden glanced at the sea, then at Snuffy, then back to the sea. "How did he know where to find me?"

Gideon interrupted. "I think Brada gave it up at some point."

"My guess as well," said Snuffy. "I sure as hell didn't know where you were, Sam. Sorry about that."

"Forget it. When I asked Carrea who sent him he wouldn't say."

"Have anything to do with the girl's father?" said McFadden.

"Can't say for sure, Sam," said Gideon. "Could be coincidence. It did come on the heels of my call to her mom, but I'm just making a wild guess. Whoever Carrea is, he just wanted us gone. That much was clear."

Snuffy finished his coffee and put down the mug. "I couldn't wait to quit Cabo, Sam. Scary place this time around. I'm just happy to have my boat back."

McFadden shot a look at the compass and the GPS. The swells had dropped again, along with the wind. Snuffy reached over and tapped the throttles. The hull's acceleration was slight but McFadden felt it nonetheless. He said, "Explain what you meant about Carrea doing our homework for us with respect to the credit cards Connor and his friends were using."

"I told Carrea what we were doing in Cabo," said Snuffy. "He asked for our list and made some calls. Nothing as far as a positive ID of our boys turned up if that's what you're asking."

McFadden said, "But someone was using those cards in Cabo."

"We may never figure that out," said Snuffy. "That suggests to me that the answer lies at their last stop—the one place we know for sure Connor and the others showed."

"Punta Carocos," said McFadden. "Parrish's beach hostel." He braced himself against the back of Snuffy's chair, the satellite phone in hand. "Time to check in with Wolfman and let him know we're heading his way." He punched in the access code and number. The call was brief—bad news, all of it. McFadden's face showed it.

"What was Wolfman's sitrep?" said a worried Gideon.

"Bad and getting worse. Been shooting and scooting all day."

Gideon slammed a fist against the control panel. "What's our ETA?"

Leaning over the GPS, Snuffy said, "Four hours if this sea holds."

"Not good," said McFadden. "Another hour and we might be too late."

Chapter 66

Preacher moaned in pain, unable to raise his left arm above his head. His bloodied left side swollen and tender to the touch, was hot, always a worrisome sign. Despite his wound being cleaned and packed with sterile gauze, plus some antibiotics working their way through his system, the former SEAL was in rough shape. Wolf was worried. One hour ago, against his better judgment, he had dropped Maria on the outskirts of Los Colinas to contact an old friend of her father's. She had not returned.

Had she been captured? Was she dead or lying wounded in the brush? He needed an answer. Barricaded in Parrish's main house, he was blind and on the defensive, unusual for him. He sat at the end of Lopez's bunk.

"Luis, I'm worried about Maria. I'm going up the hill to do a little recon. Don't want us to be taken by surprise."

"Risky, *amigo*."

Pocketing two loaded magazines, Wolf checked his Glock. "So is sitting still. Maria's been gone for an hour. Not a good sign. Can't afford to lose another set of eyes at this point."

Lopez ran a penlight beam over the sleeping Preacher. "Go. Elizabeth and I will cover for you. We'll watch over him."

"Don't let him fall into Garcia's hands if it comes to that," said Wolf. "That's the last thing he'd want." The Mexican marine nodded.

Wolf donned a black hooded sweatshirt and slipped past the steel door leading to the hidden tunnel Parrish had dug by hand in the hillside behind his family's home.

Elizabeth Parrish shut the door behind him and returned to her post at a second story window in the darkened main house.

Ten minutes later, Wolf emerged from the tunnel's mouth hidden in the abandoned olive grove above the beach. Crouching, he let his ears adjust to the sounds around him. *No threats.* Moving only when it seemed safe, he found the footpath leading to the access road and kept to the shadows. He studied every twisted trunk and clump of cactus in moonlight broken by drifting clouds. Far below and behind him, waves lapped the stony beach. Swells wrapping around the point had died that afternoon, a good thing if *South Wind* was to anchor just off the beach. The boat's predicted landfall had come and gone. *They'll be here*, Wolf told himself. *We'll get Parvin and Parrish back.*

Footfalls headed his way. *More than one person.* Retreating to the shadows, he dropped on one knee, his weapon held out in front. Two figures walking single file crossed his path not ten yards away—Maria Parrish and her contact, a short Mexican, thin and stooped, following in her footsteps.

Wolf whistled, low and steady. Maria and her companion froze.

"Pssst, Maria. Wolf. Stay there."

He stepped from the shadows and walked to them, whispering, "Were you followed?"

"I don't think so."

Wolf stared at the man by her side. "I know your face."

"Jorge Ruiz," she said. "He—"

"Works for your father," Wolf interrupted. "I know. We were getting worried when you didn't return."

She shook her head. "Not easy. Garcia has locked down the town."

"We'd better hurry. Lead the way," he said. "I'll cover you."
Wolf hung back, watching their every step. Only when
Maria and Ruiz reached the main house and reunited with
Lopez, did Wolf relax. She and her sister huddled with their
visitor. Propped on pillows, Preacher was awake but silent,
watching from his bed. Sleep had helped.

Ruiz glanced at the wounded American, then Lopez. He
said, "*Cómo está tu amigo?*"

Lopez said, "*Usted habla Inglés, verdad?*"

"*Sí, Mayor*. I speak English if you wish."

"Good. It is for the benefit of my friends." Smiling at
Preacher, Lopez said, "Wounded, as you see. But he is
one tough *hombre*."

"I know," said Ruiz. "People are talking about the price
El Jefe pays for doing battle with your friends, Major. We
do not say this out loud, of course. With our own eyes we
have seen it."

Flashing a thumbs-up, Preacher grinned from his bed.

Maria said, "What he says is true. I think Garcia is worried
about losing control of Los Colinas. It is his own fault."

"What do you know of their father?" said Wolf. "And
my friend as well."

Slow to speak, Ruiz rubbed his jaw before answering.
"They are alive. But I think some of Garcia's men want to
kill them for what has happened."

"We didn't start this war," said Wolf. "But we'll end it."

Ruiz shrugged, his watery eyes shifting from Wolf and
Lopez to the Parrish daughters. "No, you did not begin
this fight, but I fear for *Señor* Parrish."

"And my friend," said Wolf.

"Yes, your friend, as well. I also fear for my family."

"Garcia has often threatened Jorge and his nephews,"
said Maria.

Wolf got up and stood by Preacher's bunk. "I think we have to take Jorge at his word. Do you know how many men Garcia has with him?"

A shrug. "A handful at this time, I think. Perhaps five."

"Would he be willing to trade six of his men for *Señor* Parrish and our man?"

"Forgive me, *señor*, but I do not think you hold six of his men."

An awkward pause followed Jorge's accusation. Wolf kept going. "Would he negotiate? Maria and Elizabeth need their father returned. And my friends and I want *Señor* Parvin back with us, unharmed."

"Ah, you wish me to ask Garcia this, eh?"

Wolf said, "Yes, we would be grateful. Both parties know you."

"Maria tells me that is why you sent her to me."

"Yes. It is worth the risk, I think," said Wolf. "To stop the killing."

Ruiz took an offered bottle of water from Elizabeth and drank. "Forgive me, *Señor* Wolf, but it seems you are the ones doing the killing."

"In self-defense," snapped Wolf. "You know this is true."

"So you say."

Maria sat next to the old man. "Will you help my family, Jorge?"

Wolf said nothing, opting instead to let Maria and her sister work their magic with Ruiz. The women sat on either side of him, their eyes pleading. Reluctant, but won over, the carpenter nodded.

"Ah, such a thing you ask. What can I do, *pequeña hija?*"

"Speak to my father. See that he is well. Ask the same of *Señor* Wolf's friend. Tell Garcia this is a reassurance we need."

"It will be dangerous but I will try," said Ruiz.

Wolf added his non-negotiable, couched as a request, "Tell me what you see when you visit them. We need to know what the inside of the jail looks like—where our friends are being kept. Where Garcia and his men stay when they are there. Will you do this?"

Ruiz's eyes bored into Wolf's. "So, there is to be more killing, eh?"

Backing away, Wolf said, "Not if it can be avoided."

The old man got to his feet. "What about this trade you speak of? After all that has happened you still wish to make this offer to *El Jefe?*"

"Of course," said Wolf. "When you make this proposal, study Garcia carefully to see if he gives you an honest answer. I rely on your instincts, Jorge. After all, I have yet to meet the man."

Ruiz gestured to the battered Lopez. "But I see the major has. What does he say to me about trusting *El Jefe?*"

Lopez touched his shattered eye socket and shook his head.

"I thought as much," said Ruiz. "I will go to *Señor* Garcia. I will do as you ask. I hope he believes me. I also hope that I return with the answer you seek."

"We'll see," said Wolf. "Maria will take one of the bikes to return you close to Los Colinas. It is faster and we have little time."

"Very well," said Ruiz. "I leave on this mission with a heavy heart."

Lopez shook their visitor's hand. "*Vaya con dios, hermano.*"

"My wish as well," said Wolf, a hand on Ruiz's shoulder.

A sad smile from the reluctant messenger. "*Decir una oración por mí,*" he said from the doorway. He went into the growing dusk, Maria at his side. Wolf and Lopez watched them go. In minutes, the buzzing of the outbound dirt bike filled the air, then faded.

A tearful Elizabeth went upstairs to resume her post without being told. Wolf checked on Preacher, left him in Lopez's care, and scrambled through the tunnel again. Back among the olive trees above, he knelt at the base of a gnarled trunk—one shadow among many—to await Maria's return.

Chapter 67

Shifting between rage and despair, a mercurial Miguel Garcia kicked a moaning Max Parrish. *El Jefe* to his dwindling collection of *sicarios* and coerced *campensinos*, Garcia felt his control over them slipping. Curling into a fetal position to blunt the blows, Parrish rolled into the corner of his cell. The muscled Garcia, squat, his right eye wandering from a long-ago burro kick—the animal's last mortal act—aimed his boots at his prisoner.

Screaming, "Call off your dogs or I cut you into small pieces before your daughter's eyes!" Garcia loomed over the cowering Parrish. "Then I turn both your girls over to my men for their pleasure. Your little *putas*, eh? Maybe first I make you watch, then I kill you. *"Entender?"*

Waving a pistol, Garcia backed away, his chest heaving from the effort. "Talk, you piece of shit! Who are these men?"

Garcia's handpicked sheriff, Tito Mendez, sat idly by, watching his boss work. Responsible for the jail, Mendez was a sadistic toady who catered to Garcia's moods. Illiterate, and slow, Mendez excelled at only one thing—mimicking his *patrón's* cruelty. Parrish and Parvin had been chosen targets, the latter caught after refueling the van during a village reconnaissance with Lopez. As with unwary travelers before, Mendez and a squad of motorcycle toughs had intercepted them. Given to playing professional lawman, Mendez, who reverted to the thug he was during the traffic stop, led the assault on both men. Only Garcia's arrival on the scene prevented Lopez and Parvin from being beaten to death.

Recognizing a chance to increase the pressure on his nemesis, Parrish, Garcia interrupted the brawl. He ordered Mendez to jail the American as bait and send the bloodied Lopez on his way to lure the resort owner. The plan initially worked—Garcia's ploy netting Parrish. But leaving two Americans unaccounted for was a crucial mistake that turned the situation on its head.

In the next cell, Mike Parvin, hands tied behind his back, eyes swollen into slits, wiggled into a sitting position against an adobe wall. One of two, ten-foot square cages of floor to ceiling chain-link fencing sunk into a cement floor, Parvin's space was shared with two local men unlucky enough to have crossed Garcia's path. Unshaven, filthy from sleeping on the bare floor, Parvin and cellmates were both witnesses and victims of Garcia's escalating anger.

When Parvin had refused to talk despite the torture, Parrish had been pulled from their midst to suffer his turn. He underwent a savage beating from Mendez, then a second one at Garcia's hands after Wolf and Preacher's daylight raid. When his *patrón* tired, Mendez continued the punishment. Made of stern stuff, neither Parvin nor Parrish talked despite their pain.

As of this hour, with six of his men missing, along with their motorcycles, Garcia's world was showing signs of unraveling. Three more hires had died in yesterday's battle, two of them by an ancient weapon— of all things. There was talk of *espíritu*—spirits.

"*Imbéciles!* Do spirits ride motorcycles and shoot guns? These are men who do these things!"

Despite the tirade Garcia's hired *sicarios* took notice and grumbled openly among themselves. His press-ganged *campesinos*, three in number, were anxious, bordering on being useless in the wake of these losses. None of them were willing to attack Parrish's seaside resort in the wake of those who had done so and not returned.

What to do?

And then, like a gift, Jorge Ruiz arrived.

Chapter 68

Shuffling to the jail in the heat of the day, Ruiz shook a white handkerchief in one hand held above his head. At the jail, a nervous rooftop replacement waved an AK-47 at the carpenter, halting him at the entrance. One of Garcia's hired guns opened the door, jerked Ruiz inside, and ushered him at gunpoint to a side room, claustrophobic and filled with cigar smoke.

Miguel Garcia had jammed his bulk behind the sheriff's wooden desk like a bear cornered in its den. A gnawed cigar smoldered on the edge of the desk. Two pistols and a plastic bowl filled with 9mm rounds sat on the desktop. Garcia was loading magazines. A displaced Mendez, toying with a silver handgun, sat in a broken office chair beneath a filthy barred window set high in the wall. Aiming his gun at Ruiz, the sheriff pretended to fire. The carpenter flinched. Mendez laughed. Garcia pointedly ignored Ruiz until done loading.

"So, Jorge," he said, "why do you turn up on my doorstep, eh?"

Ruiz cleared his throat. "I come to see *Señor* Parrish, *Jefe.*"

"He comes to see the prisoners, Tito. Do you give permission?"

Mendez got to his feet, waving the silver pistol at Ruiz. "And what is the purpose of your visit? If I don't like your answer, I turn you away."

Backing from Mendez, Ruiz addressed Garcia. "I bring a message from the Americans who make this fight with you, *Jefe*."

Garcia put aside his handguns and waved Mendez back to his seat. "You have spoken to them?"

"Not by choice. For some reason they contacted me, *Jefe*." Heaving himself from behind the desk, Garcia stood nose to nose with Ruiz, his good eye fixed on the messenger. "What do they want? Why do you speak to them? They are dogs, enemies, Jorge Ruiz."

Staring at the floor, his posture submissive, Ruiz said, "They told me to see to *Señor* Parrish and the American, their friend."

"And why do they want you to do this?"

"They want to see if they are alive. They know I work for *Señor* Parrish. They say to me they wish to make an offer to you, *Jefe*."

Turing his back on Ruiz, Garcia masked his excitement. Over his shoulder, he said, "They are cowards to send a *peón* such as you to speak with me. Do they know who I am?" Pistol in hand, he whirled on Ruiz.

"*Sí, Jefe*. They know who you are. That is why they make an offer."

Mendez snarled from his chair. "Lies! They want to trick us."

Garcia silenced his acolyte with a wave of his hand. "Let him speak. What could these men offer me that I cannot take if I wish to do so?"

"They hold six of your men, *Jefe*. They wish an exchange."

"A sign of weakness," screamed Garcia. "They are cowards."

Ruiz said, "Perhaps, *Jefe*. But they have killed three of your men."

"They told you this?"

Bowing his head, Ruiz said, "No. This is known, *Jefe*. The people have seen this happen. They know."

Garcia paced. "You think I care? I have men enough to wipe out these *gringos* if I wish."

"I am to see *Señor* Parrish and the American with my own eyes, *Jefe*. This is what they tell me to say. They will not make their offer if I do not return with word that these men are alive. Please, *Jefe*. These *gringos* will kill me if I do not speak with *Señor* Parrish and the other man."

"Why should I care?" sneered Garcia. "But for the sake of argument let us say I agree to make this exchange. I also have demands, Jorge Ruiz."

"I'm listening, *Jefe*."

Garcia flashed a malevolent smile. "Of course you are, Jorge."

"These *gringos* must leave, go away immediately. If they do not leave I will have them killed...along with Parrish and the one I hold."

Ruiz nodded. "I understand."

Raising his pistol, Garcia's eyes narrowed. "And for good measure I will kill his daughters as well."

"I understand, *Jefe*."

Garcia prodded Ruiz's chin with his pistol. "And then perhaps I will kill you and your cousins."

A downward look and nod. "I understand, *Jefe*."

"You will tell them everything I have said."

"As you wish."

"Good," crowed Garcia. "Now go, visit the prisoners to see for yourself that they are alive." He turned to Mendez. "Tito, show this skinny dog your prisoners. We wouldn't want the *gringos* to think we have not treated these two as they deserve, eh?"

Mendez pushed Ruiz out the door and down the hall to the cages. A deputized *sicario*, armed with an AK-47, slouched on a stool, his weapon trained on the cells.

At the sound of footsteps, Max Parrish rolled on his side and propped himself on an elbow. Acknowledging Ruiz, he gave a weak wave to his handyman. Next door, Parvin glanced at their visitor through puffed eyes. His cellmates shot pleading looks at Ruiz. Mendez prodded Ruiz's back with his pistol.

"Seen enough? Tell the *gringos* their friends are well cared for." He laughed, along with the guard and Garcia, who had entered the cellblock.

"See, Jorge Ruiz, they are content. They are alive and happy, no?"

"*Gracias, Jefe*. I will tell the *gringos* what I have seen."

Garcia gripped Ruiz's shoulders and locked eyes with him. "Look at me, Jorge. You will tell these fools this. I say when and where we will make this exchange. They will do as I say or these men die."

"I will do as you say, *Jefe*."

Relaxing his grip, Garcia playfully patted Ruiz's cheek. "Of course you will, Jorge. Your life depends on it, as does your family's."

With a tilt of his head, Garcia summoned his guard dog and sent Ruiz out the door with his message.

Mendez watched from the jail's half-opened door until Ruiz was lost to sight. "Perhaps I should follow him," he said to Garcia. "I could kill him when he meets with the *gringos*."

"This is why I make the decision, Tito. Fool, of course they would like to have us follow Ruiz. We would walk into their trap. I'm too smart for that. It is we who set the conditions and the trap, not them. Tell Mateo to climb from the roof. And tear Diego from his whore at the cantina. I want everyone here. I have to make a plan to ambush these *gringos*."

"Will we be taking Parrish and this Parvin to make such a trade?"

"Of course. They are the bait, fool."

"Are they to be killed?"

"Yes, but it is the *gringos* who will do the killing."

"I don't understand, *Jefe*."

Garcia focused his good eye on Mendez, unnerving him. "You wouldn't. Go, do what I told you. The hour is late and I need to see who is with us."

"Before I go, may I have one request, *Jefe*?"

"You try my patience, Tito. What is it?"

"I want to be the one to kill the American we now hold."

Rolling his one good eye, Garcia said, "If you don't follow my orders, Tito, I will kill him myself, and then you for making me repeat myself. Now go before I change my mind and feed you to the *gringos*!"

Chapter 69

Halfway down the gravel road leading from Los Colinas, Jorge Ruiz heard the rumbling of a motorcycle. He halted as Maria Parrish had instructed. She burst from undergrowth behind him and skidded to a stop beside him. "Get on," she ordered. She scanned the tree line and cactus on both sides of the road, then accelerated toward the sea. Ten minutes later, Ruiz dismounted at the steps to Parrish's main house. Wolf and Lopez waited at the top of a short flight of stairs.

"You made it, *Señor* Ruiz. I trust your meeting with Garcia was successful. Let's meet inside."

They sat together in what had been the Parrish's great room, now turned into fortified combat headquarters. Heavy wooden tables had been turned against the windows. Mattresses were piled in one corner for use as needed. Buckets filled with water and sand sat ready to quench any signs of fire.

Maria came from the boat shed where she had parked the bike with the others. She took a place at the table, next to Lopez.

Wolf leaned across the family's long dining table. "Did you see Parrish and Parvin?"

Ruiz nodded. "I did. They have been beaten badly, *señor*, but they are strong men. If you free them before Garcia has a chance to kill them, you will have done well."

"How many men does Garcia have?"

Ruiz took a long moment to answer. His response, he knew, would be critical. "There is another man on the roof to replace the one who was killed. I saw just one *sicario* inside the jail. He guards the prisoners. They have Kalashnikovs. I do not know these two. They are not from Los Colinas."

"Four," said McFadden. "Hardly an army is it?"

"Are there more, Jorge? Perhaps others in town?"

Ruiz shrugged. "My nephews would know, I think."

"What about Garcia and his police chief, Mendez?"

Another thoughtful pause. "Both there, both armed with pistols." Wolf made notes on a sheet of paper. He pushed it across the table to Ruiz. "Will you draw for us the inside of the jail, where the cells are, any other rooms or hallways?"

Ruiz hesitated. "We must know what to expect," said Wolf. "It becomes a trap for us, otherwise. Do you understand what I'm asking?"

"*Sí*, I will try."

"Draw as if you plan to build a house," said Lopez.

The plan of the jail emerged, line by labored line until Ruiz was satisfied with his version. He handed the diagram to Wolf, who studied it.

"In which cell is *Señor* Parrish?"

Ruiz marked the paper. "Alone in this one. All the others are together in this second one. There are two of my people with *Señor* Parvin."

"A complication?" said Lopez.

"Could be. We have to get into both at once to make it work."

"Who keeps the keys?" said Lopez.

"Mendez," said Ruiz. "But he does only what Garcia says."

Lopez said, "Have to get those keys."

"Or take the cages apart," said Wolf. "I think there might be a way."

Eyeing the drawing, Lopez tugged at his beard. "Care to explain?"

"Later," said Wolf. He focused on Ruiz. "Tell us how our offer was received, Jorge. What does your heart tell you?"

"He pretends to be interested but I think he will use the time to prepare an ambush to kill you and your friends, *Señor* Wolf. You cannot trust him. And once you are dead he will kill those of us who helped you."

Wolf reached for Ruiz's hand. "*Amigo*, believe me when I tell you that Garcia will not succeed. He does not know who he is dealing with."

A faint smile showed on Ruiz's lips. "I pray that you are right, *señor*. There are many people who also make this prayer."

Chapter 70

"Are you willing to risk taking a message to Garcia telling him we accept his willingness to make this trade? Of course he'll want to set the conditions of our meeting, but I can live with that in order for him to think he has the upper hand."

Preacher, who had listened to the discussion without saying a word, rallied from his berth. "Pride goeth before a fall."

Wolf pumped his fist. "I'm depending on it."

"*Sí*, I will take your message. It is what comes after that I fear."

Wolf, who had not let go of Ruiz's hand, locked eyes with him. "I understand. I too, am worried about Garcia's reaction. But I tell you this, Jorge, to do nothing is worse...for us and for you and your family. And for the people of Los Colinas."

Ruiz shook his head in agreement. "Then you know my heart."

"I do," said Wolf. "*Señor* Parrish has told us how Garcia has harassed him for years in order to get his land."

Near tears, Ruiz lowered his head. "And now this is his chance. I think he will kill my friend. I think you know this, *Señor* Wolf. "

Tension filled the room, everyone waiting for Wolf's response.

"It is a gamble, Jorge, one we must be willing to take. That is why we will move first."

Rising from the table, Ruiz shrugged in surrender. "Very well. I will take your answer to Garcia and wait for his reply."

"If he does not give you his answer right away tell him you must see to your family and will return. Go home and gather your wife and children. Maria will be there to take them to a safe place."

"But if he sends for me and I do not return to hear what he has to say he will know something is wrong."

Wolf said, "I can't force you to go back to him."

Ruiz bowed his head. "I have to do this to make this plan succeed."

Wolf placed a hand on the carpenter's shoulder. "Very well. Tell him you will speak with us. His answer won't matter at that point. But you and your family must leave Los Colinas."

"*Entendre*—I understand."

Wolf offered his hand to Ruiz. "Thank you for your help. Remember to look after your family, Jorge."

Taking Wolf's comment as a sign that the discussion was finished, Maria left to get the motorcycle for a return to the village. Following her, Ruiz paused on the threshold, waiting for Parrish's daughter.

"Remember Lot's wife," said Preacher. "No looking back."

Ruiz shot a puzzled look at the bandaged SEAL. Wolf waved away the warning. "He just meant to say, do what we agreed to without fail."

"*Entendre*—I understand."

Maria Parrish pulled up, her bike idling. Ruiz paused on the steps as if having second thoughts. He turned to Wolf. "There is something you should know before I go."

"Yes, I'm listening."

Ruiz tugged at his sleeve as if trying to find the right words. "There is one in town I will send to you tonight."

"Who?"

"Emiliano."

"And why should I know this man?"

Ruiz locked eyes with Wolf. "He is a man who holds secrets."

Impatient, Wolf said, "We all have secrets, Jorge. What does your friend know that would interest me?"

"He is not my friend, *Señor* Wolf. He keeps to himself, you see."

Wolf said, "Ah, *Lobo solitario*, eh? A lone wolf like myself."

Ruiz missed the irony.

"Forgive me, Jorge, it's just a saying we *gringos* use. Tell me about this man—this Emiliano."

"I know why you are here. Emiliano has the answer you seek."

"We have to worry about Garcia. Don't you agree?"

"Of course. But first, listen to what Emiliano has to say, yes?"

Ushering Ruiz to Maria waiting on the motorcycle, Wolf said, "I'm not going anywhere until tomorrow. If you think it's important, I will see this man."

Wolf walked Ruiz to Maria's bike and shook his hand as he mounted the motorcycle. The two roared away, Ruiz's words fresh in Wolf's mind. When Wolf returned Preacher sat up in his bunk, his eyes on his friend. "What was that about, Skipper? Ruiz jumping ship on us?"

"Not at all. He was wound up about a guy named Emiliano. Said he was the keeper of secrets. Also said he knew why we were here."

"Maybe he's setting us up," said Preacher. "You think about that?"

"I read people well," said Wolf. "Ruiz was telling the truth."

"So, you've thrown down the gauntlet using poor old Jorge as bait. Care to share tomorrow's game plan with the major and me?"

"I'm expecting Sam and the others on *South Wind* tonight."

"Sure. But what's our strategy?"

"A page right out of Nathan Bedford Forrest's Civil War playbook."

Preacher grinned. "I like it—'Get there firstest with the mostest.'"

Chapter 71

Ruiz was right. Emiliano, *guardián de los secretos*—the keeper of secrets—appeared at dusk on the steps of Parrish's hostel like a penitent in threadbare white cotton. A wiry wrinkled brown gnome with few teeth planted in a flat face, Emiliano drove a pickup almost as old as its owner. Wolf welcomed Emiliano and ushered him inside. Quizzed about his age by a suspicious Preacher, Emiliano admitted only to seventy years, though he looked ancient. Soft-spoken, he was given to few words, as if using them would exhaust his God-given quota. But face to face with the *gringos* who had challenged Garcia, he was as direct, if brief, in his gratitude as his fellow townspeople were reticent in theirs. After, Emiliano, as translated by Lopez, made a startling promise.

Lopez said, "If you are willing, he says he will take you to find those you seek. But you must go with him tonight."

Preacher wasn't convinced. "How do we know this guy wasn't in on it? Maybe he had something to do with the killings."

Ever the diplomat, Lopez rephrased the accusation, softening the words. Ignoring the skeptical Preacher, the two Mexicans chatted. An animated Emiliano drew a map in the air. Facing Wolf and Preacher across the table in the lamplight, Lopez's eyes widened at the telling.

"All these years he has watched Garcia and his *sicarios* at work. They routinely dumped those they murdered in the brush. Emiliano says he would take the bodies away and bury them in the hills—always in one spot, hoping some day to tell what he knew."

Wolf said, "Why didn't he tell what he knew?"

Lopez scoffed. "Tell who? Who would listen to him? The army wasn't interested and the police were part of the problem. Emiliano gave the victims a decent burial to spare them the indignity of being ravaged by animals."

"One man?" said an incredulous Preacher. "He did this by himself?"

Lopez relayed Emiliano's answer. "Yes, he was alone

"How many did he bury?" said Wolf.

"Forty-seven. He remembers men, women, some children."

"How many years has this been going on?"

"Since Garcia returned. Maybe eight or ten years he thinks."

Preacher said, "Ask him if our missing boys are among them."

The old man either hadn't heard the question or he deliberately ignored it. Lopez repeated McFadden's words to no avail. Silence.

"What's the deal?" growled Preacher. "Why'd he shut down?"

Lopez appealed again and got a terse reply. "*Hay que ir esta noche.*"

Wolf signaled for silence. "I get it," he said. "For some reason he wants us to go with him tonight to find the answer. Maybe in some weird way this is his way of letting us in on what he's been doing all these years."

Preacher said, "You're on to something, Wolfman. We shouldn't spook this guy. We should take him at his word."

"Oh, so now you're suddenly a believer?"

"Something about him."

Lopez gripped Wolf's hand. "Preacher is correct. Do what Emiliano asks."

"Tell him we would be most grateful," said Wolf, through Lopez.

"I'm coming with you," said Preacher. "You'll need me."

"You're in no shape to go," said Wolf.

"I've still got one good arm, Skipper. I'm going."

Lopez, still hobbled from the effects of his beating, leaned over the table. "What about my *adelitas*?"

Wolf reached for Lopez's elbow. "Not Parrish's daughters, Luis. Think of what we might find. Besides, the three of you must stay here in case Garcia sends his dogs. We can't afford to lose this base."

Lopez slumped to the bench. "Honor demands it."

"For once, Luis, put your exaggerated sense of honor on a shelf for just one night, okay? I need you here to cover my back."

"Is that an order?"

"If push comes to shove, then yes."

"Then I accept, but only under protest."

Wolf got up from the table and bagged several bottles of water. "Protest duly noted, Major Lopez."

Chapter 72

Wolf and Preacher armed themselves and crowded into Emiliano's truck. He drove a pickup, its bed an omen of their mission—a lantern, machetes, shovels, pickaxes, and garden trowels piled on worn quilts and burlap bags. Sobered by the sight of the digging tools, Wolf and Preacher braced for their mission. Driving by feel, and without lights, the old Mexican unnerved both Americans by following an invisible road into the hills above Los Colinas. After forty minutes of grinding gears they crested an eroded mesa and were rewarded with a spectacular view of the moonlit sea. To the north, what few lights burned in Los Colinas belonged to the Pemex station's dull halo and a handful of houses.

Emiliano's truck lurched to a halt. He got out and lowered the tailgate. He fired a kerosene lantern and handed Wolf and Preacher each a shovel.

Throwing ragged quilts and burlap bags over his shoulder Emiliano grabbed the light and a spade.

"*Sígueme.*"

"*Sí*, we follow," said Wolf.

He led them to a windswept corner of the mesa. Removing his hat, he swept his arm over a shallow sunken semi-circle of earth. "*Todos ellos están aquí.*"

Leaning against a shovel, Wolf said, "He says all of them are here." He shook his head. "Hate to say it, but my gut says that might even include those two surfers from California."

Preacher let out a low whistle. "Why say that? They left just days ago."

"Something about our friend tells me that."

"If you're right that's two more families we'll have to contact."

Emiliano set the lantern at a low mound wearing withered blossoms. Wolf caught Preacher's eye. Scuffing the soil with a boot, he stared at the site. "Is this what I think it is?"

Catching the question in Wolf's voice, the Mexican nodded.

"Ask him about Connor and the others," said Preacher.

Wolf tried. *"Hermano, están cuatro chicos americanos aquí?"*

A hurried nod, a tapping of the ground with a shovel's blade.

"He buried them, Preacher," said Wolf. "He knows what we're after."

Their guide held up four fingers and pointed. *"Aquí."*

Preacher paused, *"Un momento por favor."* To Wolf, he said, "What do you want to do, Skipper?"

"He brought us here for a reason, Preacher."

"But we can't just start digging can we? This is a crime scene. We don't have forensics training. Imagine what we might find."

Watching the two, Emiliano squatted beside the lantern, waiting.

"We found what we we've been looking for," said Preacher. "Take his word for it and leave the rest to the FBI and the Mexican government."

"What do we have, really?" said Wolf. "If we want proof we'll have to dig for it. That's why we're here. I say we dig."

"Hold on," Preacher said, shaking his head. "We disturb this site and we're messing with evidence."

Wolf held up a pick and shovel. "Why do you think he brought these? If we want to find the missing, dig. If the government arrives and takes over the investigation we'll never know what happened. They may even move the grave for all we know. We should dig while we still have time, *amigo*." Wielding the pickax, Wolf bit into the ground, breaking up the packed soil. Dilemma solved, Preacher abandoned his protest and followed suit with his good arm, tossing aside shovelfuls of dirt despite his misgivings. Casting his shadow in the lantern's yellow light, Emiliano moved between them with a long-handled spade, deftly defining the grave's outline. Trading off and on for water breaks, the trio worked for thirty minutes, deepening the hole.

Wolf stopped. "I have a sandal and a foot," he said.

Chapter 73

Emiliano hurried over and bent down, trowel in hand. He scraped away more dirt, revealing a desiccated foot and lower leg protruding from rotting denim.

"Let me," said Wolf. He reached for the tool. "*Te ayudo or te puedo ayudar?*"

In minutes a shrunken outline emerged. Preacher dug with the small gardener's spade Emiliano had given him. Stepping into the grave, the Mexican handed two brushes to the Americans. Sweeping dirt from a head, Wolf said, "From the pictures we have, this looks like it could be the Farrel kid."

Working in shifts under Emiliano's direction, Wolf and Preacher unearthed two more bodies in stages of decay like the first. Propping elbows on his shovel, Wolf took a break. "We need to document this as we go. Preacher, take GPS readings. We might need this down the road."

Wolf and Emiliano found the fourth body, smaller than the other three. "Has to be Connor," said a watching Preacher above them. "Tell me what you see, Wolfman."

Digging and removing dirt until they had revealed the body's outline, Wolf and Emiliano paused in their efforts. Sitting on the edge of the excavation, Wolf reached for a bottle of water. Preacher pocketed his GPS and used a brush to sweep dirt from the face. Moisture and time in the soil had ravaged the body. Moving the lantern over the face, Wolf saw wisps of blonde hair and enough of the features remaining to identify Sara Ward's only child. He turned away, his eyes moist.

"Connor?" whispered Preacher, taking the lantern from Wolf.

Shoulders sagging, Wolf nodded.

All work stopped. Preacher and Wolf abandoned the gravesite to their guide. Avoiding eye contact, Wolf focused on the moonlit horizon. Emiliano held up a hand. Silence settled over the lonely grave and its four occupants. A long moment passed, the wind shaking the trees on the slopes, the distant hiss of waves far below the mesa, the only sounds. Wolf brushed dirt from his hands and walked a short distance away, his back to their final discovery. Preacher waited a decent interval and joined him. "What now?" he said.

Glancing back, Wolf said, "If I thought it would do any good I'd say bundle up the remains and take them back to the states with us."

"And how would that work?"

Wolf squinted in the lantern's glow. "It wouldn't. We'd never get past customs. Don't even want to think about what would happen if we turned up with four sets of bones. What we do have though, is the exact location where they lie. Plus, we've got a credible witness."

"You know the families will want their kids back home."

"Roger that. Wouldn't you?"

Preacher nodded.

"I have a suggestion," said Wolf, "but you may not like it."

"Knowing you, probably not. I haven't liked any of this. We were almost killed and we're still a long way from home. What's one more outrage at this point?"

Chapter 74

Wolf was right. Preacher didn't like his suggestion.

"We need to gather some of the identifiable stuff from each body. Personal effects. We should also take one bone for DNA tests if needed. You agree?"

Pacing, Preacher wiped his brow with the back of his hand. "Oh man, that makes us some kind of grave robbers. You'd really do that?"

"Only as backup."

"Can you imagine the circus if the media got hold of this? You can't guarantee some family member might take exception to us mutilating their son's body. One outraged parent will blow the whole deal."

"True," Wolf said, "but look at the possible downside. How can we go back and tell the families we found their sons but have nothing to show for it."

"We'd turn over the personal belongings."

"And where would we say we found them?" Throwing up his hands, Preacher said, "Not the same."

Shaking his head, Wolf said, "Hey, no bodies, no crime."

Preacher temporized. "GPS plotting? Witnesses?"

"All good to have. But only if...and it's a big IF...Mexican authorities show up and do the right thing by consulting with the FBI. They do that, fine, end of story as far as I'm concerned."

"You don't seem convinced that'll happen."

Wolf shrugged. "I'm just saying—"

Preacher surrendered. "Okay, go for it. You're in charge of bagging bones. I don't want anything to do with it." He walked away.

Wolf called to Emiliano, pantomimed what he wanted to do, but failed. On his own, Wolf went to work in the lantern's glare. Severing shriveled tendons and ligaments was not easy but he went down the line, removing one patella from each corpse with his knife. Wolf penciled names on each bony disk and bagged the fragment in burlap, along with a scrap of notepaper identifying to whom they belonged. Eager to be done, he worked silently but methodically, watched by Preacher and Emiliano.

Once finished, Wolf, covered in sweat, stepped from the grave. Hands trembling, he put away his knife. "Hard work, not nerves," he told the watching Preacher.

"I would never accuse you of nerves."

Emiliano stepped forward, his arms draped with four worn quilts. He and a somber Preacher covered each body head to foot with the makeshift burial shroud.

Wolf turned to Preacher. "Maybe a few words before we cover it up. What do you think?"

"The least we could do." Head bowed, he stood at the head of the grave, hands folded in front of him, his prayer brief, voice low. Emiliano crossed himself and began backfilling. Preacher and Wolf joined in. The faded quilts rapidly disappeared beneath the dirt. When finished, Preacher and Wolf smoothed the fresh mound.

El guardián de los secretos went to his pickup for potted flowers. His was a last touching gesture. Extinguishing the light, Emiliano placed the tools in the truck's bed. With Wolf and Preacher crowded in the cab, he descended the mesa, driving by feel and glimpses of rutted track in the fickle moonlight.

Chapter 75

Punta Corocos

A gentle onshore breeze carried the faint sound of marine diesels to Wolf's hiding spot in the olive grove. McFadden and crew had arrived in time, after all. Considering the situation, *South Wind*'s appearance was a godsend.

Someone's prayer, perhaps Jorge Ruiz's or Lopez's, had been answered, Wolf thought. Maybe Preacher had put in a word. After all, prayer is his thing, not mine.

The trawler, dark except for running lights, slowed as it entered the bay. The engines idled. He heard chains rattle as anchors were run out. Wolf left his listening post and returned to the tunnel.

Good. We can move Preacher on board, out of harm's way. Having Snuffy and Gideon just doubled our firepower. He went down the passage to share the good news.

Lopez met him at the escape route's steel door with a smile. "You heard them?" said Wolf. The marine nodded. Parrish's younger daughter came down the stairs, relief written on her face. Even Preacher had revived. He sat on the edge of his bed, grinning, ready for the coming fight. "Second half. Put me in, coach," he said.

"Stand at ease, Iron Man," teased Wolf. "I'm heading to the beach to meet Sam and the boys."

"Ask them what took so long," said Preacher.

"I will. And we'll get you aboard as soon as possible," said Wolf.

"Belay that," huffed Preacher. "Staying right where I am."

"We'll see about that."

Rising on shaky legs, Preacher said, "Not an issue. I'm staying."

Wolf smiled at the bravado. He called to Elizabeth. "Keep an eye on these two until I come back." Then, he was out the door, hurrying to the beach, where *South Wind*'s inflatable had landed.

After embracing McFadden, Wolf pumped both fists in the air. "Just in time, Sam."

"That's what Custer said to Crazy Horse, Wolfman."

The two laughed. Wolf threw an arm around McFadden's shoulders. "We're not going down that road, Dawg. With you here the situation's changed." Wolf's expression hardened. "We've found the missing, Sam."

"What? When?"

"Just tonight. Preacher and I found the graves. A lot of graves."

"Positive ID?"

"It's them all right," said Wolf. "All four. Bagged some personal gear and bone fragments for safekeeping. It's done, Sam."

"What about those two surfers we met at Parrish's place?"

"They're probably up there with the rest. They'll have to wait their turn."

Speechless, McFadden bowed his head. Wolf let him absorb the news. Up the beach, Gideon and Snuffy dragged the dinghy above the high water mark and buried an anchor in the stones. Gideon reached them first and Wolf took him aside to tell him about the discovery on the mesa. He sank to the stones, head on his knees.

McFadden regained his composure. "Snuffy should know. I'll break it to him."

"Appreciate it," said Wolf. "I hate being the bearer of bad news."

McFadden lingered on the beach waiting for the tardy Snuffy.

Wolf walked Gideon to the house. "Just so you know, Preacher's been hurt."

"Hurt as in—"

"Caught a round in his left hip in our last go around. The bullet kept going, lodged under the shoulder blade."

"Nick a lung?"

They went up the steps. Wolf shook his head. "Don't think so. He's breathing okay."

"He's lucky," Gideon said. "Knowing Preacher, he's probably looking for a fight."

"He is. Says he's ready for the next round."

Gideon asked about Lopez. "He's on the mend." Wolf, glanced back at *South Wind*. "Wonder how Snuffy's taking all this." The two paused on the porch.

"He'll get through this," said Gideon, "I think he knew all along but didn't want to say it out loud. Had some rough moments coming north but my guess is he's still game to finish this. Tonight's news will hit him hard. You know, the finality of it all."

Wolf looked back at the beach. McFadden and Snuffy were a single unmoving silhouette. "Wish I had better news," said Wolf.

"It is what it is," said Gideon. "We knew this was a possibility."

Snuffy and McFadden hadn't moved. Wolf turned away at the top of the steps. "We're gonna need all hands on deck. In your phone call you said the Cabo connection turned out to be a dead end."

"'Fraid so," said Gideon. "Snuffy and our guardian angel Carrera ran it down. I've been thinking, Wolfman. It looked like everything pointed here, and now your news settles it."

McFadden left Snuffy behind and joined Wolf and Gideon on the porch of the main house. "He'll be along eventually. Just needs some time by himself."

Gideon went inside to a subdued reunion with Preacher and Lopez.

Wolf and McFadden faced each other. "What's the latest on Parrish and Parvin? Your call made it sound like we have a fight on our hands."

"No way around this, Sam. Our guys are lined up against a wall and we're the only ones who can help."

Nodding, McFadden said, "Just so you know, we hashed this out on the way here. All of us are on board with this. Even before you hit us with the news we kinda knew this is where our MIAs ended up. Whoever this Garcia guy turns out to be, he's the one with the answers."

Wolf exhaled. "I had a bad feeling about this place, Sam. Right now we're in a fight for survival. I hope we get those answers, but the first thing we gotta do is make it through tomorrow."

"Sounds like we're against that wall you mentioned."

Pausing with his hand on the door latch, Wolf said, "Let's go inside and brief our little army about what we're facing."

"Sounds bad, Wolfman." said McFadden.

"Bad as I've seen, Sam. But having you guys here raises our odds considerably."

The two went inside to a war council.

Chapter 76

Downing his fifth, or seventh, or tenth tequila, a glassy-eyed Juan Diego wiped his beard and licked the excess from the back of his hand. Bellowing, "*Mas!*" he waved the empty shot glass overhead. His bored server, a plump heavily made up twenty-something weary of the *sicario*'s pawing, sighed. Taking her time, she strolled to the table Diego had commanded for the past five hours. Out-drinking, out-shouting, and out-cursing the regulars, he had backed into one of the cantina's claustrophobic corners like an ugly gargoyle. With a loaded pistol stuffed in his waistband,

Garcia's hired gun had intimidated everyone who dared darken the doorway.

Summoned from his lair, a dilapidated trailer in the hills outside Los Colinas, Diego had loudly lamented abandoning his lucrative highway trolling. Soft targets were Diego's specialty—tourists, travelers, the occasional trucker, *gringo* surfers, and unarmed *campensinos* caught in his highway web. Only one week before, Diego had narrowly escaped from a hastily planned robbery gone wrong up the coast.

Diego had fled the debacle in his truck, accompanied by only Mateo, a cold-blooded but undependable *sicario* wannabe. When victims shot back, Mateo was the first to bolt the scene. Still licking his wounds, the memory ate at Diego. Tequila helped, but did not heal, the shame.

His new assignment—settling scores with *gringos* for a gunfight that had ended badly for Garcia only the day before. Bottled up in the backwater town, Diego and Mateo took turns sleeping in the jail or Diego's truck. Promised thousands in pesos, they were holding the line, a thin one at that, for *El Jefe*. Along with one other *sicario* and Los Colinas' incompetent police chief, Mendez, they were it. Rumor had it that eight of their kind had disappeared or been killed. Tequila helped dispel the fear.

Diego yelled for attention.

The cantina's lone server moved in slow motion. Diego stifled his frustration with another rejection of his advances.

"*Ah, mi putita*," he said. "You are like a butterfly. So graceful."

Ignoring him, the woman filled his glass and turned to leave. He grasped her hand and grinned. She tried to shake free as if a cockroach had touched her flesh. Diego's grin disappeared, replaced by an ugly scowl. "*Puta!*" he screamed. A tug-of-war began. He won, pinning her to his lap, both arms wrapped around her. Squirming to avoid his lips and foul breath, the sober server proved stronger than the drunken Diego. Upended in a pile of petticoats and denim, the two struggled on the concrete floor. Diego struck her once, bloodying her nose.

Poised to hit her again, Diego's wrist was caught in a vise-like grip. Mateo had slipped inside the cantina unseen. Shocked, Diego roared at the interruption. The woman escaped, leaving Mateo holding her tormentor.

"FOOL!" screamed Diego. "What are you doing?" Reaching for his pistol, he slashed at Mateo's hand, freeing himself. Scrambling to his feet Diego lashed out at the younger man, who backpedaled to the door.

"Garcia wants us. He sent me to find you. We have to go! *El Jefe* sent for the *federales.*"

Momentarily distracted, Diego looked for his victim—gone.

Pistol still in hand he warned Mateo, "Do that again to me and you are dead, *hermano!*"

Holding his wrist, Mateo shrugged at the threat, one he had heard often in the heat of the moment. Diego's warning had lost its currency long ago. "We go to the jail. *El Jefe* wants all of us there to hear his plan. We are going to kill some *gringos* today."

Diego shook his head, trying to focus through the tequila haze. Shooing Mateo ahead of him, he followed his fellow gunman from the cantina, his gait unsteady. The whore's insult burned in his brain, along with Mateo's action.

She will pay, then Mateo, vowed Diego. *First, we kill the gringos.*

Chapter 77

Jorge Ruiz had yet to show. Maria Parrish kept her eyes on the main street. Ruiz was supposed to have told Garcia that Wolf had agreed to a hostage swap. She warned Ruiz's family about what was to come.

"When Jorge returns, you all must leave," she said. "Believe me, he will tell you this himself."

Ruiz's wife, a plain, taciturn woman, twice Maria's age, had accepted the news without showing emotion. Her two sons, both in their late teens, heard Maria's plea with the same passivity their mother showed. The family's youngest children, a boy of eight and a girl not yet ten, showed no signs acknowledging the gravity of the situation.

"Papa is coming," said the oldest son at the front window.

Showing no signs of panic, Ruiz walked slowly, as if time did not matter. Maria knew differently. Wolf had been adamant about the timing of his plan to free her father and his friend before meeting with Garcia.

Ruiz walked in the front door and sat down, his face lined with worry. "I have Garcia's message for the *gringos*. He will meet with them at the church. I tell you, Maria, they cannot succeed against Garcia."

Maria said, "You must trust them, Jorge. And you must remember *Señor* Wolf's words. While there is still time you are to take your family and flee to safety."

Shaking his head, Ruiz said, "I will stay."

"But you heard what *Señor* Wolf said."

"*Sí*, I heard. But I could not live with myself to do this. Am I to leave my people to their fate? Am I to go away with my family so they may be safe? What would people think of me? What of my self respect?"

"Your family needs you. This is Wolf's fight. He makes it his."

"So he has. And I intend to do my part."

Maria pleaded with Ruiz. "Please, do as asked."

"And what of you, my young friend? You have risked much yourself. If you do this, so can I. But I ask of you a favor. Don't refuse me."

"What do you ask?"

Taking Maria's hands in his, Ruiz got to his feet. "Take my wife and family with you. Take them to the hills until this is decided. Look after them. I will send for them if God wills it."

Nodding, Maria wiped tears from her eyes. Taking her reaction as their only clue, Ruiz's two youngest rushed to their father. Bound by habit, their mother and two older brothers kept their masks in place. Ruiz hugged each child in turn, and then he and his wife shared a chaste embrace with their sons. Steeling himself against their leaving, Ruiz gave final instructions to his family.

"Go with *Señorita* Parrish. Do what she tells you. Take only what you can carry," ordered Ruiz.

When they had gone, Ruiz opened a stout, upright wooden chest his father had made for the newlyweds thirty years before. Opening an engraved silver box, he took out a black velvet bag—inside a pearl-handled, army-issued 1911 .45, one of the most reliable and powerful automatic handguns in Colt's armory. He loaded the pistol with a single magazine, kissed a wooden crucifix, and headed to the town church where Garcia had ordained the meeting would be held. If he hurried, Ruiz would reach the church before Garcia or the *gringos*. *It would be enough*. With his family safe, he would be free to deal with *El Jefe*, something he should have done three years earlier. *Do not dwell on that now,* he told himself. *I will redeem my town, my people, and my honor. God willing.*

Chapter 78

Gideon dropped off Wolf's slowing bike and sprinted to the hulking front-end loader. Climbing the rusting yellow machine, he played with the controls, then jumped down to examine the battery.

"I was told these machines were recently used to grade the roads. Tell me it's workable," pleaded Wolf, "I'm counting on you."

Ignoring Wolf's pressure, Gideon burrowed into the engine compartment, tugging at wires, wiping caked oil and grime from connections. Conscious of their vulnerability, Wolf wheeled the dirt bike in a quick U-turn to cover Gideon's effort. He idled in the big machine's shadow, pistol in his left hand, in case one of Garcia's thugs showed.

A spark, a string of curses, a metallic whining, and then a reluctant diesel engine came to life. "We have liftoff," yelled Gideon. He leaped into the operator's seat and grinned at a jubilant Wolf. "Ready when you are, Skipper."

"Wait," cautioned Wolf. "Tango on roof not yet down."

Gideon tied a bandana over his nose and mouth and goosed the front-loader's throttle. Belching oily black smoke, the big machine shook as if protesting being awakened.

Two hundred feet away, Preacher, left arm in a linen sling, steadied Parvin's crossbow in a tree's crotch. Longer than his previous shot against a similar target, Wolf's preemptive strike hinged on this single shot. Defying stabbing pain, Preacher centered the weapon's scope on the rooftop sentinel. Releasing the safety, he whispered a quick prayer and squeezed the trigger. Covering the distance in less than two seconds, the deadly shaft hit Mateo Muñoz just below his left shoulder blade, piercing his heart. Stunned, the dead man stared at the bolt's razor tip protruding from his chest. Mateo staggered, and then fell to the tarred roof, the Kalashnikov slipping from his hand, discharging as it hit the roof.

Wolf had seen it all. "Tango down," he yelled. "Hit it, Gideon!"

Grinding gears, the Marine lurched forward, the machine's gap-toothed bucket low and menacing. Wolf rumbled alongside in low gear, pistol in his hand. As they neared the rear of the jail, a lone figure carrying an AK-47 ran into their path. The man fired at the rig's cab. His first burst, low and scattered, ricocheted off the yawning bucket in fiery sparks. Lead fragments hit Gideon's left forearm, shoulder, and scalp. A second burst hit the cab. Gideon, blood flowing from his wounds, ducked below the controls, aiming at the back of the adobe building sight unseen. Wolf accelerated, firing at the shooter.

The gunman took three rounds in the chest and fell back. "Second tango down!" screamed Wolf.

With the threat removed, Gideon sat up, wiped blood from his eyes and corrected his aim. "Roger that. Opening the door, Skipper!"

Braced for the collision, Gideon opened the throttle wide.

The front-end loader hit the jail's rear wall, smashing the adobe blocks in a thundering explosion of fragments. Gideon tried reversing the hulking machine. The gears locked, refusing to cooperate. Abandoning the beast, he climbed over the bucket, and staggered into the gaping hole, searching for survivors.

Chapter 79

"PARRISH! PARVIN!"

The force of his attack had crumpled both cells. A pair of legs, bent at odd angles, showed beneath a mountain of adobe bricks. Surprised by the extent of the damage, Wolf followed, his pistol ready just in case.

"Right behind you, Marine!"

First in, Gideon found Parrish and Parvin cowering in crumpled fencing that had been cells. Barely recognizable and choking in swirling dust, the two linked hands with Gideon and headed for daylight. Covered head to foot in powdered adobe, a third silhouette, gray and stunned, clawed at the piled bricks, trying to free the broken corpse. A cursory pat down by Wolf determined the survivor was not one of Garcia's watchdogs. Ignoring garbled protests, he pushed the man outside where Gideon waited with the dazed Parrish and Parvin.

Despite the danger, a crowd of people spilled from the town's woodwork, somber at the sight of the smoking jail and the body in the dust. Wolf led his charge to Gideon, and then trotted to the circle of the curious, parting them. Nudging the body of the gunman he had shot, Wolf studied the brown pockmarked face.

Something familiar.

"Damn, I recognize this sonofabitch," he said aloud. "The big dog from the firefight north along the coast." The fallen man's weapon was gone, unsettling Wolf.

Scanning the ring of townspeople, he said, "We've got a missing AK. Not sure what that means." He tossed Gideon a spare set of van keys Maria had given him. "Take Parrish and Parvin back to the beach. Clean 'em up and hunker down."

"Will do. What's next for you?" said Gideon.

"Gonna pick up Preacher. No sign of Garcia. He's still out there."

"Oughta let Sam know what's happened."

"He knows," said Wolf. "You could hear the jail go up fifty miles away. No way he didn't hear it."

"If Garcia's anywhere close, that means he knows as well."

"Yeah, it's not finished. I'm heading to the church to back up Sam."

"Let me go with you. He'll be expecting you."

Wolf shook his head. "Negative. You need to get patched up. And our guys need looking after. Get yourself cleaned up and come back for us. I'll have Sam and Preacher with me. Get back here as soon as you can."

"With a busted wing Preacher won't be much help if you step in it."

"You don't know Preacher."

Chapter 80

Gideon was right. Garcia had heard the collapse of the jail and seen the rising column of dust from his vantage point at the top of the church steps. *Not a good sign*, he thought. *The gringos will know I did not mean to trade Parrish and the other. Mateo would not have died without a fight. I hope the gringos paid heavily.*

He glanced at the church's lone bell tower where Mendez waited. *It has come to this. Am I to be dependent on fools like him?*

Mendez called down to him. "*El Jefe*, two *gringos* coming. Should I shoot them now?"

"Wait until I am inside the church. When they reach the steps, kill them."

Garcia slipped into the chapel. Pausing at the foot of the nave, he pulled both pistols from his belt and let his eyes adjust to the dim interior. The terra cotta image of Christ on his cross hovered above the simple wooden altar. The priest's abandoned high-backed chair sat by itself, the door beyond it left open when he ran.

You proved yourself a coward, priest, but you were wise to leave. I would have shot you and blamed it on the gringos.

Aside from four strait-backed, caned seats and three rows of primitive benches, the sanctuary was deserted. Except for Mendez in the bell tower, Garcia was alone. Shadows cast by a rack of flickering votive candles danced on a thick adobe column to his right.

He crossed the rough tiles, leaned over the rose-colored glass holders, and blew out the tiny tongues of flame. Coils of smoke drifted in Garcia's wake as he retreated to the single curtained confessional. Backing in, he sat with weapons pointed at the arched entry where the *gringos* would have to come. Anyone attempting to use the door beside the altar would be easily spotted.

Mendez will be able to kill or at least wound one or both from his nest in the tower before he is killed. When they rush to take shelter in the church I will finish them.

Silence enveloped Garcia. Expecting the end tested his nerves.

They can't see me, he thought. *They will be easy targets, outlined in the doorway by the sun at their backs. I must be certain, steady.* His breathing slowed. The minutes crawled by. Hidden behind the privacy curtain, Garcia sweated in the stifling wooden box. Leaning forward, he pushed the heavy crimson drape aside with the muzzle of the pistol in his right hand. Focused on the entrance, Garcia felt another's breath on his neck. He froze.

Death whispered to him. *"El Jefe."*

Garcia's head exploded.

Seconds passed. The box filled with gunpowder's biting scent. Jorge Ruiz stepped from the confession booth, studied Garcia's shattered skull, and then knelt. Crossing himself, he spoke to the clay Christ.

"Perdóname, Señor, porque he pecado en su casa."

He wept, and then, thinking of Mendez above, fled in the priest's footsteps.

Chapter 81

McFadden heard the shot. He changed position, pointing his pistol at the bell tower, he sprinted to a low wall encircling a dusty garden. Crouching on one knee, he risked a look. A burst of fire chipped the lip of the wall, showering him with adobe scraps. Preacher, still carrying the crossbow, had followed McFadden. He caught a glimpse of a figure in the tower's arches and flashed his index finger, signaling *one man*. McFadden got it and waved. "Cover me," he yelled.

Preacher dropped the crossbow and fired three shots at the sniper's perch. One round struck the bronze bell. Using the opportunity, McFadden gained a blind spot below the tower and fired two shots at an exposed left arm holding an AK-47. A scream of pain and the rifle disappeared. Across from McFadden, Preacher waited, steadying his right arm against a slanting wall, silently daring the sniper to show. A burst of gunfire, followed by three shots, erupted in the tower. Silence.

A bloodied Wolf showed, holding a Kalashnikov. "All clear!"

"Wolfman, you hurt?" shouted Preacher.

"Negative! Not my blood, sailor!"

McFadden crabbed sideways, his pistol leading the way through the church door. Ten anxious minutes passed before he and Wolf reappeared. McFadden waved Preacher forward. "Two shooters inside," he said. "One in the bell tower courtesy of the Wolfman, one on the floor."

"Wasn't me," said Wolf, carrying the AK-47. "Already dead when I came in the back."

"Garcia one of them?" Preacher said.

McFadden shook his head. "Never had the privilege. Better ask Parrish or Parvin."

"Or them," said Wolf on the top step, gesturing to scattered gawkers. "Who is willing to identify Miguel

Garcia?" He stood on the top step, facing the plaza. He waved the Kalashnikov at a knot of onlookers. "Who knows Garcia?" No takers. He repeated his question. No one answered.

McFadden said, "Try Spanish, Dawg."

"*Quién conoce a Miguel Garcia?*"

No takers. The crowd thinned, leaving a handful behind. At the rear of the line, Jorge Ruiz pushed his way through the remnant to the bottom step.

"I know him, *Señor* Wolf."

"You're not supposed to be here. But thank you. Come with me."

The two went into the church to the wooden confessional. Garcia lay on his back, half his face intact and his skull in pieces like broken crockery. Ruiz stared at the body.

"Garcia?" Wolf said. Ruiz nodded.

Wolf pointed at the corpse. "I did not shoot this man, Jorge. I did kill the one in the tower because he tried to murder my friends. But this one—I did not kill."

Ruiz looked at Wolf. "I know. This man, I killed, *Señor* Wolf."

The remark caught Wolf by surprise. "I thought you did not want more killing."

"This is true. But things changed. We knew his family for many years. But when he returned he was different. How does that happen?" Ruiz shrugged. "Things became worse. *Señor* Parrish, an honorable man, did not like what was happening. But what could one man do? We turned our backs to the wind. Things sometimes are evil, you know?"

Wolf said, "I do know. Seen it happen. Even in my own country."

Ruiz looked at Wolf. "You must go. The *federales* are coming."

"When?"

"Perhaps yet today, certainly *mañana*."

"How do you know?" said Wolf.

"A woman from the *cantina* tells me this."

"Did Garcia send for them?"

Ruiz shrugged. "Almost certainly. He was depending on them to help him in this fight. It will not go well for you and your friends."

McFadden came inside, interrupting. "Maria's here. She wants to see her father."

"Tell her he's safe," said Wolf. "Gideon took him to the beach along with Parvin."

"Hope he's coming back for us."

Wolf said, "He is. We're done here I think."

Ruiz caught Wolf's eye. "Ah, *mi familia?*"

"Also safe. Ask Maria where she hid them."

Ruiz went out the door and went down the broad steps to Maria Parrish. Eager to be off, she waited for him on her idling motorcycle. Preacher and McFadden joined Wolf.

"What now?" said Preacher.

Wolf tugged at his bloodied shirt. "Gonna toss this and get a clean one."

"I meant, what did Ruiz have to say?"

Eyes on the carpenter and Parrish's daughter, Wolf spoke without looking at his friends. "Said we should get out of Dodge before the *federales* show."

McFadden frowned. "Hell, we know that. But what about our missing boys? Are we supposed to go home with just scraps of evidence?"

Preacher jumped in as well. "We come all this way and we end up with a bag of bones and some personal effects. How's that gonna play?" He waved his good arm over the rooftops. "These yardbirds knew where they were all along. Even Ruiz knew."

"Probably so." Wolf exhausted, shrugged. "Look, it doesn't matter who knew what, or when. We have the evidence our kids were murdered. We're not giving that up. I sure as hell don't want to wait around hoping the Mexicans do the right thing. I say we make ourselves scarce until we sort things out."

Chapter 82

Gideon returned with Lopez in the passenger seat. With the van idling at the foot of the church steps, the major yelled through his open window. "This would be a good time to leave, *amigos*."

Wolf cleared the AK-47 and smashed it against the church's steps. He tossed the broken weapon aside and ambled to the van, along with McFadden and Preacher. The three climbed into the back seats. Gideon hit the gas and raced past the jail ruins and the *sicario's* corpse.

McFadden said, "How are Parrish and Parvin?"

"Cleaned up like you wanted. Two happy campers right now."

Wolf stared out his window. "Not out of the woods yet," he said. "Ruiz told us we have to leave. All of us. Before the *federales* show."

"I will stay behind," said Lopez.

"Oh? And how would you explain all that's happened?"

"That I stumbled into a war."

McFadden joined the discussion. "That's not going to fly, Luis. For starters, you had no reason to be here. Your story won't hold water. At least come with us until we see how this ends."

Wolf leaned forward between the seats. "You're going with us, Luis. That's an order."

Gideon headed toward the beach. When the van reached
the eroded incline leading to Parrish's resort, Wolf called a
halt. Off to one side, where brush and cactus lined the dirt
road, Emiliano's ancient pickup sat with its tailgate down.
Backed into ruts, the truck wore a patched canvas tarp tied to
its sides—the keeper of secrets nowhere to be seen.

"What's going on?" said Preacher. "That's Emiliano's
truck."

Wolf said, "So it is." He told Gideon to stop. "A little
unfinished business." He climbed from the van. "I'll
handle this, Sam. You guys go on ahead."

Preacher said, "Handle what? What's Emiliano doing here?"

"Taking out some trash. Move out, Gideon!" ordered
Wolf, tapping the van's side. The vehicle began its
swaying descent, McFadden and the others, puzzled, stared
at Wolf waving in the van's dusty wake.

Backtracking from the truck's tailgate Wolf followed the
trail of flattened brush and hacked cactus. He passed two
mangled motorcycles on their sides in matted weeds where he
and Preacher had dumped them days before. Twenty yards in,
he met Emiliano. Dragging a putrefying corpse wrapped in yet
another of his quilts, the little man passed without glancing up
from his burden. Wolf grabbed a fistful of fabric and pulled
along with the Mexican, easing his task. When they reached
the lowered tailgate, a gust of onshore wind lifted the canvas
tarp, scattering a cloud of flies. The carnage Wolf and
Preacher had wrought just days before was now a stiffened
tangle of bare limbs and bloated torsos. The gagging stench of
rotting flesh slapped Wolf in the face like a reminder.

Breathing through his mouth, he helped Emiliano tumble
the body into the truck's bed. Covering his nose and mouth,
Wolf counted six bodies.

"*Y aun al impío merecen una fosa*," said Emiliano, lashing
the tarp.

"You say even the wicked deserve a grave? Who am I to argue?" Rewarded with a shy smile and nod from Emiliano, Wolf palmed a roll of cash in the Mexican's hand and pointed to the hills. "*Para ellos*—For them. *Mis jóvenes amigos*—my young friends."

Left alone on the edge of the road, Wolf waited until Emiliano drove away, then headed to the beach below.

He found McFadden on the seaside patio, quizzing Parrish about how the ex-pat was going to handle the inevitable questions when the *Policía Federal* showed.

"It's a work in progress," Parrish was saying. "Not to worry, Ruiz and I are going to be telling the same story if they ask. Our tale is one of survival. A triumph of sorts against outside forces for the good people of Los Colinas. How do you think that will play?"

Wolf had arrived mid-conversation and expressed his skepticism. "You mean the good and passive people who stood by?"

Parrish did his best to sell the scenario he and Ruiz had outlined, "Garcia had friends in the government," he said. "When they find out what happened there may be hell to pay in the short run."

McFadden put a hand on Parrish's shoulder. "Then you and your daughters should head north with us until things settle down."

"Thank you, *amigo*, but I'm not leaving. After what I went through I'm more than ever determined to stay. With Garcia and Mendez dead I have a chance to return to normal."

"Their kind is always replaced," warned Preacher. "Never fails."

Parrish waved away the caution. "Thanks, but I'll take my chances. My wife's family connections with the presidential palace—*Los Pinos*—might pay off after all, and

I want to be here when they do. We built this place with our own hands."

McFadden wasn't buying it. "Too many loose ends," he said. "Hardest thing to explain is what the hell we're doing here."

"*IF* you're still here, you mean," said Parrish. "You've got maybe a twelve-hour grace period, Sam. Ought not to waste it talking to me."

"He's right," said Wolf. "Pack up. We should move while we can."

Chapter 83

Like dusty migrating beasts trailing a cloud of dust, three black *Policía Federal* pickups with the familiar wide white stripes and seven-pointed star on their hoods, rumbled into Los Colinas. In the lead vehicle, an officer standing in the truck's bed with two others, signaled, sending one truck left, another right, blocking intersections. Parking his idling vehicle in the middle of town, the officer wearing black fatigues, facemask and bulletproof vest dismounted. Carrying Galil assault rifles, two *policía* shadowed him, dressed alike in black, all but their eyes obscured by black hoods painted with ominous white death masks. Hovering on either side, they provided security as he scanned the town's deserted plaza.

"*Quién está a cargo?*" he bellowed through a bullhorn. Impatient, he repeated himself, then tossed it to his driver and stomped across the main street to the remains of the jail.

Jorge Ruiz witnessed all this from the shadows of a deserted store. Once a shop of a family of weavers, the one-story building was now home to an army of scavenging mice. Despite his wife's pleadings Ruiz had crept back into town. One of a handful of more courageous inhabitants, he kept his distance as the *federales* poked about in the jail's rubble and climbed over the pinned machinery. He stood immobile as the curious police made the discovery of Garcia's fallen *sicario* in the alley alongside the collapsed jail.

The head police officer, a stunted martinet with an exaggerated sense of rank, returned to his vehicle and radioed for instructions after his find. His second-in-command, a barrel-shaped sergeant, ordered a squad to dismount the trucks and collar what men they could among onlookers. Those not quick enough to disappear were hauled before the group's leader and quizzed about the destroyed jail and the corpse.

A sullen *campesino* mumbled his version of what had happened. Dismissed, his place was taken with another, who proved equally unhelpful. A white-haired widow in a black shawl was ushered to an interview. All this time Ruiz had been focused on the interrogations, unaware of two privates probing the backsides of Los Colinas' few buildings. He didn't hear the masked pair approach from behind.

"You there," barked the larger of the two, a corporal. "Come with us."

Trapped, Ruiz stepped from the shadows and raised his hands.

"Never mind that," said the policeman. "Tell our *comandante* what you know of this."

Ruiz lowered his arms. "What does he wish to know?"

The shorter *policía* leveled his rifle at Ruiz, prodding him toward the parked pickup. "Fool. Tell us what happened here."

"*Bandidos*," said Ruiz. "There was a gun battle between men who do not live here and others."

The corporal nudged Ruiz's elbow with his weapon. "Save it for his questions." Accompanied by the two, Ruiz shuffled to the parked vehicle. The commander was about to send the widow away when the pair arrived with their catch.

"Sir, we found this one watching from a distance."
The widow, relieved to see Ruiz, smiled and nodded.
"Do you know this man?" the policeman asked her.
Bobbing her head, the old woman managed a toothless smile.
"Very well, you may go," he said, waving her away. Hobbling
through the plaza without looking back, the woman rejoined
a small knot of villagers drawn by the show.
The officer eyed Ruiz. "Identify yourself."
"I am Jorge Ruiz, sir."
Hearing the deference in Ruiz's voice, the officer drew
himself to attention, hands clasped behind his back. "Tell
me, *Señor* Ruiz, do you live in this miserable little town?"
"*Sí*, I live here, though I cannot agree with the
description of Los Colinas as a 'miserable little town.'"
The hooded men snickered, prompting a rebuking glare
from their leader. Chastened, the men stepped back, eyes
on the ground. Behind the mask, the officer's eyes
narrowed, a warning Ruiz caught. Hands at his back, the
policeman circled the carpenter. "Have you ventured much
beyond Los Colinas, Jorge Ruiz?"
"No, sir. This is my home. I have lived here for two
generations."
"Well then, Ruiz, let me correct you. I have traveled a
good deal. I have even been abroad." He stopped, eyeing
Ruiz. "Los Colinas is a wretched little town, and at this
moment I am not in a good mood. And perhaps you've
noticed that my men are not in a good mood. But because I
am a good officer, a professional, I follow orders when given
them. My men, in turn, follow my orders without question.
My orders were to leave more important tasks and come to
this wretched town and investigate rumors of wrongdoing."
Ruiz kept silent, not sure what direction the lecture
was going to take. Are we to feel the weight of this little
man's authority?

"Your fellow citizens are either blind or deaf...or both. One hears the gunfire but sees nothing. Another sees ruins of a jail but says he heard nothing. The old woman tells of *bandidos* shooting each other in the middle of the day." Having circled Ruiz, the masked man stopped in front of him and said, "Which is it? Or are you an idiot like the others?"

"What the *señora* said is true. We heard shooting. There was an explosion as well. When things got quiet we left our homes and found the streets as you see."

"And the jail?"

"As you found it."

Arching an eyebrow at Ruiz, the policeman pulled at his death mask, pondering the answer. "So, you admit to hearing this battle you speak of. You see the results and yet no one, including you, knows who did the shooting, correct?"

Ruiz nodded.

The officer hit him with an open hand. "FOOL," he screamed. "You think we don't know what has happened here? I've a mind to arrest all of you for lying."

Give him Garcia in the church, Ruiz thought. *If he discovers that on his own all of us might pay for our silence.*

Playing the simple *peon*, he took a step back, hand to his jaw. "Please, sir, we are not liars. I believe those who began this fight fled." He pointed to the church. "They left behind two of their dead there."

Chapter 84

All eyes turned to the adobe bell tower. The sergeant, who had been standing off to one side during the questioning, stepped forward, brandishing his pistol. "Shall I investigate?"

"Immediately," said the officer. "See if this is yet another lie."

Signaling to four *policía*, the sergeant and the men jogged to the church, weapons at the ready. Ruiz watched them bound up the steps and disappear inside. Moments passed in an uncomfortable silence.

A lone recruit showed in the entrance and hustled back to his commander's truck, where Ruiz and the officer waited. A hurried whispered report and the patrol's leader waved two more of his men forward. He sent them back with the runner and then demanded of Ruiz, "How do you, the only witness out of all your fellow citizens, know about the two dead in the church?"

"I saw the end of the fight, sir."

"Ah, so now your memory improves and you tell me you saw this battle after all, eh?"

"Only as it was ending, sir. I tell you the truth."

"So you say." Calling over his two bodyguards, the officer ordered them to watch Ruiz. "This man is under arrest until further notice. He does not move without my permission."

Leaving Ruiz and his captors behind, the leader hurried to the church. Halting at the top of the steps, he glanced at the bell tower. Two conscripts were lowering a roped body to the ground. The policeman looked back at Ruiz, anger in his eyes. A third *policía* exited the church and guided the body to the ground. The patrol leader stepped inside the church.

In his place, the sergeant emerged and called for a wheeled cart. Two townspeople were drafted to find one and bring it to the church for the slain. When they did as asked, they were told to load the bodies. Leading the procession, the officer and his men returned, followed by the cart with its bloody cargo. The officer ordered it parked by his truck and dismissed the escort. He called Ruiz to his side.

"Do you know these men?"

Ruiz leaned forward, studying the swollen faces of Garcia and Mendez. He shook his head. "No."

"They are not familiar?"

Again, a shake of the head. Ruiz said, "They may have been with the other one, the one killed in the street."

"Look closely. Your life depends upon it."

His hands trembling, Ruiz stared at the two. "It is possible I may have seen these men before, though I can't be sure."

Drawing his pistol, the officer tapped Garcia's shattered skull and lowered his voice. "Let me help your memory, Ruiz. This is Miguel Garcia, a son of Los Colinas. And this other son of a whore is Tito Mendez, chief of police."

Clearing his throat, Ruiz whispered, "It is possible. But in their condition—"

The officer's pistol struck the side of Ruiz's head, felling him.

"You piece of—You don't think I know these two? Who's going to pay me what I'm owed now, you? I want the names of those who killed them. I think you know who did this, Ruiz. You don't tell me, I kill your family in front of you. Understand?"

Groggy from the blow, Ruiz nodded.

Holstering his weapon, the officer waved over his bodyguards. "Get him up," he said. "Tie him up and throw him in the back."

Wolf will know I had no choice, Ruiz thought. He stayed down to avoid more punishment, though he knew the *gringos'* fate was sealed if he gave in. *But my family*. He crossed himself, silently begging for forgiveness for what he was about to do. The bodyguards lifted him by the arms.

"I know, I know," he rasped. "Spare my family."

The policeman grabbed a fistful of Ruiz's hair and pulled back his head. "Of course. I am not a monster. A wise man saves those he loves."

Ruiz shook his bloodied head. "No, I am a coward."

"Just weak. One who cares for his family," sneered the officer, releasing Ruiz. "So, tell me, who were these men and where are they?"

"Parrish's place. The beach."

"Of course," said the patrol's leader, his eyes widening. "It would have to be him. Those *gringos*." Pointing west, he yelled across the plaza to the driver of the second pickup. "The resort by the sea. No prisoners. Tell the others!" The bodyguards dropped Ruiz at their feet, one sprinting to the third truck to relay the order.

Towering over the prone Ruiz, the officer delivered a painful kick to his prisoner's abdomen. "This is your lucky day," he said, "I'm going to let you live with your shame." He pressed the Glock's muzzle against Ruiz's forehead and pulled the trigger. A loud click. Ruiz fell back.

His tormentor laughed. "Next time for real. If you are lying I will return and show you and your family no mercy." He climbed into the passenger's seat, chambered a round in his pistol, and did the same with the Galil between his knees.

He snapped at his driver. "What are you waiting for? Drive."

Eyes fastened on the rear view mirror, the recruit behind the wheel said, "We have visitors, *Jefe*."

Twisting in his seat at the sound of diesel engines, the head policeman looked back and cursed. Trailing a wall of dust, six tan army Humvees swept into the plaza and split into two columns, flanking the *Policía Federal* pickups.

Chapter 85

An army captain wearing camouflaged fatigues, flak vest, pistol belt, and helmet eased from the first Humvee. Right hand on his holstered pistol, he walked toward the lead truck and halted midway. Steel gun shields top the armored utility trucks swiveled, bristling with M-60 machineguns aimed at the surrounded *Policía*. The army officer's every step was covered by heavily armed soldiers who climbed from the command vehicle and took up position behind sand-colored Humvees.

"Who is in charge?" he challenged.

After a few face-saving moments the lead *federale* shrugged, climbed from his truck, and swaggered to stand opposite the army officer.

"Senior Captain Humberto Huerta," said the helmeted soldier, saluting.

The policeman played one-upmanship for yet another thirty seconds before returning the salute. "Surely you appreciate my position."

"Which is?"

"I cannot reveal my identity or mission for obvious reasons."

"Two commanding officers cannot meet face to face? What have we here? I am to speak to a phantom, a mask?"

"It is a sensitive operation I am conducting, sir. You understand. I have my orders."

The captain gestured to himself. "I too, am acting under orders from the governor of this state. He in turn, answers to the Interior minister. However, I don't hide behind a mask, nor have I been told to terrorize civilians."

Overhearing the taunt, the armed men in black shifted in their pickups, weapons at the ready. Sensing the tension, the captain said, "We have a situation, *Comandante*."

The mask nodded. "Apparently we do."

Gesturing at the prone Ruiz, the captain said, "Is this unfortunate individual a player in your drama?"

The *federale* ignored Ruiz. "He is a troublemaker I was questioning to find out who was behind the trouble here."

"Then we are acting in concert, sir. I was sent here to take charge. To see if I can straighten out the situation. Judging from the bodies in that cart I see we have arrived too late."

"You should know that there are *gringos* involved, sir. It is my opinion that they did the shooting. My men and I were about to confront them."

"Where are they to be found, sir?"

Hesitating to answer, the masked *federale* balked.

"These *gringos*. Where are they?"

Ruiz leaned on one elbow, mumbling. "I can show you, Captain."

The *federale* said, "Don't trust him. My men and I will handle this."

"I think not, sir. This is what I'm here for. We will take care of this. You may continue with your other duties, perhaps other missions."

The scent of blood was in the air. A confrontation was building involving heavily armed men. One shot, accidental or otherwise, from either side and a bloodbath would follow. The captain gambled by returning to his armored Humvee. He paused at the passenger side door and turned, saluting the lead *federale*. "Safe travels," he said.

Chapter 86

Outnumbered, outgunned, and outmaneuvered, the masked officer stomped to his truck and executed an angry U-turn in the plaza, followed by his men. Spewing curses all the way to the main road, he tore off his mask and led the three-truck convoy to the highway, heading north.

The captain summoned his second-in-command, a tenacious no-nonsense lieutenant promoted from the ranks. "Take two vehicles and follow them for five kilometers," he said. "Make sure they keep going. If they challenge you, use your judgment. Then return. I will need you."

"But sir, they are *Policía Federal*."

Squinting, the captain pinched the bridge of his nose. "Perhaps. They certainly looked the part. How long have you served with me, Mendoza?"

"Two years, sir."

"Have you forgotten what I've taught you?"

"No sir."

"What do I always say?"

"Things aren't always what they seem."

"Good. Go. Chase our angry friends for a bit while I sort this mess."

After the lieutenant left, a sergeant was sent to photograph the bodies and organize a village burial. While that was being arranged, the captain called Ruiz to his vehicle to learn the role and whereabouts of the rumored *gringos*.

Not about to blunder into an ambush, Huerta waited until his lieutenant returned with welcome news that the *federales* had kept going, the major ordered his men into action. With Ruiz riding in the lead Humvee alongside him, Huerta left his lieutenant in charge of one vehicle at the highway junction leading to Los Colinas. Radio contact was to be maintained at all times he warned. With Ruiz guiding, Huerta led his other five vehicles toward the bluff overlooking the sea. He parked one squad on high ground, its M-60 covering the cliff and narrow road to Parrish's hostel. He positioned other Humvees at the top of the road with orders to allow no one in or out without his permission. Satisfied with his arrangements, he ordered his driver to negotiate the furrowed track to the resort. With a gunner manning the turret's machinegun, Huerta climbed from the Humvee with Ruiz and a heavily armed sergeant in tow.

Bandaged and bruised, Parrish waited on the main house's deck. Wolf, McFadden, and Parvin had hidden themselves in the tunnel with Lopez and Parrish's daughters. One hundred yards offshore in the glassy bay, Gideon, Preacher and Snuffy were aboard *South Wind* preparing to leave once their friends joined them. With the Americans' departure interrupted, a waiting game began.

The army officer stopped at the bottom of the steps and saluted. "Senior Captain Humberto Huerta, Second Military Region."

"Max Parrish, sir."

The officer gestured to Ruiz. "This man tells me of terrible things that have happened in Los Colinas. And you, *señor*, have obviously suffered as well."

"Thank you for your concern," said Parrish. "*Señor* Ruiz speaks the truth. An honorable man, he is also my friend."

Huerta removed his helmet, tucked it under one arm and smoothed his hair. "He told me there were *gringos* involved. What do you know about this, *Señor* Parrish?"

"Honorable men as well, sir."

Scanning the grounds and sea, Huerta said, "Where are these honorable men? And whose boat rides at anchor?"

Parrish came down the steps. "May I ask your intentions, Captain?"

"But of course. I was told to unravel this situation. I prefer to do this as quickly as possible and return to my normal duties."

"How can I help?" said Parrish.

"Let us not play games, señor. To do my job I need to talk with these men."

About to speak, Parrish was interrupted by Huerta. "Please do not try my patience, *señor*. I know these *gringos* are guests of yours. Ruiz has already confirmed this. I assume the boat belongs to them. If they are waiting to board, and if you do not wish to be considered their accomplice, I suggest you produce the men in question."

Parrish folded his hands beneath his chin as if praying.

Eyeing the seaside patio with its chairs and table, the captain said, "I will wait for a few minutes, *Señor* Parrish. If you have coffee prepared I will take it there. I will have a conversation with your guests. Do I make myself understood?"

"Perfectly, Captain. If you will allow me—"

Dismissing Parrish with a wave, Huerta tossed his helmet to his guard and headed for the patio. The soldier in the turret kept his eyes on Parrish as he went up the steps into his house.

With the invitation's message clear, the exodus began.

Wolf came first, followed by McFadden, then Parvin and Lopez, and finally Parrish with his daughter, Maria, carrying a steaming pot and five cups on a tray. He set them on the table and poured. He handed each man a cup and saucer. Offshore, Gideon, Preacher and Snuffy watch all this from *South Wind*'s darkened main cabin.

Huerta flashed a tight smile. "*Bienvenida, señores.* That wasn't so hard, was it? Reason prevailed. Good." He added more sugar and stirred his coffee. "Introduce yourselves. Then tell me how you came to be here and what part you played in this fight in Los Colinas."

Prompted by Wolf, McFadden cleared his throat and said, "I am Sam McFadden, sir. Three months ago, four American students traveled to Baja California Sur on holiday."

Huerta paused, his cup raised. "Ah, I remember this story. Go on."

McFadden continued. Then Wolf, Parvin, and finally, Parrish and Lopez. The coffee cooled in the cups. The tide went out. The wind died. Twice, Huerta excused himself to make radio contact with his men. Two hours passed with the captain probing their telling. He asked about the men on the boat and accepted McFadden's explanation of their roles. Lopez and Huerta carried on in Spanish. Wolf and the others caught a third of what they were saying, though the respect the two men shared was obvious.

Signaling an end to the interrogation, Huerta rose, as did Parrish and his guests. Seizing the moment, Wolf risked all with one request.

Chapter 87

"Captain Huerta, there is one thing my friends and I would ask of you. May I speak privately with you?"

"It would seem you have already asked enough. People have died at your hands in this affair. Yes, you convince me that you had no choice but I am not an *abogado*—a lawyer. I may yet have to answer for my actions as it is. This is no easy matter."

"I appreciate your situation, sir. But only you can do what I'm about to ask. Will you hear me out?"

"Very well. What do you want?"

Wolf said, "We know where the graves of our missing students are located." He waved beyond the cliffs. "A man who lives here took us there to see for ourselves. We have coordinates of the sites. We saw the graves. There are others buried there. We were told many were victims of Garcia and his *sicarios*. Will you pursue this for us? The families of our missing would be most grateful."

"You ask too much."

Wolf offered a folded slip of paper. "This marks the site, sir."

Huerta looked at the creased note as if it were toxic. "Perhaps *Señora* Parrish will be your champion. She has contacts with *Los Pinos*. My sources tell me it was she who got the governor to move on the troubles here. Ask her." He returned the note to Wolf without opening it and walked away.

McFadden grabbed Wolf's elbow. "What the hell was that all about?"

"I asked him to look into the graves we found," whispered Wolf.

"Might as well ask him to loan us some of his troops to start digging while you were at it."

Wolf ignored the jab. "It was worth a try, Sam."

"The hell it was. How about we leave that to the FBI?"

Wolf said, "Oh, yeah, that ought to work. We're gonna need a sit down before we even think about doing that."

Eyes closed, McFadden rubbed his forehead. "That, I'm willing to do. I just want to clear out, okay? I want to get the hell out of here without any more last minute snags."

Wolf scowled. "Fine. I get it. But when we get back—"

McFadden waved him into silence. He and Wolf watched Parrish and Lopez huddle with Huerta on the patio. The conversation grew more animated, worrying both. The officer shot an angry look at Wolf and headed to his waiting Humvee. About to slip in the passenger side door held by a private, Huerta was intercepted by Parvin. Carrying a flat camouflaged bag, he spoke to the officer, handing him the bag, and then snapping a salute. The Mexican returned the gesture, shook Parvin's hand, and climbed in the idling Humvee. His driver wheeled about and charged up the hill.

At the top of the cliff two other vehicles fell in behind Huerta's and disappeared from view.

Wolf and McFadden hurried to Parrish and Lopez.

"What was that all about?" said McFadden. "Looked like he was ripping you a new one."

Parrish smiled. "On the contrary. He wrapped up things. Told us he's satisfied with our stories. He's returning to La Paz to make a full report. As far as he's concerned Garcia and Mendez crossed some cartel people."

Wolf said, "How's he gonna explain those *sicarios* we took out?"

"The hazards of the trade," said Lopez. "I believe he'll report it to his superiors as such."

"What about the grave sites?" said McFadden. "Wolfman stepped in it big time by asking Huerta to look into it."

"Worth a try," said Parrish. "You'll have to run it past the FBI when you get back. We'll do what we can from this end."

McFadden clamped a hand on Parvin's shoulder. "I saw what you did, Mikey. Nice touch with the captain."

Wolf said, "Gave up your crossbow didn't you?"

Parvin shrugged. "Thought it would buy us some goodwill. Didn't you guys recognize him?"

"The captain?" said Wolf.

"Yeah. That roadblock south of Ensenada, remember?" He glanced at Preacher. "Where you almost gave away my crossbow."

"Of course." Preacher closed his eyes and looked up, smiling.

"Just might have saved our collective ass," said Wolf. "I gambled on getting Huerta's help with the graves but it pissed him off."

"I know," said Parvin. "Wasn't sure what was happening but it didn't look good. Decided to grease the rails for our departure."

"Good instincts," said Wolf. "I misplayed it. We owe you."

Parvin grinned. "You can buy me a new crossbow to make up for my loss."

"You got it."

"And maybe let me do a little fishing on the way back."

Wolf said, "I'll talk to Sam. I'm sure he'll agree."

Clapping his hands, McFadden yelled, "Okay, we've got a boat to catch." He looked at Wolf. "I'm beat. Getting too old for this."

"Hell, Sam, you don't look a day over sixty."

With the crisis apparently solved, Lopez announced he would stay behind to fully recover as he originally proposed. Wolf and McFadden bequeathed him the van to find his way back to Ensenada. Lopez embraced Wolf and shook the Americans' hands. Parvin and McFadden made the rounds with their goodbyes.

"You coming, Wolfman?" said McFadden.

"Go ahead, I'll be right behind you." He turned to Parrish. "Got a few minutes?"

Chapter 88

Parrish waved his girls toward the beach. "I'll join you to say goodbye." He and Wolf were left alone. The two men walked along the rocky beach, Parrish limping. "What's on your mind, *amigo?*" he said.

Wolf grinned, disarming the resort owner. "Don't think I don't know what you pulled, asshole."

Shocked, Parrish halted. "What are you talking about?"

Arms crossed, Wolf faced Parrish. "Pretty slick, Max. We come rolling in here looking for our missing and you fucked us from the get go."

"That's it?"

"No, that's not all of it. Once you figured out what our mission was you decided it was too good an opportunity to pass up, huh? Get some former Spec Ops people to fix your little problem for you, right?"

"What have you been smoking?"

"Probably the shit you were handing out. You were battling Garcia and losing. Looked like you were gonna have to cash in the farm and leave your little slice of paradise, huh?" Wolf leaned into Parrish, inches from his face. "You sent Lopez and Parvin into town knowing they'd get their asses handed to them by Garcia's thugs. You almost got 'em both killed, you sonofabitch."

"You forget that I ended up in the jail with Parvin?"

"Gotta hand it to you, Max. Took balls to risk that. Made for a good cover. Had me fooled up until the end."

"I don't have to listen to this."

Wolf grabbed a fistful of Parrish's shirt. "Yes you do. You risked my guys. I coulda been killed. You set us up to go to war with Garcia for you. We ended up killing off your worst nightmare and you come out smelling like a rose."

Parrish pushed Wolf away. "Fuck you. What about Ruiz? He's the one who killed Garcia, not you."

"A fluke. You counted on one of us taking him out first." Forming a fist, Wolf circled Parrish. "You even used your wife in this plan. Got her to send the army. Lucky she did. *Los Federales* had your number and ours. They woulda shot your own daughters, asshole. Think about that!"

In the distance, McFadden was shouting for Wolf. Parrish stepped back, pointing down the shore. "Your friends are waiting."

Wolf shook a fist at Parrish. "When they come looking for our boys you'd better lead them to the graves and be first in line with a shovel, so help me—" He stomped away, trailed by a wary Parrish.

Wolf put his anger on hold, gave each of the daughters a hug, and scrambled into the rubber boat. Last to leave the beach, he left behind camping gear, clothes, surfboards, and the van for Lopez. In place of the belongings Wolf carried hallowed cargo—bones and personal effects from each of the missing.

Wading in the shallows, Maria and Elizabeth pushed the inflatable into deeper water, giggling as they did. Their father lingered, waiting until Wolf and friends were farther out. The three, arms around each other, watched the men climb over *South Wind*'s stern. When the dinghy was winched aboard and stowed, the sound of muscular engines broke the bay's stillness.

Maria and Elizabeth stood with their father, watching until *South Wind* weighed anchor. Parrish and his daughters waved until the boat was lost to view.

Chapter 89

At first paralleling shore for most of an hour, Snuffy Larson plotted a new heading, taking *South Wind* thirty miles off the coast. "No way any of us are going to end up in some Mexican jail," he vowed. "Been there, done that."

"Amen to that," said Parvin. "I'm not going back without a fight."

Below decks, a bandaged Gideon put his medic's skills to work. Preacher's dressings were exchanged for fresh ones. Parvin's wounds were cleaned. Doctoring done, Gideon stopped in the galley for fresh coffee and took three mugs of fuel topside. Wolf and McFadden sat with Snuffy in the open bridge, enjoying the salt air. Heading northwest, *South Wind* ran along waypoints programmed to take them out of Mexican jurisdiction. When they hit international waters Snuffy and Wolf switched to the enclosed bridge.

Wolf passed the word. "Won't need much help from you guys," he said. "Catch some shut-eye if you can."

"I love it," said Preacher. "Wake me when I'm needed."

"Get plenty of sleep," said Gideon. "You'll need it when we finally hit San Diego."

Preacher went forward through the passageway, found an empty berth in the bow and crawled in. Not long after that, Parvin folded. McFadden returned topside to call Reggie with an update. Neglecting to mention his role in the firefight and Wolf's grim burial discovery, he sounded upbeat about the return leg of their trip.

"Finally heading home," he told her. "I want a hot shower, a shave and a cold beer, though not in any particular order."

"That's it?" she teased.

"Sorry, Reggie. Being with the guys can change a man's priorities."

They shared laughter, and then she confessed, "I've never been so lonely or worried about you, Sam McFadden."

"Sorry about the loneliness," he said. "As for worry, no need to be," he lied. "Except for the possibility about running out of cold beer or eating bad food it's been a rather uneventful trip."

When she pressed for details about the missing, McFadden begged off by promising to tell all when he returned. Admitting missing her, he soothed Reggie with a declaration of love and signed off. With all the good spots claimed, he made a bed from two blankets in the darkened main salon. Gideon was already asleep, head in arms, playing cards scattered across the galley table.

On the darkened bridge, Snuffy turned the helm over to Wolf and stretched across a padded bench. *South Wind* plowed through deep waters at a steady fifteen knots. Two radar screens glowed with a squall's shadow to the north, one hour away. They hit it early. The chop turned angry and the wind picked up. To lessen the pounding, Wolf dropped to twelve knots, then ten. Jostled awake, Snuffy kept Wolf company until dawn. The rain moved on as gossamer curtains, leaving behind a gift of groomed swells. Trading places, Wolf surrendered the helm and sprawled on the bench, soon adrift in deep sleep.

Two hours later, Sam McFadden came up from the galley to join Snuffy on the bridge. He found a radio station pumping out scratchy mariachi tunes. Snuffy grimaced at the choice. McFadden said, "Yeah, probably not." He picked up an English speaker reciting small craft warnings for the southern California coast. Snuffy approved with a smile.

Well beyond Mexico's reach and out of sight of land, *South Wind* headed due north. The two made small talk about the weather. Snuffy gave McFadden the wheel and plotted the next day's waypoints. The final approach would take them east, then south of Point Loma into San Diego's harbor. *South Wind* was berthed in a crowded marina just above North Island. Letting Wolf sleep, they spoke in low voices about what they would do after they reached San Diego and cleared customs and immigration. The four graves on a wind-swept mesa in Baja were on Sam's mind.

"When are you going to tell Sara about Connor?"

Snuffy stared beyond the *South Wind*'s bow. "She'll want to know, of course. I have absolutely no idea what I'm going to say."

"When's the last time you two talked?"

Inching the throttle forward, Snuffy said, "Two days ago. Told her we were still nosing around in Los Colinas. Didn't talk long."

"What's your gut tell you?"

A deep sigh. "She knows."

McFadden focused on the horizon. "Yeah. A mother's intuition. She's gonna need a shoulder to cry on."

"She can use mine as long as she wants, Sam."

An awkward silence followed, both men alone with their thoughts.

McFadden smothered a cough and said, "Glad you'll be there for her."

"Me too."

Hoping to lighten the mood, McFadden glanced sideways at Snuffy. "Do you remember the first time the Wolfman and I met Connor?"

Snuffy laughed, a hopeful sign. "That day at Pacific Cliffs. Wolf cleaned Tank Limmer's clock, and later, you guys had breakfast at my house."

McFadden said, "Connor ate enough for both of us. Great kid."

"He was that. Great mom, too."

Catching the smile on Snuffy's face, McFadden said, "You should marry that girl, Snuffy."

"The thought has crossed my mind."

"And—?"

"Just might have to do that, Sam. Have to get through this first."

McFadden went back to the horizon. "Breaking the news, right?"

Voice wavering, Snuffy said, "Yeah. Anybody but Connor. Why him?"

"No answer for that."

Snuffy said, "Any regrets about going?"

Taking his time to answer, McFadden finally said, "Leaving Lopez behind."

"His decision, Sam."

"I know. Just didn't seem right. Didn't much care for Preacher getting hit, or Parvin getting the shit kicked out of him, or Gideon getting cut up."

Snuffy put a comforting hand on McFadden's shoulder. "Or the two of us spending time in Cabo's hell hole."

Shrugging, McFadden said, "I have to say it. I wasn't sure how that was gonna end. We owe Gideon for calling the girl's parents. Her father pulled some strings somewhere."

"True. Like to know how he managed to spring us from jail in Cabo San Lucas. Might be worth asking."

Tilting his head at Snuffy, McFadden said, "Ain't gonna poke that sleeping dog. Best leave it alone for now."

"Once we clear Customs what do we do?"

McFadden yawned, his arms touching the overhead. "My plan is to cut the guys loose eventually. But first, Wolfman has to get Preacher to an off-the-books clinic to take care of his wound. In the meantime, Gideon and Parvin need to disappear for a while. I'll use the sat phone to book them all into the Best Western on the harbor. They're due a little R&R. Hell, everyone is."

Snuffy faced McFadden. "What about the...you know, evidence?"

"Wolfman and I are working out how to handle that."

"Sara will want to know right away."

McFadden leaned against the bulkhead. "She deserves answers."

"And the other families?"

"All of 'em. This is on Wolf and me. You guys can't be part of the conversation. That will put you in the clear if you're asked about it. *Capiche?*"

"*Capiche.*"

Gideon came up the ladder to the bridge. "Chow's on. Want me to take over for you, Snuffy?"

"Naw, you guys go ahead. Ask Parvin to spell me when he's done."

"Your call," said the Marine.

McFadden said, "Be right down." He turned to Snuffy. "Remember what I said about handling things."

"Got it. You and Wolf."

Chapter 90

The boat hit the last waypoint and turned east into a warm mid-morning sun, as eager as the men aboard to reach home. Nursing San Miguels, the beer of choice from Snuffy's galley stash, Wolf and McFadden sat in fighting chairs in the stern's cockpit. A sturdy cardboard box containing the tagged bones and personal belongings of the missing students remained locked away below.

"Snuffy asked me what comes next," said McFadden. "I told him and the other guys that you and I would decide. Said, for practical reasons, that they didn't need to be involved."

"Plausible deniability, huh? That's good. You should run for office, Dawg."

"I'm serious."

"At ease, I get it. So, what do you see as the next move?" said Wolf, raising the bottle to his lips.

"As agreed. We turn over the GPS info and effects to the FBI along with the names of our witnesses in Los Colinas."

Wolf said, "Okay. But with one change."

"Which is—?"

He lowered his bottle. "I vote for anonymity."

"We've been over this, Wolfman. They won't look based on some phantom's hunch, even if they have the coordinates in front of them."

"Hmm, not sure that's true. Ever see those news clips when cops go digging up some backyard or farm after getting a tip?"

"That's at home," McFadden snorted. "We're talking Mexico. New ball game."

Wolf stretched in the chair, his face to the sun. "I'm thinking of the risk we'd be taking. We'd be way too exposed, Sam. Might be charges"

Swiveling in his chair to face Wolf, McFadden said, "We're sending these guys home once we tie up things in San Diego. We both knew we'd have to do this at some point. We can't sit on evidence the families need to know about. What happens when Snuffy tells all to Connor's mom? We have to be on the same page, Wolfman. We knew this was a risk."

Wolf sat up. "Think of Reggie, Sam. If this blows up in our faces we might end up facing charges. I'm entitled to have second thoughts. It's my ass on the line, too."

"You think I don't know that?" said McFadden. "The last thing I want to do is put Reggie through this. Same goes for you."

"I'm with you, Sam, but I think we can go one of two ways with this. Do an anonymous drop to the media. Of course, I'd meet one on one with Crystal Hamm and lay it all in her lap. She's been reporting this story about Connor and friends from day one. Man, she'd love to wrap it up with an exclusive."

"How does that work? She shows up with the whole nine yards and immediately she's asked where she'd get the stuff."

"They can't touch her. She'd protect her sources. First Amendment."

McFadden said, "Lot of good that would do her. She and her bosses would get hauled into court until she talked. You thought about that?"

"I know her, Sam."

McFadden laughed. "Yeah, maybe in a Biblical sense."

"Hey, cheap shot, Dawg."

"My bad. You don't want her facing that. She'd be hung out to dry."

Wolf tried his other idea. "Or maybe we find a good lawyer, a criminal hot shot made of Teflon. He can go to the feds for his anonymous clients. He could even allude to them being righteous-minded Mexican citizens who wanted to do right by the families. That would play."

"Long shot. Your Crystal Hamm media idea would have better luck."

Wolf offered McFadden another beer but he declined. "Think about it, Sam. I could make the pitch to Crystal alone. We can give her cash to get a lab to do DNA testing on Connor's bone fragment. His mom agrees to do the match. It would take some time, but when it comes back positive we've got a winner! She keeps her mouth shut until Crystal drops the bomb. The other families get first peek at the story before it airs. Think of the pressure that puts on the feds and the Mexicans."

"Possible. I'm not signing on yet," said McFadden.

Propping his feet on the rail, Wolf said, "Hey, it's just a thought. Gets the ball rolling."

"How confident are you Crystal wouldn't fold?"

"You kidding? This would be a sure-fire Emmy for her and the station bosses. It would make her rep with the big leagues."

McFadden faced Wolf. "I don't know."

Wolf threw an arm around his friend. "Hey, Sam. It's the best way to go. We should tell Snuffy what we're thinking, though."

"Yeah, he'd need to get Connor's mom on board with this."

Wolf said, "I'll do it. Snuffy and I go way back. Better it comes from me." Heading for the cabin, he paused and looked at McFadden. "One more thing, Sam. This is on me. No arguing, okay? Once we hit San Diego you're out of the picture. I'm the only one walking point for our team."

"You got it."

Wolf smiled. "Good, it's settled. Now go call Reggie."

Chapter 91

After they cleared Customs and Immigration, the team went to ground in San Diego for three days of rest as planned. Wolf took Preacher to the after-hours clinic and stayed with him during his surgery. Snuffy went back to Pacific Cliffs to comfort Sara Ward, Connor's mom. Sam had been right—she knew. Inconsolable, she clung to Snuffy, not letting him out of sight for two days until exhausted. She finally slept.

Parvin and Gideon, booked in separate rooms at the Great Western Island Palms Hotel overlooking the marina, erased their sleep deficit and stuffed themselves at McFadden and Wolf's expense. Trading bedside duty with Wolf, the pair kept an eye on Preacher as he healed in a room he shared with Wolf. At week's end, Parvin flew back to Reno with the bonus McFadden had promised, along with extra cash for a new Excalibur crossbow. Preacher finally headed back to his log home on Lake Superior's North Shore. His healing wound still tender, the retired Navy SEAL, at his wife's insistence, swore off future adventures with Wolf. Maverick Gideon finished out the month before flying to Florida to join a nephew's landscaping firm north of Tampa. The lure of hard work drew him, along with an offer of a cottage on the water for as long as he needed it.

Connecting with Crystal Hamm, the Fox affiliate's lead reporter proved more delicate for Tom Wolf. Still cool because of his inattention to her during his earlier Hawaiian sojourn, she played him for a full day before granting an audience. Sworn to secrecy, she devoured the news about the Baja mission's conclusion. The exclusive he delivered restored Wolf's standing in her heart. Funded by Wolf and McFadden, she contacted a reputable private lab known for its medical scholarship, particularly its DNA expertise. Persuading Connor's mother to cooperate took more doing, but with Snuffy's coaching and her empathetic approach, Crystal Hamm got what she wanted—an agreement to provide a blood sample and a powerful interview lasting hours. Working overtime, the lab announced a perfect match with Connor's remains. The other three families, anxious for closure, fell in line.

Her news editor endured the station boss and company lawyers' hovering in the newsroom or in hushed conferences in the paneled boardroom. The suits delayed the story until all the families, their lawyers on hand, were on board. It came down to the wire. Saturated with promos and slick teasers prior to ratings week, Crystal Hamm's story arrived on a Sunday night, jolting San Diego.

McFadden paid the expedition's bills and resumed his businessman's role as a gun range owner. He gave up little to Reggie until the news of the discovery of the four missing California college students broke that evening. Wolf called thirty minutes before the news special aired.

"I suppose you've been watching all the hype," he said.

McFadden took the phone to the pool deck, out of Reggie's earshot. "Who hasn't?" he said. "You in town?"

"Staying out of sight at Crystal's townhouse. Got the blinds down. Waiting for the shit to hit the fan."

McFadden laughed. "Not in your DNA to keep a low profile, Wolfman. Is she with you?"

"Nah, she's at the station waiting to do a live panel with talking heads when her news special wraps up."

Wandering to the hillside railing, McFadden stared at San Diego's glittering skyline. "You hanging around for a while?"

"That's why I'm calling, Dawg. Eat your heart out. In the morning I'm heading to northern California. Got a friend who needs a forty-foot sailboat ferried to Florida. I'll be out of touch for a long couple of months. Off the grid. Wanted you to know."

McFadden let out a low whistle. "Man, when you want to disappear you really know how to do it style. Appreciate the heads up. Crystal Hamm going with you?"

"Your line tapped?"

"Don't go all paranoid on me, Wolfman."

Raising his voice, Wolf shouted in McFaddens' ear. "Hey, whoever's listening, I'M GOING TO DISNEYWORLD!"

"If anyone was listening you probably broke their eardrums."

"Good. Crystal promised to join me once she wraps this story. She busted her ass on this one, Dawg."

"Any fallout?"

"Ah, the feds raked her over the coals about her sources but she and her lawyers stonewalled 'em. Floated the sympathetic Mexicans angle but they're not buying it. They will probably want to talk to us at some point." "Tell her, atta girl for me. As for the feds, we can handle it."

"I'll be in touch," said Wolf. "Hey, show time. Catch her act and say hi to Reggie for me."

"Roger that. Watch your six, Wolfman."

"Always."

McFadden came in from the patio and slipped next to Reggie on the couch. Between commercials, the drumbeat for the Baja story stopped just short of overkill. Then, in a dramatic opening, a somber Crystal Hamm emerged from a shadowed set, an enlarged map of the Baja Peninsula glowing behind her.

"Good evening. Tonight we bring you a story of four families..."

Chapter 92

First carried live by the Fox network, CNN and the mainstay networks later picked up the story. Dominating the 24/7 news cycle, Crystal Hamm's report went viral, bringing out the worst in hysterical net bloggers and conspiracy theorists who flooded talk radio with bizarre plots woven from thin air. The next day the White House dusted off its original Oval Office condemnation of the murders and trotted out the president's press secretary with an update. Congress fulminated as usual, its members deploring violence south of the border with sound bites and canned indignation.

Mexico's four commercial networks delivered the bomb-shell to a nation long inured to such news. That four American youth had been murdered and buried on their soil became a short-lived *cause célèbre* before it faded. *Los Pinos*, the Mexican presidential palace, issued a stern warning about lawless factions and sent the army and *Policia Federal* into the countryside, raising dust and tension. Embedded media delivered the usual photos and live reports, but in the end, Mexican life resumed as usual—with fratricidal wars.

Denied permission for weeks, then months, the FBI was finally able to field a forensics team, after pressure on Mexico City from the White House. The Mexicans and Americans invaded Los Colinas with an army of experts. Arriving at the wind-swept mesa the teams found no graves—Mexican or American. Signs of recent digging, yes, but no bodies. Finger pointing began at once, both sides accusing the other of a cover-up. Coordinates were checked and rechecked. Satellite photos were shared and compared. Cadaver sniffing dogs roamed, pawing here and there without success. Those who lived in the tiny town were rousted and hustled before angry government investigators in hastily erected tents, but no one could give the strangers the answers they wanted.

A search for Jorge Ruiz was fruitless. He and his family had wisely decamped when Wolf and McFadden sailed away and no one knew where he had gone. Even the much-sought-after Emiliano, the rumored keeper of secrets, disappeared, leaving his rusting truck behind on the mesa. There were whispers of a *Policia Federal* raid that had come in the night—like avenging wraiths bent on restoring their honor—but no proof. The army's Captain Huerta gave a sworn statement to superiors without mentioning the mysterious *gringo* visitors. Four months later, he was killed in an ambush along the border. Major Luis Lopez, recipient of one of Wolf and McFadden's bonuses, returned to a modest hillside condominium overlooking Ensenada which he shares with an aged aunt. Wolf calls once a year.

Thanks to Salvatore Magano's intervention from Reno, Kelsey returned to her mother's Lake Tahoe home, though without her boyfriend Phillip, who was discharged from the Cabo San Lucas hospital a day before her release. He seemed to have vanished. Blamed for his disappearance, Salvatore Magano remains estranged from his daughter.

The ex-pat American Parrish fared much better than many. His beach resort became an abandoned shell, sold to a group of private investors who managed to keep their names out of the spotlight. There are plans for condos, a marina and a breakwater along the point, a project that will create an even more sheltered bay at the expense of the surf. Parrish, suddenly wealthy, joined his wife in Guadalajara, far from the sea his daughters loved. Capital gossips claimed his wife's uncle had found the family a walled estate with a mansion, pool and room for horses to run. His daughters moved to California to chase their dreams. When finally interviewed— long after public interest waned—Parrish could add nothing to the mystery of the missing.

There was no question the four Americans had been murdered. The lab results proved it, as did belt buckles, clothing, a keychain, two pairs of glasses, and footwear. Dispirited and at odds with each other, the teams from both nations took to their helicopters and trucks and went home empty-handed. Seeking official closure, the bereaved families, Sara Ward and Snuffy at their head, began a costly courtroom marathon. Encouraged by an army of lawyers on both sides of the border, the quest for justice ultimately led nowhere.

In the end, there was only the wind and the sea in the Baja. In the hills above Las Colinas there remain scars in the soil where men and machines had been at work. Any evidence of the rumored graves has long since been erased.

Made in the USA
Monee, IL
26 July 2024

61902413R00144